DEAD WRONG

CROSSROADS QUEEN
BOOK 4

ANNABEL CHASE

Copyright © 2023 by Annabel Chase

All rights reserved.

No part of this book may be reproduced in any form or by any electronic or mechanical means, including information storage and retrieval systems, without written permission from the author, except for the use of brief quotations in a book review.

Published by Red Palm Press LLC

Cover by Trif Designs

❦ Created with Vellum

CHAPTER 1

I watched the snowflakes from the second-floor balcony of Bluebeard's Castle, the monstrous money pit I called home. I'd climbed out of bed early, anticipating a beautiful sunrise—yesterday's had expanded across the horizon in ribbons of orange and gold—and was surprised to see specks of white falling from a gunmetal gray sky. There'd been no snow in the forecast. In fact, the winter temperatures had yet to dip below freezing until now.

I loved snow from a warm distance, preferably while holding a mug of hot cocoa with marshmallows. The fat, squishy ones. Not the small ones that resembled rabbit pellets. I had my standards.

"Pretty, isn't it?"

I glanced at Ray and nodded, too sleepy to chastise the ghost for interrupting my private moment. Arguably, he wasn't breaking house rules because he was outside on the balcony. Ray had been quiet of late, and I wondered whether he regretted his decision to stay tethered to this earthly plane. When I first moved into the Castle, I helped all the spirits in the adjacent cemetery cross over. I wasn't keen on neighbors, living or dead. Only Ray Bauer and

Nana Pratt had asked to stay. Why I'd indulged them, I'd never understand. It wasn't like me to be soft when hardness was required. Pops would've been so disappointed in me. One of my grandfather's key lessons had been to do what was necessary, even when easier options presented themselves.

"It's one thing to be strong, Lorelei, but you also need to be tough," Pops had said on more than one occasion. "There are those who would take advantage if they knew the truth about you." He didn't like to say the words out loud, as though afraid there were listening devices hidden in our modest house. At the time, I'd dismissed his behavior as paranoia, but now I understood. I'd seen the types of supernaturals he feared and agreed with his assessment. I only wished he were still alive so I could tell him.

I zipped up my hoodie to stave off the cold. "Where's Nana Pratt?"

"Wandering around outside. She likes that she can't feel the temperature."

I smiled. "One of the perks of being dead."

He looked at the ground below. "The moat's starting to freeze."

"Not much of a deterrent in the winter months, is it?" Fresh water was a somewhat recent addition to the moat. I'd bartered with a woman in town known as Big Boss. Fatima Fayez seemed to have contacts in every industry. One teensy tiny favor for her and voila! I had a working moat.

Okay, that teensy tiny favor turned into a huge debacle, but still. The moat was the important part. I chose to block out the minor detail where I ended up on The Corporation's radar. I was fairly certain I'd escaped the evil organization's notice, except for their employee, Naomi, who later witnessed my special skills during a fight to the death. The upside was that neither fighter died. The downside was that I'd drawn the wrong kind of attention in the process, and I'd made an enemy of Vincenzo Magnarella, a local mobster with a short temper and long fangs.

"Might be fun to skate on the moat once it's solid," Ray suggested.

"I'll let you do the honors. Getting near frozen water seems like a bad idea unless it's in a cocktail." I caught sight of Nana Pratt lingering near the front gate. "She looks tense for a ghost. Is she still mad about the tree?"

"It's your house. She'll get over it."

Nana Pratt had lobbied for a Christmas tree in the house and was dismayed when I rejected the idea. She refused to accept my argument that indoor trees were fire hazards, and I'd poured all my savings into this house and couldn't afford to lose it because of a holiday tradition gone awry.

"I'm not a Grinch," I announced.

Ray cast me a sidelong glance. "I never said you were."

"No, but I could hear you thinking it."

"Listen, I need to choose my battles wisely," he said. "I was on Team Halloween. I can't force you to celebrate every holiday."

"Good, because it won't happen. If you try to guilt me into buying those little candy hearts for Valentine's Day…" I paused. "Actually, I could be persuaded to do that, but I draw the line at sending cards."

He nodded sagely. "Fair enough."

"How many inches do you think we'll get?"

He observed the sky. "Hard to say. Snow isn't too heavy right now, but it depends on whether it picks up during the day."

"What's the most snow you ever had in Fairhaven?" If Pike County, Pennsylvania was anything like the county where I was born and raised, the town was no stranger to snow.

Ray didn't hesitate. "A hair over thirty inches in February 1978."

I whistled. "That must've been fun to shovel."

"The whole town shut down. It was kind of nice to have everything grind to a halt. Time seemed to stand still. We huddled in front of the fireplace and played games by candlelight."

"Sounds peaceful."

His head bobbed. "It was. Forced socialization. Speaking of which, if the roads stay clear, why not venture out tonight?"

I squinted at him. "Are you trying to get rid of me?"

"I'm trying to help you. Being alive isn't the same as living. I never understood that until I met you."

"So glad I could teach you something."

Ray sighed. "I didn't mean it like that. I'd like to see you thriving, that's all."

"I appreciate your concern, but I'm a big girl, and I don't need it."

"Everybody needs a squad. Look at that Taylor Swift. She has a great support system in place."

I turned to face the ghost. "Should I give her a call and see if she has room for one more?"

"I was only trying to give you a real-world example. No need to be a smart aleck. If you don't want to venture out, then you should invite one of your friends over for a game of Scrabble."

"Nobody will want to be out in this weather."

"You could visit the little vampire. He doesn't live too far."

The little vampire was Otto Visconti, a blind vampire with a Napoleon complex who'd been cursed to prevent him from drinking human blood. One drop and he'd burst into flames, or something like that. The 'what' was clear, but the 'how' was murky.

"I'm not in the mood," I said.

Ray gave me a long look. "I guess your gentleman caller isn't back yet."

I exhaled in annoyance. "Kane isn't my gentleman caller. He isn't my anything." I retreated into the house and stormed downstairs to heat the kettle and try to forget the name Kane Sullivan.

Six weeks had passed since I'd shown the prince of hell my true colors. Six long weeks of uncertainty. When I first discovered he'd taken off without a word, I stayed close to home, licking my wounds. Eventually, I returned to the Devil's Playground to see whether Josephine Banks, his right arm and nightclub muscle, would reveal his whereabouts.

It had been a wasted effort. The vampire seemed to delight in telling me she was under strict orders to keep his location restricted to his inner circle.

The message was clear—I wasn't his inner circle. I wasn't anything to him.

I knew my revelation would shock the mysterious demon, but I never expected that it would send him packing. We'd developed a bond during my time in Fairhaven, or so I believed.

My mistake.

I should've known not to get too close to anyone. It always ended poorly.

My skin tingled as I poured hot water into a mug. It was too early for a visitor, but the ward didn't lie.

"It's that handsome werewolf," Nana Pratt blurted as I opened the front door. The ghost was on the porch, excited by the prospect of company.

The look on Weston Davies' face told me this wasn't a social call. The fact that the alpha of the local Arrowhead Pack also actively disliked me might've also been a clue.

West removed his knit cap. "Good morning, Lorelei."

"Your face says otherwise. Come in."

He wiped his boots on the mat before stepping inside. A wolf in the wood but a gentleman in the 'hood, apparently.

"Would you like tea? I just made myself a cup."

"Sure." He unzipped his coat and hung it on the new coat rack, a gift from Gunther Saxon, the mage assassin, who was aghast to have nowhere to hang his pricey outer layers. "Where are you with the renovations?"

"Somewhere in the murky middle."

Unsurprisingly, the aforementioned money pit required extensive renovations. I'd bought the pile of bluestone sight unseen, apart from a handful of online photos. The five-thousand-square-foot house had been built as a summer 'cottage' during the Gilded Age by a tycoon named Joseph Edgar Blue III. Blue lost interest in the house after his wife's death. It was finally abandoned when his son and heir squandered the family fortune, and no one could afford the Castle's upkeep, along with the rising property taxes. The house's position atop a hill meant I could see the town below and the river that bordered it to the east, as well as the forest to the south. As far as I was concerned, the view was the building's best feature.

West followed me into the kitchen and sat at the small table while I reheated the kettle and steeped his tea bag. He didn't seem eager to tell me the reason for his visit, so I didn't press the issue. I applied the most important skill I learned in England—I talked about the weather.

"Didn't expect to wake up to snow today," I said, flinging the soggy tea bags into the trashcan with awkward zeal.

"No, it came as a surprise to us, too." He drummed his fingers on the table. "Usually, Rosalie can smell it before it starts."

"Neat trick." I set a mug in front of him and sat at the table. "Any milk or sugar?"

"No thanks. I'm trying to cut back on sugar."

"Aren't we all?" I sipped my tea and savored the two

teaspoons of sugar I tasted. I was trying; I just wasn't successful.

He took a sip from his mug. "We lost one of our own last night. Chutney."

I didn't recall meeting anyone named Chutney. "I'm sorry to hear that. I guess you're not knocking on everybody's doors to deliver the sad news."

His face remained solemn. "Just yours."

Lucky me. "What can I do for you, West?"

"Would you be willing to contact his ghost and tell us what happened?" Like everyone else in town, West was aware that I could communicate with ghosts, but that was the extent of his knowledge.

"You don't know how he died?"

"Yes and no."

Very illuminating. Glad the alpha of the Arrowhead Pack was as forthcoming as ever. "Was he ill?"

West shook his head. "He was out running with a few members of the pack last night, before the snow started."

"He died in his wolf form?" That was unusual. Werewolves were stronger and more resilient in their animal forms.

West nodded. "He ended up in pieces on the ground."

"An attack by another animal?" I didn't want to contemplate what might be bigger and stronger than a werewolf and roaming in the woods by my house. Then again, I lived near the crossroads in Wild Acres, so anything was possible.

"An attack is the likely scenario, except nobody saw anything, and it looked more like he..." West seemed to be struggling for the right words. "It wasn't a leg here and an arm there. His body was more like confetti."

Werewolf confetti didn't sound very celebratory.

"I can't think of anything that would cause that," I said. There was always the chance that an unfamiliar monster or demon had wandered through the crossroads at an inopportune moment for Chutney, a wrong place and wrong time scenario.

"Somebody suggested spontaneous combustion," West said.

Not a theory that occurred to me. "Is that even possible?"

West shrugged. "It wouldn't be my first thought, but at this point I see no reason to rule it out, given the state of the body."

"I can see why you'd like to ask Chutney what happened to him." I hesitated. "Are you sure you want me to do this?"

"When it comes to my pack, I'll do whatever's necessary." And by 'whatever's necessary,' he meant ask a favor of me. West had made no bones about the fact that he wished I hadn't moved to Fairhaven.

"Lie down with dogs and get up with fleas, right?"

"You know you don't have to say everything that pops into your head." He tapped his temple. "Think of your head like Vegas. What happens there stays there."

"For someone asking a favor of me, you could try being nicer."

He closed his eyes, as though collecting himself. "You're right. I'm sorry. Would you mind coming with me now? I'm worried the snow will make it harder."

"Weather doesn't impact ghosts in my experience, but it could impact your investigation."

"We did a sweep for evidence last night," he said, "but I think it's worth doing another one. It's impossible to know whether we found all of his remains."

With that image in my mind, I had a little trouble swallowing my tea. "You hated coming here to ask for my help, didn't you?"

He gulped the remainder of his drink and set the empty mug on the table. "I'd rather come here to kick your ass at Scrabble, that's for sure."

"We don't have to be at odds, West."

"We don't have to be friends either."

Got it. The werewolf still didn't trust me. That was fair, because I was most definitely hiding important information from him. He had an excellent sixth sense, I'd give him that.

"Not that it should matter either way, but Chutney left behind a wife and two kids. Even if you don't do it for the pack, it might ease their suffering to know what happened to him."

Clever wolf, playing the family card. He knew from previous conversations I'd been close to my grandfather. My fault for oversharing and exposing a weakness. If Pops could see me now, he'd be disappointed that I'd lowered my guard enough to reveal personal details that were now being weaponized against me. Kane leaving town was bad enough. I didn't need the extra reminder that sharing led to caring.

"You met his son the last time you were at the trailer park," West continued. "Chatty kid with the bowl haircut."

I remembered him. He knew I'd lived in London before arriving in Fairhaven and asked if I was fluent in British. Cute kid. And now a devastated one.

"I can try," I said, "but no promises."

West offered me a ride in his truck, which I accepted. I was mildly concerned that my ancient truck, affectionately known as Gary, wouldn't operate in the wintry conditions. I'd find out eventually, but I was happy to live in blissful ignorance for now.

"Where'd you learn to be so distrustful of strangers?" I knew it was the pot calling the kettle paranoid, but I couldn't help myself.

He kept his gaze fixed on the road. Flakes were now falling at a more rapid pace, and his wipers were having trouble keeping up. "What makes you think it's all strangers and not just you?"

"Ouch." I knew wolves tended to be wary of outsiders, but sheesh. "If I recall correctly, you were an outsider once upon a time. Maybe try to remember how that feels." When we first met, West told me that he'd come from another pack but neglected to offer any details.

West's fingers tightened on the steering wheel. "I've been established here for a long time. Fairhaven's a small town. We have to look out for each other."

The most recent census identified the town's population as three thousand people, which meant it hadn't increased significantly from its early days. Fairhaven came into existence as a crossroads village that bordered the Delaware River and Sawmill Creek. During Colonial American times, a crossroads village was a settlement that was situated where two or more roads intersected. It provided identity and vitality to the surrounding countryside, as well as a sense of community. Fairhaven still possessed all those qualities and then some.

He parked the truck at an access point to the woods. "You should've worn gloves."

"That's what pockets are for." I climbed out of the truck and made a show of stuffing my hands into my coat pockets.

I followed West into the woods, feeling like Snow White trailing behind the huntsman with blind trust. Snow White's sweet and kind demeanor had saved her from execution, but I had something better.

Weapons.

I pulled down my knit hat so my ears were covered. I'd been prone to earaches as a kid, and I wasn't interested in reliving that experience. My grandmother had been amazed that someone with my abilities could still suffer from ordinary ailments. Like my parents, my grandparents had been all human, and they'd often been stunned by my body's balance between child and goddess.

Snow blanketed the ground, although it was only a thin

layer. If there was still evidence to be found, West's keen werewolf senses could manage it.

He stopped in the middle of a copse. "This is where we found most of him. Do you think his ghost would be around here?"

"If he hasn't crossed over yet, I'll find him." I stood quietly and waited for West to leave.

He seemed to realize I wasn't moving. "Oh, you want me to go?"

"I don't perform for a live studio audience."

"How about if I search for clues over there?" He pointed in the direction of a row of evergreen trees dusted with snow. If Nana Pratt had her way, I'd cut one down and drag it home after I was finished.

"As long as you're out of earshot, I don't care where you go." It wasn't simply the pressure I was avoiding. It was the chance I might say or do something that would reveal I was far more than a ghost whisperer.

I waited for West to disappear from view and focused on my surroundings. Snowflakes landed on my coat and immediately melted. I ignored the wintry conditions and concentrated on connecting with Chutney. Of all my powers, this was the one that came most naturally to me, probably because it was the one supernatural skill I'd chosen to hone. In London, I'd worked as a finder of lost heirs and used the ability to earn a living. It also helped that communication with spirits was my most innocuous ability. As far as I was concerned, everything else involved the violation of boundaries. When I was younger, Pops worried that I'd lose control or go too far and end up unable to live with the consequences of my actions. I understood his fears. He was a mere mortal, saddled with the task of raising a goddess with incredible powers—Melinoe, goddess of ghosts and nightmares. I couldn't imagine what it was like for him to discover his only granddaughter was an anomaly, a danger to herself and others. To his credit, he dedicated his life to training me. I owed him a debt of gratitude I'd never be able to repay.

I swept the area in my mind, searching for any sensations that indicated the ghost was afoot. "I command you to come to me, Chutney."

Leaves rustled and detached from their branches as a gust of wind blew through the forest. I listened for any sign of Chutney's ghost but heard only the normal sounds of the forest. Hooting. Scampering. Chirping.

No Chutney.

I tried again. "Chutney, this is the goddess of ghosts speaking. I order you to appear before me."

No response. Odds were good that Chutney had already crossed over. If I'd been torn to shreds, I would've hightailed it out of this realm, too. Too traumatic.

West poked his head in the clearing. "Any luck?"

Weston Davies, patience personified. "He isn't here."

The alpha joined me in the copse. "You're sure?"

"Yes."

Somewhere nearby, a twig snapped. The sound elicited a ferocious growl from West as his head spun to the left.

"It's us. Don't shift," a voice pleaded. The werewolf I mentally referred to as Beefy Bert emerged from behind a tree, followed by another member of the pack, Anna Dupree.

"Sorry, we didn't know you'd be out here," Anna said. She scowled at the sight of me. "Why are you with her?"

"Her name is Lorelei," West said.

Anna knew my name. She also knew I was capable of more than communication with the dead. I'd met her at the local dive bar when I first moved to town and subdued her with one of her own nightmares. The werewolf had wisely kept that information confidential, mainly because I said what might happen to her if she didn't. Anna had an attitude problem, but she wasn't an idiot.

"We've been scouring the woods for hours," Anna said. "Nobody knew where you were."

"Bert and Anna were with Chutney last night," West told me.

That explained the disheveled hair and the dark circles under their eyes.

"Did you notice anything strange last night?" I asked.

"Other than the fact that our friend was no longer in one piece?" Anna challenged.

West let loose another snarl that made the hair on my arms stand on end, so I could only imagine how it impacted Anna. The she-wolf lowered her head.

"I'm only here to help," I said.

Anna lifted her head. "Help how? You're not a wolf. What do you think you can do that we can't?"

I took a step closer to her and looked her directly in the eye. "I would be more than happy to show you what I'm capable of." A snowflake landed on the tip of my nose, which somewhat lessened the intimidation factor.

"Why not let her help, Anna?" Bert said. "Any more of this snow and we won't be able to find those tracks."

West perked up. "What tracks?"

"No tracks," Anna insisted. "Bert was seeing things last night. He was high."

"It was a beautiful night, and I was running through the woods on all fours. I was high on life."

West's nostrils flared. "What did you see, Bert?"

The other two werewolves exchanged uneasy glances.

A young man in a yellow and black tracksuit trotted over to us. "Are you guys talking about what Bert saw?"

"Where'd you wander off to?" Anna asked.

"I thought I found a piece of Chutney, but it turned out to be a chunk of that buck we saw. Big fella." He held his hands about a foot away from his head. "Antlers out to here."

"Xander was with them last night, too," West explained.

I pivoted toward Bert. "Is the buck the animal you saw?"

Bert shook his head. "I think it was a lost dog."

"And I told you it couldn't have been," Anna said. "Otherwise, we would've smelled it."

Bert pinned her with a fierce gaze. "You calling me a liar?"

She rose to the challenge. "Did you smell another animal, Bert? Because the only scents I picked up last night were evergreen mixed with the shit you took behind the bushes."

Bert snarled. "I told you that wasn't me."

Her hands moved to her hips. "Then I guess Chutney took a giant dump right before he died."

I tried to steer them back on track before they tore each other to shreds and joined Chutney. "Can you describe this dog, Bert?"

He scratched the back of his head. "Pretty big. Bigger than you'd expect. Thin tail. Long hair around the face."

"Sounds more like a lion," I said.

He gave his head an adamant shake. "Nah. Couldn't have been. It was wearing a collar."

West's face hardened. "You were close enough to see a collar, but not close enough to take it down?"

"The collar was shiny," Bert protested. "It glimmered in the moonlight."

"I was going to say it glittered," Xander murmured.

"I don't care if it glowed bright orange and had the Chanel logo as a buckle," West seethed. "Why didn't you go after it?"

"Because," Xander began, taking great interest in the ground, "we were too distracted by Chutney."

"Then he exploded," Bert continued, "so we forgot about the dog."

"Could've been one of those Australian shepherds," Xander said. "Or a Burmese mountain dog."

"Or it could've been a lion," I repeated.

"We get a lot of wildlife in this forest," West said, "but lions don't generally feature."

I gave up. "Okay, so what kind of dog looks like a lion in the dark?"

"Moonlight," Xander corrected me.

I was ready to send Xander on a one-way trip to the moon so he could see the light up close.

"We all smelled the buck," Anna said. "If there was another animal nearby, we would've smelled that too."

"We all smelled it, but Chutney was the one who tracked it," Xander said. "I was so jealous. That buck had been evading us for weeks."

"Chutney's hunting skills were next-level last night," Anna said. "It really sucks. He was so proud." The werewolf chewed her lip. "One second he was running through the woods and the next second…" She made an exploding noise. "Fur everywhere."

"At least he went out with a bang," Xander said, prompting a disapproving growl from Anna.

"That had to be hard to witness," I said.

"I only wish I understood what happened," Bert said. "It was like he triggered a land mine."

West looked at me. "We swept the area already. There was no evidence of any explosives. No traps either."

"Do you think something came through the crossroads and attacked him?" I asked.

Bert shrugged. "It's always a possibility, but we didn't see anything actually attack him."

"Plenty of monsters have cloaking abilities," I said. Especially in a dark forest. "Has anybody searched today?"

"We've been searching for pieces of Chutney, but I think we found all we're gonna find at this point," Anna said. "If you think there's more, knock yourself out."

That wasn't a scavenger hunt I wanted to join. "I wasn't talking about Chutney. I meant the mysterious animal. You're wolves. Can't you track it?"

"The snow and the lack of a scent make it harder," Bert said.

"Harder, but not impossible," I countered.

Anna grunted. "I wouldn't bother. Even if Bert's right, it wouldn't be the first lost dog in Wild Acres and certainly won't be the last."

"Aren't you concerned the dog won't make it another night in subzero temperatures?" I asked.

Xander answered for them. "Sometimes you gotta let nature take its course. Survival of the fittest and all that."

I glanced at West, expecting their compassionate leader to kick the legs out from under Xander and insist he care about the fate of lost dogs, but West only repeated his earlier statement about their sweep of the area.

West nudged my arm. "Come on, Clay. I'll give you a ride back to that pile of blue stones you call home."

"It's a work in progress," I said, once I was buckled in the passenger seat.

"It's a work in something. I'm not sure progress is the right word."

"This cold weather is slowing me down," I said. "Snow makes me want to curl up in a ball under a blanket and wait for the thermostat to hit sixty."

West grinned. "You picked the wrong place to settle if you're looking to avoid winter. Should've headed farther south."

"This hair isn't cut out for heat and humidity." My gaze drifted in the direction of the Devil's Playground as we drove past the access point, and I forced my attention back to West.

The werewolf seemed to notice. He glanced at me with a look that bordered on sympathy, which I didn't love. "Last I heard, Dantalion and Josie are still running the place."

I kept my tone neutral. "Makes no difference to me. I prefer Monk's."

"Yeah, me too." He paused. "Nobody knows why Kane took off. Don't suppose you'd know the answer to that."

"Why would I? He and I don't know each other very well." Of course, Kane knew more about me than I'd prefer, but there was no putting that goddess back in the bottle. I'd told him my identity, and now I had to suffer the consequences of a runaway demon.

West parked outside the gate to the Castle. "I owe you one, Lorelei."

"Why? I didn't do anything."

"You came with me when you could've stayed home. You didn't have to do that." He nodded toward the house. "If you still need help with your budget planning, say the word."

"Thanks, but Nana Pratt is on the case." The ghost had expressed her displeasure when she learned I'd also sought assistance from the werewolf. Ray said she wanted to feel useful, so I told her she was hired as my official bookkeeper.

"How about I drop off a few bags of salt later? If this weather keeps up, you'll need them."

I glanced at the snow-covered bridge that led to my front porch. "I would appreciate that, thanks."

I exited the truck and took my sweet time walking to the house. The last thing I needed was for the werewolf alpha to see me fall flat on my ass. Between Kane's absence and the pack's distaste for me, I was already up to my eyeballs in humiliations galore.

CHAPTER 2

My conversation with West motivated me to tackle a simple project in the dining room. I was fully functional, and the day was still young, so I figured I might as well make the most of it.

The walls in the formal dining room had the misfortune of being covered in a textured, metallic mural that contravened my minimalist aesthetic. In other words, it had to go. I'd been giving it the stink eye for months, but that didn't seem to have any effect. If only I possessed the kind of magic that allowed me to circumvent manual labor, my life would be hunky dory. Of course, someone less ethical in Melinoe's goddess shoes might use her powers to make a team of ghosts perform all the work in the house. That someone would not have been raised by Pops.

I shook my fist at the air. "I curse you for this hideous wallpaper, Joseph Edgar Blue III."

During the years the house sat vacant, the paper had peeled away from the walls in multiple places. I started with one of those and attempted to strip off the section.

"I wouldn't do that if I were you," Ray advised.

I turned to observe the ghost. "Rules, Ray."

"It's bitter cold outside."

"Yes, but you can't feel it."

"I see snow, and I feel cold. I can't help it. You should see Ingrid. She's shivering."

"I thought she was enjoying the great outdoors because she was impervious to cold."

"She changed her mind. It's a woman's prerogative."

I had two octogenarian ghosts that acted like tweens. "Tell her to manifest a coat." The ghosts could change their appearance at will, although they tended to stick to the clothes in which they were buried.

"No need. She followed me into the house. She's in the foyer."

"It's not much warmer in there." I concentrated on pulling a swath of paper, but it shredded into slivers with most of it remaining stuck to the wall. As usual, one simple task was quickly becoming one monumental pain in the ass.

"You're going to make it worse," Ray said.

"I don't recall asking your opinion." I paused. "But if I did, what would it be?"

Ray observed the mess of the mural. "You should steam it off. What's the sudden rush to fix the dining room anyway? You planning on hosting dinner parties?"

I gave him a pointed look. "Do I strike you as the kind of person who throws dinner parties?"

"No, you strike me as the kind of person who doesn't get invited to any because they know you won't show up."

"You're very astute, Ray."

"When you spend years as the quiet man in the recliner, you notice things."

"You make yourself sound lazy." What I knew about Ray suggested the man had been far from lazy during his lifetime.

"Not lazy, just introverted. Where's your drop cloth?"

"I'm not painting the wall until the mural is off."

"I don't mean for paint. I mean for the debris once you

start scraping off the parts that won't budge." He motioned to the streaks of paper that remained stuck to the wall after my peeling effort. "Makes a real mess."

Nana Pratt entered the chat. "Why bother with all that work? Glue down the parts that stick out and paint over it. Save us all from your bellyaching."

I leaned against the wall. "If my bellyaching is that problematic for you, I'd be more than happy to issue you a one-way ticket to the Other Side."

The elderly ghost seemed to realize she'd overstepped. She backed away until she was safely in the doorway. "I only meant to offer an alternative."

"No shortcuts." Ray shook his head firmly. "If you're going to do up this house, you're going to do it right or not at all. Once you steam it like I told you, I can help you with the scraping. All I need is a putty knife." He looked over his shoulder at Nana Pratt. "This would be good practice for your fine motor skills, Ingrid."

"I'm game," Nana Pratt said. She surveyed the once-grand room. "Can you imagine the lavish parties the original owner must've hosted?"

According to local lore, Blue had been partial to hosting parties that featured mediums toting scrying glasses. He'd milked the hell out of living next door to a cemetery, and his guests loved the drama of it. I'd be hosting no such parties. I would've preferred that no one discover my connection with ghosts, but the residents of Fairhaven had proven themselves too wily for my own good.

I followed Ray's instructions regarding the steamer. Apparently, there were actual steamers dedicated to this job, but he said I could use the steamer function of my iron in a pinch. I had no intention of driving downtown to the hardware store. Hewitt's was likely teeming with people eager to buy all sorts of winterizing equipment and necessities, so the iron would have to do for now.

"You should throw a housewarming party when the renovations are finished," Nana Pratt said.

"Absolutely," I said, knowing the renovations could easily take another decade at my current pace.

"You might meet somebody special if you have a party. Lots of people meet their spouses that way," she continued.

"I don't need to meet somebody special," I said. "I am somebody special."

Ray nodded his approval. "All women should have your confidence."

Nana Pratt blew a raspberry. "That isn't confidence. That's called deflection."

"Have you been thumbing through that psychology book?" Ray asked.

I craned my neck to look at them. "I have a psychology book?"

"You brought it home from the library last week," Ray said. "I put it on hold."

I hadn't even noticed it in the stack. The librarian had them ready and waiting for me, and I carried them home on autopilot. "Why did you want a psych book?"

"I'm interested in learning about subjects I didn't get a chance to study when I was alive," Nana Pratt said. "Women in my generation didn't really go to college."

"Neither did I," I said. I'd barely made it through the multiple high schools I'd attended.

I returned my attention to steaming. It took effort to hold the iron close to the wallpaper without touching it. My shoulder and arm muscles would complain tomorrow. And if I had to hear Ray say, "patience, grasshopper" one more time, he was going to find himself outside with one.

I was relieved when it was time for scraping. The ghosts were happy to step in and try their hands at home improvement. I watched Nana Pratt struggle with the putty knife until I couldn't take it anymore.

"No, like this." I mentally seized control of her hand and turned it so that the blade was in the correct position.

Nana Pratt looked down at her ethereal hand. "How did you do that?"

I knew exactly what she meant, but that didn't stop me from playing dumb. "Do what?"

"You controlled her like she was a Roomba, and you used the remote," Ray said.

"I was being helpful."

Nana Pratt peered at me. "How can you control me like that, Lorelei?"

"If I can help ghosts cross over, is it so crazy to think I can help them do other things as well?" I knew it was a bullshit response, but I didn't know what else to say.

Ray's voice was gentle and encouraging. "Why not tell us the truth? It isn't like we can tell anyone. You're the only one we can talk to."

"I wouldn't tell even if I could," Nana Pratt said. "It's obviously an important secret to you."

"It's best if you don't know the details."

"But why?" Nana Pratt pressed.

Because I was trained from childhood to protect my secret. Because the truth risked my life and the lives of those around me. Because Kane discovered my secret and immediately ran away from me. When even the prince of hell rejects you because of who you are... I shook off the negative line of thought.

"Because," I said simply.

Ray moved to stand beside Nana Pratt. "Lorelei, if it's us you're protecting, there's no need. Nobody can hurt us when we're already dead."

"There are many ways to hurt the dead. You have no idea." My response sounded more ominous than I intended.

"You would never hurt us," Nana Pratt said. "I know that."

"Not intentionally, no." I gestured to the wall. "Can we get back to work now? This mural isn't going to remove itself." Although I wished it would.

"Isn't there a magic spell that will change the mural without all this work?" Nana Pratt asked, as if reading my mind.

"I'm sure there is, but I try not to engage with witches unless absolutely necessary."

"You seem to like the Bridger witch well enough," the old woman pointed out.

I looked at her. "Spells cost money. Right now, I have more time than money, so manual labor it is."

Ray resumed scraping. "You really won't tell us?" he asked softly.

Years of conditioning were too difficult to undo with a simple request. Pops had ingrained the need for secrecy deep into my psyche for my own good.

"No," I said. "Let's change the subject."

"What did your werewolf friend want this morning?" Nana Pratt asked.

I told them about Chutney, and Bert's alleged sighting of a lost dog.

"Why haven't you gone out to look for it?" Ray asked.

"Because Bert's the only one who thought he saw a dog, and because I'm not a wolf."

"No, but your grandfather used to take you hunting. You know how to track."

I lowered my arm. "Are you trying to get rid of me again, Ray?"

"Of course not, but Ingrid and I can carry on with this work while you search for the dog. It's freezing outside, and with snow on the ground, a dog will struggle to find food."

And now all sorts of unpleasant images were flashing in my mind starring a potentially imaginary dog and his quest for survival. Clearly, I'd watched *The Incredible Journey* too many times.

I switched off the iron and set it on the floor. "You really don't mind if I go?"

"As long as you don't mind us staying in the house while you're gone," Ray replied.

"Stay out of my bedroom, and we're good."

They both nodded. "Put on an extra layer before you leave," Nana Pratt advised. "Otherwise, as soon as the sun goes down, you'll catch your death."

I hurried upstairs to change, adding an undershirt and a pair of thermal leggings for good measure. I also wore my fluffiest, warmest socks and stuffed my feet into boots. If the dog was still out there, I was determined to find it.

I walked to my truck and prayed the engine would start. I hadn't driven the truck in the winter months, and this could be the season I discovered the hard way just how ancient Gary was.

Outside the gate, I noticed three large bags stacked on top of each other. True to his word, West had dropped off the salt. I'd have to carry them to the house when I returned home. I was too focused on the dog now, that somewhere between the dining room and the truck, I'd named Benji.

Relief swept through me as the engine sprang to life. Victory! I glanced at the Castle to see two silhouettes in the window. My roommates really wanted me gone. Maybe they were throwing a party and inviting all their ghost friends. At least I could command them all to leave if I arrived home later to a rager.

As I drove toward Wild Acres, my thoughts turned to Chutney. What could have killed him? There were three other werewolves in the vicinity at the time, and the only possible sighting was of a stray dog and a buck.

I stopped at an intersection and glanced in the direction of the Devil's Playground. Nope. Not going that way. The prince of hell could rot in … well, hell.

My truck fishtailed here and there, but the road conditions were decent. I'd seen the plows out earlier, so I had faith that Gary could manage. Nevertheless, I drove cautiously, because of the ice and also in case the dog or any other animal decided to take a leap of faith in front of my truck. Gary's response time was reflective of his age. One slick patch on the road, and I'd take out the dog and myself in one swift maneuver.

I reached my destination and parked the truck at the head of the trail for the Falls. If I were a desperate dog, I'd head for the nearest water source. I hoped the animal was smart enough not to venture into a partially frozen river though.

Magical energy crackled as I drew closer to the waterfall. My powers were strong no matter where I was in the world, but this area seemed to magnify them. I could practically feel my skin buzzing with pent-up energy.

No dog. No tracks, although the snow played a role in that. Anything that had been on the forest floor was covered by now. I should've searched for the dog after my conversation with the wolves this morning. I felt a twinge of guilt for not giving it more consideration, especially after I'd mentally chastised Xander for his lack of compassion.

The only animals I saw during my search were deer, rabbits, foxes, and squirrels. I thought of the dead buck and wondered whether he'd been related to the young deer I spotted. I shut out the thoughts and ventured closer to the crossroads, where I spied two werewolves huddled against the base of a giant oak tree. They were hunched over their respective phones, immersed in whatever was happening on the small screens. Their clothing was far less layered than mine, a benefit of the lupine blood that coursed through their veins.

I kept waiting for them to notice me, but their noses remained buried in their phones.

I cleared my throat as I got within two feet of them. "You know, I could be a terrible monster that walked straight through the crossroads and killed you both because you weren't paying attention."

The brunette I recognized as Bree deigned to look up at me. "I was aware of you. I just put you in the not-a-threat category and kept playing."

Her companion didn't bother to glance up. "I don't need to see you to know you're the chick from the Ruins. You have a very distinct smell."

I tried not to get my hackles up. "Do I?"

"Usually, it's sweat and bacon. Today there's a little soap mixed in. Did you shower right before you left the house?"

"Yes," I lied. As a matter of fact, he smelled the soap from the spray mixture I used to steam clean the mural. Damn werewolf senses. "What's so important on your phones that you can't be bothered to acknowledge me?"

The one who wasn't Bree held up his phone to show me. "Cat videos on TikTok. I'm not allowed to watch them at home, so I save them all for when I'm on duty."

"TikTok is banned in your house?" I asked.

"No, cat videos are. My brother thinks it's weird for a werewolf to enjoy them, but these cats are flippin' hilarious." He turned the phone around. "I follow this one orange Tabby." Laughing, he shook his head. "He's always getting stuck in random places around the house. So funny."

Bree tapped on her phone. "I'm playing Duolingo, but it's so cold that my phone battery is close to dying. If I don't finish, I'll lose my four-hundred-and fifty-three-day streak."

"Speaking of dying," I said, immediately aware of what a terrible segue that was. I'd properly chastise myself later. "Were either one of you on duty last night?"

At the mention of last night, their faces turned somber.

"No, thank the gods," Bree said. "It was hard enough hearing about Chutney. I wouldn't have wanted the visual."

"Did the guards hear what happened?" I asked. There was no better way of asking whether they heard their fellow pack member explode.

Bree knocked her knee against her companion's. "Meathead's brother did."

Meathead nodded. "Ivan said it sounded like gunshots. He couldn't leave his post, so he called West to report it."

"Any idea if Chutney had health issues?"

Bree barked a laugh. "You think he blew up because of a health issue? I'd love to know the diagnosis for that."

"I have no idea what happened to him. That's why I'm asking questions."

Meathead peered up at me. "I didn't know you were a cop."

"I'm not. West asked me to help out." Okay, he didn't ask me to interrogate his guards, but still.

Meathead continued to look at me, as though trying to make up his mind about something. Finally, he said, "Okay then."

"I take it there hasn't been much excitement at the crossroads tonight."

"It's so cold and miserable, even the monsters would rather be elsewhere," Bree said.

"You haven't seen or smelled any signs of a lost dog, have you?"

"Thankfully not," Bree replied. "Tough conditions for a small-town dog. Is he yours?"

"No." I cut a glance at the crossroads. "How about a lion?"

They both started laughing.

"I don't even know what a lion would smell like," Meathead said. "Peanuts and popcorn?"

Bree snorted. "Only if it escaped from the circus."

"Or the zoo," Meathead added. "The zoo has all kinds of tasty snacks."

Bree's face hardened. "I would never set foot in a zoo. It's unnatural to keep animals locked up."

Meathead lowered his head. "Yeah, I know, but the snacks."

"Go see a movie if you want good popcorn," she snapped.

These two were about as helpful as a chocolate teapot. "Stay warm, you two. I'm going to keep looking." It was getting darker by the minute. It occurred to me that I had to travel alone through the woods to reach the trailhead where I'd left my truck. I hoped to make it back in one piece, unlike Chutney.

My phone buzzed as I slogged through the forest. I slowed to a stop and used my teeth to tug off a glove so I could answer. "Hey, Otto."

"Good evening, Lorelei. Why do you sound like you're outside?"

I glanced at the towering trees around me. "Because I am outside."

"Did you decide to walk here? It seems like an unpleasant evening for a stroll."

I closed my eyes as the realization settled in. Otto had invited me for dinner and a game of Scrabble afterward, and I had agreed. I opened my eyes to look at the clock on my phone. I should've been there twenty minutes ago.

"I'm so sorry, Otto. I got caught up in a project, and now I'm in the woods."

"Dare I ask the reason?"

"It's a long story, but there might be a lost dog out here, and if there is, I want to find it."

"I didn't peg you for an animal lover."

"If it were summer, I wouldn't be as concerned, but this weather is dangerous for a domestic dog."

"Is anyone helping you in the search?" He paused to sigh. "Why did I bother to ask such an inane question? I bet you didn't ask for assistance."

"I asked. No one was available on such short notice." Fine, it was a bald-faced lie, but I hated that Otto thought he knew me so well. Never mind that he was right.

"Does this dog belong to someone you know?"

"I don't know. It might not even be a dog. It might be a lion."

"I see. Now I'm starting to think you're simply blowing off our engagement. If you made other plans, you need only say so."

I was beginning to feel the cold standing in one place. It was time to move again. "I promise you, Otto. I'm out here searching for a wayward animal. I'm sorry I forgot our plans, truly. How can I make it up to you?"

"No need to grovel. It's unbecoming. We can simply reschedule once the crisis has passed."

"How about I bring a special dessert to make up for this snafu?"

"I'd much rather hear you sing."

"Never gonna happen, Otto." The vampire was a skilled pianist. When I made the mistake of revealing my musical talents, he became fixated on exploring them. He grew even more intrigued when I refused to indulge his request. Music and I had a complicated relationship, and that was the most I was willing to admit to him.

"One song of your choosing," he persisted.

"No means no. Bye for now."

I tucked away the phone and continued my search. There was still no evidence of a dog. I was beginning to think Bert had been delusional at the time of the incident. Maybe he'd eaten some hallucinogenic berries. Thanks to the crossroads, nothing would surprise me in this forest.

I heard the crack of a twig behind me and whirled around. I saw only darkness and the outline of trees. "Who's there?" I demanded.

No response. As much as I wanted to dismiss the sound as

another woodland creature, my well-honed instincts told me otherwise.

"Come out where I can see you," I demanded.

Another crunching sound alerted me to movement to my left. A splotch of red flashed in the inky void. A woolly hat.

"Who's there?" a voice asked.

"I asked you first."

"No, you didn't." She sounded indignant as she approached me. Pale features shone in the sliver of moonlight.

"Sage?"

She squinted at me. "Lorelei?"

My body relaxed. "What are you doing out here?"

The fae waved her bow and arrow in the air. "Luckily for you, not shooting first and asking questions later."

"I'm looking for a lost dog."

"What does it look like?"

"It has a shaggy head and a thin tail. Other than that, no clue."

"You don't know what your dog looks like? Wait, when did you get a dog?" Sage had been to my house to help revive Ray's daughter when she was in a supernatural coma.

"It's not my dog."

"Then why are you out here searching for it?"

"Because it's lost, and the weather conditions are terrible."

Sage observed me for a moment. "Huh."

"What, huh?"

"Nothing. If it helps, I haven't seen a dog, and I've been out here for an hour."

"How have you not caught anything?" I asked. "I've seen plenty of other animals scampering around out here." Just not the one I wanted.

"If I was in the mood for fried squirrel, I'd be in luck. Gran happens to love squirrel on a stick, but since she isn't the one out here in the frigid cold, she'll have to take what she can get."

"I'm surprised you waited until this late to hunt."

"I would've been out earlier if I'd known someone was going to raid our food storage."

"Someone broke into your cabin?"

"No, the outbuilding where we keep most of the meat. It's outdated, I know, but we're fae, we tend to do things the old-fashioned way."

"Was it animals?"

"Oh, no. The thieves were of the two-legged variety. Saw the boot prints to prove it. I tracked them as far as the road. I figured I'd better get us dinner before Gran threw a hissy fit. She gets hangry when her blood sugar drops."

"Did you call the police?"

"Not yet, but I will in the morning. By the way, your friend went that way." She pointed past me. "With any luck, they tracked down your dog."

"What friend? I'm out here alone."

"Really? I'm sure I saw another silhouette when I got here." She pulled a face. "I could be wrong. Wouldn't be the first time."

I thought of my earlier instincts and fought the urge to shudder. Maybe Vincenzo Magnarella was finally making good on his threat. The vampire mafioso made it clear that he'd be seeking vengeance for my role in destroying his blossoming avatar business. Other than outing myself to Kane in the process, I harbored no regrets.

"If you're a fan of venison, I spotted a few deer that way," I said, indicating the section of forest closer to the Falls. I felt a smidge of guilt over Bambi, but I appreciated that Sage and hangry grandmother needed to eat.

"Thanks, you're a godsend," the fae said, continuing past me.

She had no idea.

CHAPTER 3

I put one boot in front of the other and strode to the entrance. This visit was purely for information gathering —information related to Chutney's death, not Kane's disappearance. Kane could stay away for the rest of eternity, and I'd be fine with it. The demon had made his bed of nails and now he'd have to lie on it, although the sadist would probably enjoy that. Make it a bed of puppies.

I joined the line behind two whispering women. They seemed to be checking out the butt of the guy in front of them. The tight leather pants made it easy for them. You could tell everyone in line was supernatural because not a single one of them bothered to wear a coat.

Finally, it was my turn. "How's it going, Larry?"

The bouncer looked startled to see me. "I need to see some ID."

I stared at him. "You've got to be kidding me."

"Rules are rules. Come on, you're holding up the line."

"It would move faster if you didn't make me show ID when you know perfectly well who I am."

"Listen, every night I admit magic users. Witches, mages, fae. It'd be all too easy for one of them to use a glamor to look like you or someone else, enter the club, cause a heap of trouble, and leave. Suddenly, you're banned and you don't know why. That's why I ask for ID."

Okay, that actually made sense. "Fake IDs are simple to make," I grumbled, digging through my handbag for my license.

"They are, but I find someone will use one or the other, but never both. They don't tend to cover their bases." Larry wriggled his fingers as I produced the ID. He nodded and handed it back to me. "Have a good night, Miss Clay."

I slipped the ID into my handbag and entered the nightclub. The interior was awash in red and green. In the middle of the room, an oversized Christmas tree hung upside down from the ceiling. Gold and silver ornaments gleamed in the dimly lit space. Bulbs flashed off and on, providing the dance floor with festive strobe lights. The Devil's Playground took the holidays more seriously than a corporate chain store.

I spotted a pair of broad shoulders behind the bar. My heart sank when I realized they belonged to Dantalion.

As luck would have it, a vampire vacated a stool as I approached. I swooped in to claim it. "Hey, Dandelion."

The demon's piercing blue gaze darted to the left and back to me. "Lorelei. I didn't expect to see you here."

"What can I say? This place is growing on me like a fungus."

He raised a perfect eyebrow. No caterpillars on that devilishly handsome face. "What can I get for you?"

"You're tending bar? What happened to Cole?"

"Got in a fistfight while trying to buy the last snow shovel."

"That's the holiday spirit. I'm in the mood for a French 75 with gin."

The vampire on the stool beside me leaned over. "I am French," he said in heavily accented English, "and I am at least seventy-five. I lost count years ago."

Dan rolled his eyes.

"I've heard better pickup lines at the DMV," I said.

The vampire sniffed me. "You smell interesting, like I very much want to bite you, but more out of fear."

I pushed him upright by the forehead. "And you smell like bourbon."

Giving up, he turned back to the guest on the other side of him.

Dan placed a bubbly flute on a coaster in front of me. "On the house."

"You don't have to do that."

"Kane wouldn't charge you."

I wasn't so sure about that, but I bit my tongue. A free drink was a free drink. "Have you heard about any strange happenings in Wild Acres?"

"Nothing too out of the ordinary. Why?"

"The pack lost someone under bizarre circumstances."

"That's rough. I haven't heard anything. You'd have to ask Josie. She's more on top of security issues."

Officially, Josephine Banks was Kane's director of security. Unofficially, the vampire was his muscle and his keeper—and she'd made it clear she wasn't particularly keen on me. If this were high school, she and West could start a club.

I swiveled on the stool for a better look at the crowd. Instead of Josie's sour face, I saw a group of familiar ones seated together at a premium table alongside the dance floor, including Gunther Saxon. Gun was a member of La Fortuna, an ancient society of mages that used tarot cards to channel their magic. He was also a member of the local Assassins Guild, an elite organization supervised by the prince of hell himself. In fact, it seemed like half the Assassins Guild was here tonight. Had there been a meeting without their fearless leader?

Gunther spotted me and waved me over. I shook my head

and turned back to Dantalion. "This is perfect, thanks," I said, taking another sip.

My handbag vibrated with an incoming text. I retrieved the phone from the interior pocket. The message from the mage assassin was brief and to the point.

Why aren't you coming over? I'm understimulated.

I smiled. Only Gun would be understimulated in a busy nightclub. *Looks like plenty of entertainment happening around you.*

Vaughn is telling a story and it's taking 4ever. Ready to kill him just to make it stop.

You know the rules. The local assassins were banned from killing within the borders of Fairhaven.

Dantalion moved to the opposite end of the bar to serve a demanding demon, so I took my flute and joined the assassins.

"Look, everyone! It's Lorelei!" Gun opened his arms in a welcoming gesture.

I perched on the base of his velvet lounge chair. "Why are you being weird? You knew I was here." I noticed the excessive volume of empty bottles and glasses on the table. "What are we celebrating?"

There was a brief moment of silence. Vaughn raised a bottle of champagne. "A successful month."

"Congratulations," I said. "Where's Cam?" Gunther's cousin, Camryn Sable, was also a member of the guild who happened to have a massive crush on Vaughn. I hated to think she was missing out on this golden social opportunity.

"Cam had plans tonight or she would've stayed," Alfonso said.

"Stayed? She was here?" I turned to Gun. "Was there a meeting?"

"I already told you I'm understimulated. Do you really think I want to talk about meetings? You know you want to dance. Why not give in?" The mage assassin shimmied his faux fur-clad shoulders.

"That looks more like a wet dog shaking off the excess water."

"I'll add it to the list of classics."

I frowned. "Classics?"

"You know, White Man's Overbite. Shopping Cart. The Sprinkler." He shimmied his shoulders again. "And now Wet Dog."

I smiled. Despite his murdering tendencies, Gun had a way of brightening up a room.

He plucked the flute from my hand. "Come, milady. We're here, and the music is tight. We might as well make the most of it."

He didn't give me a chance to object. I was propelled to the dance floor by an unseen force. My butt only made it halfway through a shimmy when a fight broke out. I couldn't see the participants, only the crowd widening around them. Gun and I were pushed to the edge of the floor in the process.

Shrugging off his faux fur and handing it to me, Gun shot to the middle of the floor before I had time to assess the situation. Trust an assassin to run headlong into danger. And trust a fashionista to leave his best piece behind. I wasn't sure what he intended to do.

Vaughn appeared beside me, holding a bottle of champagne. "What happened?"

"Seems like a fight." I couldn't see past the massive minotaurs now in front of me.

"Cool. Is Gun in it?"

"He was understimulated, so probably."

Vaughn squinted. "Who brought a wild boar to a bar?"

I looked at him sideways. "How drunk are you?"

He pointed to the dance floor where a boar was, in fact, charging his way blindly through the crowd. The dancers were either too inebriated or too distracted by the fight to notice.

The wild boar was a dense package of four feet by eight feet covered in thick brown fur. A set of sharp tusks protruded from either side of its snout. The animal seemed scared and confused by the crowd. It had probably wandered in from the woods in search of food.

Vaughn regarded the creature with detached interest. "Someone should probably do something about that."

"He's going to get hurt in that pit of flailing bodies," I agreed. Or he'd hurt someone else. The boar's tusks looked sharp enough to slice a hole straight through a dancer's thigh muscle.

Vaughn polished off the rest of the champagne in the bottle and set it down on the floor with a flourish. "I'll tell Josie."

The boar continued its assault on the dance floor, butting its head against anything that moved. I was relieved to see Gun emerge from the mass of bodies, unscathed.

"Is there a wild boar on the dance floor, or am I drunker than I thought?" he asked.

"There's a wild boar."

The fighting seemed to spread closer to us. I watched as one of the minotaurs picked up a shorter patron and tossed him casually across the room, as though disposing of garbage.

"This is getting out of hand," I said.

Gun was grinning ear to ear. "I know! Isn't it awesome?"

"Is there a tarot card you can use to remove the boar?" I asked.

"I'd rather not risk breaking any guild rules," Gun said.

"I didn't say to kill it."

"I know, but what if I did accidentally? It's more trouble than it's worth."

I considered catching the boar, but those tusks made me

think twice. If I was in the mood to be impaled, I would've let the flirtatious vampire do it.

Vaughn returned to the scene. "Can't find Josie."

"She was here earlier," Gun said. His gaze was riveted on an elf now climbing up the Christmas tree to escape the clutches of an angry minotaur. The mage clapped like he was being treated to a performance. "Bravo!"

The tree swayed from side to side as the elf scrambled toward the ceiling. If the minotaur grabbed the tree, the whole thing would come crashing down, baubles and all.

I elbowed Gun. "Use a card, please. This is only getting worse." I could feel the tempers in the room rising.

Gun fumbled through his cards, too drunk to choose one.

In the end, it was Sunny who saved the day. Kane's chimera cat landed in the middle of the dance floor with a hiss that drowned out the music. With its two-colored face of orange and black and a set of mismatched eyes, Sunny looked like a Halloween decoration come to life. The cat fixed her ire on the wild boar and backed the interloper into a corner.

Boars might be mean and aggressive, but Sunny had one major advantage.

The chimera could breathe fire.

The boar seemed to sense Sunny's power and began to whine.

The chaos died down. Even the elf jumped down from the tree and scampered away before the minotaur found him.

"Help the boar find its way out," Dan said, in a voice that sounded like he'd much rather be lording over hell than Kane's nightclub.

Larry appeared on the dance floor. He stalked toward the boar, grabbed its tusk, and dragged the animal out of the building. Whatever the bouncer was being paid, it wasn't enough.

I looked at Gun. "Still feeling understimulated?"

"The excitement level was adequate."

Someone went flying over our heads and crashed onto the table behind us.

"Fight!" a voice cried out.

It seemed the night was still young.

The flying patron jumped to his feet and brushed the broken glass from his clothing. Blood streaked his skin. He dragged his sleeve across his face to wipe it away. Pointy fangs now protruded from his mouth.

In a single leap, he hurdled over us and returned to his opponent on the dance floor.

Make that several opponents. The fight had quickly morphed into a brawl. Sunny remained on the floor with her back arched, and I worried she was about to spray them with fire. The building could burn to the ground in Kane's absence. As angry as I was with him, I couldn't let that happen on my watch.

I turned toward the bar in search of Josie. I expected to see the vampire vaulting over the counter. Instead, I saw Dantalion looking panicked. My gaze snagged on a brunette at the counter. Her features were even and pretty, stopping just short of beautiful. In a movie, she would've played the role of attractive best friend or ex-girlfriend. She wore a sleeveless black dress cinched at the waist with a gold buckled belt. Her bare arms were covered in colorful tattoos. She appeared eerily calm amidst the uproar. Her eyes met mine, and she raised a flute of champagne in salute.

I turned away from her. If I didn't do something, this whole place would be destroyed. I felt a stinging sense of responsibility. If I hadn't scared off the owner, Kane would be here right now to defend his turf.

I pushed my way closer to the scuffle. I could try to stop the beatings without using my powers. Just because Kane knew the truth didn't mean I wanted anyone else to know.

I quickly assessed the fighters for the one doing the most damage. A horned demon with hands the size of Texas seemed to be at the center of the action. There were so many bodies in the mix at this point, nobody would notice me—or so I hoped. I joined the fray and grabbed the demon's arm as he pulled back to throw another punch.

"Care to dance?" I twirled him toward me and hooked a hand around his neck, slipping into his subconscious. I wasn't interested in his nightmares. I was only interested in what might soothe the savage beast.

I quickly sorted through his mind for the right dream. It was basically like finding the file cabinet of his subconscious and rooting through the emotional drawers until I identified the one I wanted.

Found one.

The demon listened to a lullaby while being cradled in the lap of a larger, female version of himself. It was hard to tell from his point of view, but based on the size of his extremities, he seemed to be the adult version of himself.

I wasn't here to judge, only to subdue. I tugged the dream to the surface and felt his anger melt away. I looked over to see that Vaughn had the bleeding vampire in a headlock, and the other assassins had stepped in to quash the fight.

I released my hold on the demon and left the dance floor as Josie emerged from a private room with rumpled clothing and half her hair hanging loose from a ponytail. A woman with a half-buttoned blouse slipped out the door behind her and scurried away.

"Where were you?" Dantalion demanded.

"Busy." Josie surveyed the carnage. "What in the hell happened?"

"You didn't hear it? A couple bruisers decided to show off," the duke of hell replied.

I noticed a lipstick stain on Josie's neck. "You've got a smudge." I tapped the same spot on my neck.

Scowling, Josie rubbed away the mark. "Where are they now?"

"On the dance floor," Dan said.

She stood on her tiptoes for a better view. "Are they locked down with a spell?"

"No," Dan replied. "They're calm now, thanks to the guild."

The vampire snapped to attention. "They didn't kill anyone, did they?"

"No, but Sunny came close to incinerating a boar," I told her.

Josie turned her sharp gaze to me. "A boar?"

"It must've snuck in from the woods," Dan said. "If we're lucky, the wolves will hunt it tonight."

I wasn't sure how the boar managed to get past Larry. The bouncer would ID his own mother. "Too bad your boss took a vacation and left you two to clean up the mess." Petty party, table for one.

Josie's hands curled into fists. "Kane doesn't go on vacation."

"I'd hardly call where he went a vacation," Dan added.

Shushing him, Josie punched his arm. Hard.

"I don't see why it's a secret," Dan said, rubbing the injured spot.

"We don't have to understand his reasons in order to respect his request for privacy," Josie shot back. "That's what friends do."

I grunted. "Kane doesn't have friends. He has minions."

The vampire and the demon stared at me with equal ire.

Josie spoke first. "I'd be more than happy to throw you out of here headfirst."

Dantalion held up his hands. "I've seen her fight, Josie. I recommend escorting her politely to the door without touching her."

I smiled. Smart demon.

Josie's gaze flicked to the door that separated the club

from Kane's private quarters. "You've outstayed your welcome," she told me.

The dance floor was secure, the wild boar was gone, the fighters had fled the scene, and there was no sign of Gun. She was right; it was time to go.

"Nice to see you again, Josie. See you around, Dandelion."

I strode through the club with my shoulders squared and my chin held high. I refused to allow Josie's continued disrespect to rattle me. She was only protecting her boss, which seemed to be her primary function in life. Then again, I'd never known anyone who inspired the kind of loyalty and devotion that Kane did. It was impressive—and infuriating.

I spilled through the exit and into the cold night air alongside a group of fae. They seemed slightly agitated, and I debated whether I needed to interfere before they caused problems elsewhere.

"What are you looking at, princess?" the green-haired fae asked in a hostile tone.

"I really like the color of your hair. It's like a blade of grass on a spring morning."

Her eyebrows drew together. "Are you mocking me?"

"No, I'm serious. It's festive, too. I wouldn't look half as good with that color."

She examined me from head to toe. "No, not with your skin tone, but you could try purple. I bet that would look cool."

"Thanks for the tip." I trudged through the inch of snow to my truck. No goddess powers required for that one. Just good, old-fashioned flattery. Pops would be proud. He'd taught me to disarm my opponents with charm and only if that failed should I resort to weaponry. My powers were meant to be reserved for the most severe situations. I didn't always manage to adhere to that rule, especially where ghosts were concerned. Although I could control ghosts, I couldn't control when and where I encountered them. Sometimes they popped up when I least expected them.

I stood in the parking lot for a moment and scanned the area for any sign of the wild boar. White puffs left my mouth as I breathed out the frigid night air. I highly doubted the boar was the animal Bert had seen in the woods the night Chutney died. Even in the dark, its shape and tusks wouldn't be mistaken for a dog. Also, Bert described longer hair around its head, and the boar looked more like a hairy pig than a lion.

Satisfied the boar had fled, I climbed into my truck and blasted the heater. I relished the silence on the drive home. The nightclub had been overwhelming tonight. I needed to give my senses a break. The snow was still falling, and I switched the wipers to high to battle the flakes.

My stomach growled as I parked outside the gate of the Castle. No surprise given that I hadn't eaten since lunch. That would teach me to forget plans with Otto.

I passed through the gate and crossed the bridge, mentally viewing the contents of my fridge to see if I had anything that could be prepared quickly. There was always a PB and J sandwich. If memory served, I had enough blackcurrant jam to cover one slice of bread.

As I reached the front porch, I noticed a wicker basket on the doormat. If there were newborn kittens inside, I was going to lose my shit.

Summoning my courage, I lifted the lid an inch. No fluffy heads popped out. I widened the gap and the aroma of basil, thyme, and other herbs and spices filled my nostrils.

"Otto, you're not a vampire, you're an angel."

I closed the lid and carried the basket inside. My sandwich would have to wait until tomorrow. Right now, I had a stew to inhale.

CHAPTER 4

I awoke the next morning to a scraping noise. I sat up in bed and listened intently. It sounded like an injured animal was dragging itself upstairs using its claws. As soon as I pushed down the covers, I regretted it. The air in my bedroom couldn't have been warmer than fifty degrees. The house was unbelievably drafty at the best of times.

This was not even close to the best of times.

I grabbed a throwing knife from the drawer of my bedside table and traced the sound downstairs to the dining room to find Nana Pratt and Ray diligently scraping the remainder of the mural off the wall.

I lowered the knife to my side. "Good morning," I said.

Two apparitional heads turned toward me.

"Sorry," Ray said. "We didn't mean to wake you."

I couldn't be mad. The dining room was almost unrecognizable. "I can't believe you did all this work."

Nana Pratt waved the putty knife in the air. "I'm an expert now."

Ray backed away from her waving arm, as though worried she might stab him. Some human inclinations stayed with the dead.

"Any luck with the dog?" he asked.

"No sign of Benji." My hands moved to rest on my hips. "I'm seriously impressed with this. You've saved me hours of work. Thank you."

"I'd like to finish today if you don't mind," Nana Pratt said.

"Of course not. Scrape away!"

"What will you do with your free time?" Ray asked.

I shrugged. "Tackle one of the other hundred projects in the house? But right now, I'm going to eat breakfast."

Nana Pratt nodded her approval. "It's the most important meal of the day."

After inhaling a plate of scrambled eggs and bacon, I debated which task to start next, preferably one that didn't require a trip into town. One look out the window made it clear that winter was here to stay. The brief glimpse reminded me that the bags of salt were outside. I got dressed and headed outside to sprinkle salt along the walkway from the gate to the front door. A plow passed by as I finished. At the rate the snow continued to fall, the plows would have to operate around the clock.

"You need to go to the store," Nana Pratt said when I reentered the house.

"I'd rather wait until the snow stops."

"Why? You drove in the snow last night without any trouble."

I sat on the floor to remove my boots by the door. "It isn't the snow. It's the mob mentality when there's bad weather. I don't need to see people fighting over the last packet of ground beef."

Nana Pratt folded her arms. "Well, you're going to starve if you don't suck it up and get down there soon."

I rose to my feet and walked toward the kitchen. "I won't starve."

"Fine, but you should know you're almost out of toilet paper," she said.

I stopped in my tracks. "Are you sure?"

She nodded. "I checked all the cupboards while you were outside."

"You're not supposed to be snooping."

"I wasn't snooping. I was helping."

I contemplated my options. It was still early enough that the store might not be busy. "Do I need anything else?" I asked as I retrieved my handbag from the kitchen counter.

Nana Pratt seemed only too pleased to tell me. She rattled off a list of items, including a loaf of white bread.

I shot her a quizzical look. "I don't eat white bread."

She pressed her hands to her wispy cheeks. "Oh, silly me. Old habits die hard, don't they?"

Ray hovered in the dining room doorway as I put on my coat. "You should pick up a small bag of mixed nuts," he said. "The kind with the chocolate chips. That was one of my favorite snacks."

"Oh!" Nana Pratt said. "And try the gingerbread loaf. It's homemade, and this is the only time of year they offer it."

I paused at the front door to slide my feet into the boots. "Are you both trying to live vicariously through me?" I asked.

"This isn't about me," Ray said. "I think you'll like the nuts."

Nana Pratt was more in touch with her feelings. "This is definitely about me. One look at that gingerbread loaf, and I bet I can trick myself into smelling it."

"No promises." I left the house armed with a grocery list and a scraper with a brush on the end for the truck. I swept away the newly fallen snow and drove into town.

Despite the daylight, small lights twinkled in the shopfronts and lampposts. The usual wreaths on the doors had been replaced by traditional Christmas wreaths. Fairhaven did justice to the holiday season, I couldn't argue with that. Maybe I'd put up a tree next year, if only to placate Nana Pratt. I drew the line at tinsel, though. There'd be no shreds of silver paper masquerading as decorations on my tree.

Much to my relief, the stores weren't too brutal, although some of the shelves looked like they'd been raided during an apocalypse. I bought almost every item on the list, including the beloved gingerbread loaf. I couldn't wait to see the look on Nana Pratt's face when she saw it.

As I loaded the bags into my truck, the rich aroma of coffee filled my nostrils. I shut the door and glanced at the window of Five Beans. One small coffee wouldn't break the bank.

I locked the truck and wandered into the coffeeshop. The smells were even stronger and more aromatic inside. Rita, the owner, worked alone behind the counter. She seemed frazzled, not that I blamed her. The place was packed.

I stood in line behind a middle-aged couple.

"I heard it's going to snow all week," the man said. He was wrapped up warm in a plaid coat and a hat with attached earflaps.

"It better not," his companion said. "We need to drive into the city on Thursday for your cardiologist appointment. It'll be a madhouse."

"It isn't snowing in the city," another customer interjected. "My daughter lives there and she said it's been clear skies there."

"That's odd," the man said.

I didn't disagree. New York City was only a hop, skip, and a jump across the river. The weather pattern should be roughly the same.

A familiar voice reached my ears. I turned to see Chief

Elena Garcia seated at a table with a man I didn't recognize. He was tall and well-built, with an envious head of salt and pepper hair and a fabulous tan. Looking at him conjured up images of palm trees and little umbrellas in cocktails.

Once I got my coffee, I made my way over to say hello. It never hurt to stay on the good side of law enforcement.

"Lorelei Clay, nice to see you. Crazy weather, isn't it?" Chief Garcia motioned to her companion. "Have you met Lance Needham?"

"I haven't." I was still wearing my gloves, so I shook his hand without bothering to fortify my mind. "Good to meet you, Lance."

He gave me an appraising look. "You're the one who bought Bluebeard's Castle, aren't you?"

"Yes, I'm the lunatic." I figured I might as well say it before he did.

He smiled. "I used to spend time up there as a kid. Good memories."

"Lance grew up here, but he lives in Palm Beach now."

"I'm only here for the holidays," he tacked on. "Elena's been really good with keeping an eye on my folks. They're as old as the hills, but they refuse to move to an assisted living facility."

"To be fair, they're in decent shape," the chief said. "As long as they can take care of themselves, I see no reason why they should move."

"Because you've got to think ahead at their age," he argued. "One fall down the stairs and your life changes forever." He sneezed. "Can we take the decorations down now? All this mistletoe is aggravating my sinuses."

"I didn't know you could be allergic to mistletoe," I said.

Chief Garcia laughed. "Are you kidding? These days there's an allergy to basically everything. I know a guy allergic to sunshine. Can you imagine?"

That guy was likely a vampire, but I kept that nugget to

myself. "What's the world coming to?" I said, for lack of a better comment.

Lance sneezed again. "See? I'll be happier when the other wreaths are back on the doors, too. All this change is unsettling and for what? One day of excess? Not worth it, if you ask me."

And I thought I was bad. Lance was the ultimate Scrooge. I was relieved when he excused himself to use the restroom.

Chief Garcia gestured to his empty chair. "Sit, Lorelei. Drink your coffee."

I sat. If nothing else, it would be a good opportunity to ask about sightings of a lost dog. "How's the snow impacting you?" I asked.

"Oddly enough, crime is way up. I don't know what's gotten into everybody."

"It's the holidays. It makes people feel desperate," I said, recalling how I felt when I saw the price tag on the gingerbread loaf. A crime wave at the holidays sounded normal enough. "How way up are we talking compared with this time last year?"

"I spoke to a handful of colleagues, and Fairhaven seems to be an isolated case. In fact, crime rates are down everywhere else."

An isolated case. I had a feeling there was a reason for that and it started with 'C' and ended with 'rossroads.'

"Are they violent crimes?" I asked, thinking of the incident at the Devil's Playground.

"Some, but the number of robberies this month seems outrageous given our small population. There was also a murder-suicide that I wish I didn't have to deal with. The crime scene will haunt me for months—if I'm lucky."

"A domestic dispute?" I asked.

"An affair gone wrong. It seems John Landisville couldn't live without Connie Greenburg."

Lance returned to the table with another chair and sat. "You talking about Landisville?"

The chief nodded.

"Connie was married, I take it?" I asked.

"Twenty-one years. The weird thing is she and John only met a couple weeks ago, and nobody noticed they had the hots for each other. Seems awfully fast to establish the kind of intense passion that ends up in a murdery mess."

"What did Connie's husband have to say?"

"He's still in shock. He said Connie was a devoted wife and mother and that she never so much as looked at another man in all the years they were married."

"It happens," Lance interjected. "I remember my neighbors a few years back. One couple moved next door, and the husband fell in love with the wife of the house across the street. It was a big brouhaha when the spouses found out. They both sold up and moved."

"They stayed married?" I asked.

"One did, and the other couple divorced."

"But nobody killed anybody over it," the chief said.

"Thank goodness for that, no."

"There's also a large snake on the loose, according to John's neighbor. Etta Robinson is sure it's a python." The chief heaved a sigh. "I explained to her that pythons aren't native to this area."

"Speaking of loose animals," I began, "has anybody lost a large dog that you know of?"

She frowned. "No reports that I'm aware of."

"I heard there was a wild boar sighting in Wild Acres," Lance said. "That seems fairly exotic for our little town."

"A wild boar?" Closing her eyes, the chief rubbed her forehead. "I'm glad I hired Officer Leo in the nick of time, or I'd be even worse off. He's got his hands full, too."

"He sure had his hands full the other night," Lance said. "I saw him canoodling with a very attractive lady."

"Canoodling?" the chief repeated. "Is he a celebrity now? I thought they were the only ones that canoodle."

Lance let loose a wolf whistle. "She could do shampoo commercials, that one. The shine on her hair…" He shook his head ruefully. "No human has a right to hair that glossy."

"Says the man with a mane that rivals Ted Danson's," the chief commented.

Lance raked a hand through his hair. "I can't take any credit. It's pure genetics."

"I wish I had those genes," she said. "Mousy brown isn't exactly a color in demand."

He gave her head an admiring glance. "It isn't mousy at all. More like a badger."

The chief snorted. "Great. Badger-colored hair is what all the ladies are after."

I finished my coffee. "I should probably get home. I've got groceries in the car."

"What are you worried about?" Lance asked. "Nothing will thaw in this weather."

"True, but I've got a project I'd like to get started."

Lance regarded me with sympathy. "I have a feeling that house is one never-ending project after another."

"But it'll all be worth it when it's done," the chief interjected. "It's a great house you've got there."

"Thanks, Chief."

I drove home, salivating over the smell of the gingerbread loaf. If it tasted as good as it smelled, I was in for a treat.

In the kitchen, I forged a connection with Nana Pratt and inhaled the scent of the gingerbread loaf. The ghost's eyes sparkled with delight.

"I can smell it!" She closed her eyes and soaked in the sensation. "Thank you, Lorelei. This brings back so many wonderful memories."

Hope flared in Ray's eyes. "Did you get the nuts?"

I released my hold on Nana Pratt. Then I produced a small

bag from the larger one and shook it at him. "Don't worry, big guy. I wouldn't leave you out."

"They don't have much of a smell," he said.

"We're not going to enjoy the smell." I tore open the bag and popped a handful into my mouth. As I chewed, I formed a connection with Ray. I focused on the taste of each item—the almond, the walnut, the peanut, and the chocolate chip.

Ray smacked his lips. "Just the way I remember it. Delicious."

Nana Pratt looked at me in awe. "How do you do that?"

"One of my gifts that I've now shared with you." They deserved it after all that work in the dining room.

"I didn't realize a medium could share their experiences with ghosts," Ray commented.

"I'm not a medium," I said.

"No, I guess not with those shoulders," Nana Pratt remarked.

I unpacked the rest of the groceries, mulling over what I'd heard in the coffeeshop about the strange weather and the uptick in crime. There was a supernatural feel to them, but I wasn't sure how—or if—they were related.

After a decadent lunch of PB and J washed down by a glass of water, I helped the ghosts clean up the mess in the dining room. The wall already looked a hundred times better. It was amazing what one small change could achieve.

I spent the rest of the afternoon drafting a list of projects in order of priority, as well as the materials required. If I didn't already own them, I'd start in order of cheapest to most expensive. The latter was Nana Pratt's suggestion. She also looked at my numbers and said I'd need a job by February if I expected to pay my bills. It wasn't the news I wanted to hear.

I needed a distraction, so I picked up the phone and called West. "Any news on Chutney?"

"Not yet."

"I went looking for a dog last night, but I only found a hungry fae." I told him about Sage's thieves.

"People get desperate this time of year."

"That's what I said." I shared Chief Garcia's crime report.

"I'll send wolves out to patrol tonight," West said. "They can do a sweep through the neighborhoods."

"I stopped by the crossroads last night, too," I said. "The guards weren't the same ones on duty when Chutney died."

"So?"

"I was wondering if you'd spoken to them."

"Not in relation to Chutney."

His answer surprised me. "You didn't think it was worth speaking to them about any creatures emerging from the crossroads?"

"If there'd been anything strange, they would've reported it. Bert only thinks he saw a dog. Hardly a monster from another realm." He paused. "Still, I take your point. They're asleep now because they're on duty again tonight. I'll speak to them then."

I didn't wait for an invitation. "I'll join you."

"This is a pack problem, Clay. No need to insert yourself."

"It ceased to be a pack problem when you came to me for help."

"I only came to you because I thought there was a chance you could speak to Chutney's ghost. Beyond that, we don't need you."

His response bothered me, and it took me a moment to realize why. "I want to earn your trust, West. Let me help." Maybe it was because of Kane's hasty departure, but I felt a deep and sudden need for West to accept me. The alpha was a de facto leader in town. If I could win him over, then … then what? What did West's approval mean?

That I belonged. Gods, I hated that I cared, but I did.

"Fine," he said. "You can come, but they're my wolves. Let me do the talking."

. . .

I offered to meet West at an access point, but the alpha insisted on being a gentleman and picking me up from the Castle. As much as I wanted to resist, the likelihood that my truck would die en route outweighed my ego.

"Be careful," I said, as I slid into the passenger seat. "You keep showing up at my house like this and people are going to think you like me."

I caught the hint of a smile. "It's a professional courtesy. That's all." He turned up the volume on the radio, which was his not-so-subtle way of drowning out the sound of my voice. Christmas music dominated the airwaves, and he kept changing the station, hoping for a different outcome.

"I like Christmas music," I said, humming along to "Fairytale of New York" by The Pogues.

"That surprises me."

I glanced sidelong at him. "Why?"

"You're the only house in town without any holiday decorations. Would it have killed you to stick a wreath on your front door?"

"Yes, I think it would have." I leaned back against the seat. "What do you care whether I hang a wreath?"

"I don't. I only said it surprised me that you enjoy Christmas music."

Holiday tunes lacked the emotional impact of other music, which was one reason I was willing to indulge myself. There was no fear that my powers would surge to the surface when I listened to Wham!'s "Last Christmas." It was one of the few types of music I allowed myself to enjoy without concern.

Flurries scattered across the windshield and melted upon contact. I was starting to feel like we were trapped in a supernatural snow globe and an unseen hand would eventually shake us up.

He parked the truck on a flattened snowbank. I zipped up

my coat as I exited. I noticed West didn't bother with a coat. His black shirt looked flimsy, like an article of stripper clothing he could discard in a heartbeat if the situation required it. Snowflakes clung to the ends of his light brown hair. The dampness made the slight curls more pronounced. His jawline seemed to be in a permanent state of stubble. I couldn't have hacked it as a werewolf. I needed smooth skin.

"What do you think about this snow?" he asked, as we trudged through the forest.

I admired the white branches around us. "It's prettier here than on my walkways."

"I don't mean how it looks. I mean how it feels."

I cut a glance at him. "You don't think it's natural?"

"Are you telling me you do?"

"No," I admitted. "It feels off."

"Glad we can agree on something."

I jumped over a log. "Why are you so hostile toward me? I haven't done anything to you."

"You have the option not to take my behavior personally. You realize that, don't you?"

"Except I've seen how you behave with your pack. They idolize you. You don't treat me the way you treat them."

"Because you're not a member of my pack. You're not even a werewolf."

"Well, I live here now, West, and I'm not going anywhere, so you might as well get used to me."

The sound of rushing water drowned out his noncommittal response. We'd arrived at the Falls. The waterfall appeared unaffected by the weather, cascading down the hill and crashing over rocks in spectacular fashion. The scenic waterfall was the likely culprit for the town's supernatural magnetism. It acted as a conductor, absorbing the supernatural energy generated by multiple gates at the crossroads and spreading it through the surrounding area. The air buzzed with its strength.

West inhaled deeply. "This has to be one of the most beautiful places on earth, hands down."

"Is that why you stayed in Fairhaven?" I asked. "Because it was pretty?"

He gave me a dark look and continued walking until we reached the crossroads. The only indication that the supernatural gateway existed, apart from the powerful currents of energy that emanated from it, was a Nordic design for Yggdrasil, the tree of life. To the untrained eye, the design simply looked like the artistic carving on a mighty oak tree. To those in the know, however, Yggdrasil represented much more—a tree connected to the nine realms of the universe. It seemed that the Norse had vastly underestimated that number though.

A few feet in front of the crossroads, two werewolves kicked a soccer ball between them. They'd cleared enough snow so that the ball rolled across the damp ground.

"Is this a private game or can anybody play?" I asked.

The ball rolled past the feet of the stocky brunette as he stopped to stare at us. I instantly identified Meathead's brother, Ivan. They had the same prominent brow ridge.

"Sorry, West," the kicker said. "We just wanted to release a little energy without leaving the post."

"I don't have a problem with it," West said. "As long as you're paying attention to what comes in and out of that gateway, we're good."

"On that note," I began, "did you happen to see any creatures scamper in or out the night before last?"

"Define creature," the kicker said.

I held back an impatient groan.

"Anything or anyone at all," West said. "You know we've got a wolf down, and Bert says he might've seen a lost dog in the area."

"What kind of dog?" Ivan asked.

"Doesn't matter. Did you see any dog at all?" West asked.

"Any animal," I added. "If you saw an ant crawling out of the crossroads, I want to know about it."

Ivan lit up. "Hey, you're the Ruins lady. Meathead told me about your chat last night."

Beside me West heaved a deep sigh.

"Is his name actually Meathead?" I asked.

"Since his sixth birthday," Ivan replied.

"And what was it before that?"

"Dyson, but he didn't like being associated with a vacuum. Everyone kept telling him he sucked."

"Because Meathead is so much better," I mumbled.

Ivan picked up the ball and bounced it off his knees. "It is to a six-year-old."

The kicker regarded us. "To answer your question, we didn't see anything that night."

"But we thought we heard the sound of gunshots," Ivan added. "Turns out that was Chutney."

"What really happened to him?" the kicker asked. "I've heard a dozen theories, and none of them makes any sense."

"If witnesses saw a dog, wouldn't they have been able to track its scent?" Ivan asked. "Lucas and I can scent a dog from a mile away, and we haven't smelled one here recently."

"That's what we're trying to piece together," West said. "Any more questions or can I ask mine now?"

The guards lowered their heads.

"I heard what Chutney looked like when they found him," Ivan said. "There's no way a dog did that to him."

I was impressed that West managed to not lose his temper. I was ready to pick up the soccer ball and ping them both in the head with it. I was beginning to think they named the wrong brother Meathead.

"Unless a demon came through the crossroads and Bert mistook it for a dog, but I know if any living creature crossed that boundary, one of you would've reported it, right?" West folded his arms and gauged their reactions with alpha-style intensity.

"No dogs or creatures," Lucas said.

"It was a quiet night," Ivan added. "I assume because of the shit weather. Didn't even catch a glimpse of the regulars."

"The regulars?" I queried.

"You know, the squirrels and deer," Ivan replied. "In fact, the only living creature we saw that night apart from each other was Kane Sullivan."

It took me a split second to register the response. "I'm sorry. What now?"

"The demon dude who owns the nightclub," Ivan explained.

"I know who Kane Sullivan is. You're telling me he's back in Fairhaven?"

"Sure is," Ivan said. "He sauntered straight out of the crossroads. Said "good evening" to us like he was wearing a top hat and a monocle, and carried on walking like it was all perfectly normal."

The prospect of Kane's return both thrilled and terrified me. I'd decide which one the next time I saw him.

"His suit was immaculate," Lucas commented. "If I owned a suit like that—well, I wouldn't because it would be dirty and ripped by sundown. Complete waste of money."

My whole body tensed at the thought of him. "We're not here to talk about Sullivan."

Lucas cracked his knuckles. "We are if he had something to do with Chutney's death."

"I'm not worried about Sullivan," West said.

Maybe he wasn't, but I was, albeit for different reasons.

"Next time somebody enters town via the crossroads, I want that reported," West told them.

"But he lives here," Lucas protested. "We didn't think it was necessary."

"I want a complete and accurate list," West said. "I'll decide later whether the information is necessary."

"Yes, alpha," the guards said in unison. West was diplomatic and considerate, but he could be tough when the situation demanded it.

I had a hard time concentrating on the remainder of the conversation. My head was pounding, and my mouth was dry. That bastard had been back in town long enough to contact me. I would've even accepted one of those vague "hi" texts men were so fond of sending.

Except Kane Sullivan wasn't a man. He was a demon and a prince of hell and, apparently, he was above communication with mere mortals—or goddesses reincarnated.

I heard West arrive at a natural stopping point in the conversation and jumped in. "If you think of anything else, I want to know sooner rather than later, got it?"

I didn't wait for their response. I turned to retrace my steps along the trail. My mind buzzed with angry facts. If Kane came home the night Chutney died, that meant he was more than likely at the nightclub when I was there. The fact that Josephine had lied straight to my face didn't surprise me, but the others… I'd bet good money there *had* been an impromptu guild meeting. My blood began to boil.

West hurried to catch up to my long strides. "You good, Clay?"

"Just releasing a little energy like your friends." I had no interest in confiding in West. The alpha already disliked me. If he knew my secret, he'd want me gone now more than ever. "I'm sorry I wasn't more helpful."

"You ask good questions, and you get to the point. There's a lot to be said for brevity."

I squinted at him. "Thanks," I said. I heard the note of suspicion that inadvertently crept into my voice.

West must've heard it, too, because he said, "Look. You didn't have to agree to help me. I know I haven't been the friendliest guy." We reached his truck, and he unlocked the doors. "I guess what I'm saying is, I appreciate your willingness to help the pack."

"Despite your unwelcoming attitude. You forgot that part at the end."

He dragged a hand through his thick hair. "Yeah, and that."

"I'd like to know what happened to Chutney, and I'd like to know whether this mysterious animal was a figment of Bert's imagination. If you figure it out, please let me know. I may be new to town, but I still care about what happens here."

We climbed into the truck, and West switched the heater on full blast.

"You don't need to sweat for my benefit," I said, lowering the intensity.

"You're a guest in my truck. Keeping you comfortable is a show of respect." The truck bumped over a couple mounds of snow as the tires found the road.

"You respect me? That's new."

"I'm wary of you, I fully admit that, but sometimes…" He trailed off.

"Sometimes what?"

He kept his gaze on the darkness ahead. "Sometimes you remind me of me."

Interesting. "In what way?"

"You ever hear of Tony Robbins?"

"He's the self-help guru." Now I was really curious where this conversation was headed.

"I prefer life strategist. Anyway, Robbins identified six basic human needs—love and connection, significance, certainty, growth, variety, and contribution."

"Needs for survival?"

"And a life well lived." He cast me a sidelong glance. "Guess which one of those needs is my priority?"

It only took me a nanosecond to decide. "Contribution."

"Yep, and what would you say is yours if you had to rank them in order of importance to you?"

"Certainty, I guess."

He smirked. "That explains the fortress."

"Okay, you've ranked your needs. How does that help you?"

"Our lives are the least stressful and the most meaningful when our day-to-day is in alignment with our basic needs. Contribution is my number one. I feed that need by acting as the alpha of the Arrowhead wolf pack and helping the community when necessary."

"I'm not sure my life became less stressful when I bought the Castle. In fact, I'd say it's far more stressful than it's ever been."

"No shit. You know why?"

"Because I make poor financial decisions?"

He turned onto the main artery that led into town. "Because you're out of alignment, Clay. Your brain keeps trying to redirect you to your authentic self. I bet you dollars to donuts that contribution and connection are your top two needs, but you keep pushing them down in favor of something else. What I'd like to know is—why?"

This conversation was hitting too close to home. Between Kane's sudden reappearance and West's scrutiny, I was crawling out of my skin. My gaze landed on the local watering hole. Any port in a storm.

"Hey, West. Would you mind dropping me off?"

"What do you think I'm doing right now?"

"Not at my house. Here."

His gaze skated to the dive bar. "Why doesn't it surprise me that Sullivan drives women to drink?"

My whole body stiffened. "This has nothing to do with him."

"What then? You think someone here might've spotted a lost dog in the woods?"

"Or maybe they're the owner of one. I could confirm Bert's account."

He stopped the truck and opened the driver's side door. "See, Clay? Contribution. Think about it."

I couldn't get out of the truck fast enough. "Thanks for the lift."

CHAPTER 5

Monk's was the local bar favored by humans and shifters. It was often referred to as a dive bar, a description with which I wholeheartedly agreed. The outside looked like it was being held together by the power of duct tape and the collective will of its beer-guzzling patrons. The interior didn't try much harder. Half the stools were broken, and the seats on the other half had the appearance of a well-worn teddy bear.

The music was loud, but the drinkers were louder. If I strained to listen, I could hear the faint sound of "Start Me Up" by the Rolling Stones.

I skirted a yellow 'Caution: Wet Floor' sign as I made my way to the busy counter. The inclement weather seemed to have no effect on the social butterflies, or more accurately, barflies; Monk's was bursting at the seams. I felt like Play-Doh being pushed through the grinder as I squeezed between two burgeoning beer bellies to reach the counter.

"I heard he tried to win himself a free 72-ounce steak and pushed himself too far," the belly to my left was in the midst of telling his companion.

"I feel sorry for Jackie," his companion said. "According to her sister, the cleanup was the nastiest thing she'd ever seen, and she's an ER nurse."

My stomach turned as my imagination joined the conversation.

"More people die of obesity than hunger," the companion continued. "Bet you thought malnutrition would be the real killer but nope."

"I call bullshit on that. Cite your sources, Hank."

Hank pulled a face. "Try opening a book once in a while instead of reaching for the remote. Books are heavier, give your arms a better workout."

The bartender finally spotted me and made his way over. "What can I get you?"

A different conversation was my first thought, but I opted for whatever was on tap. "Surprisingly busy tonight," I remarked.

"You should see us during a real blizzard. You'd think we were giving away free sleds."

Monk's was a reasonable distance from downtown Fairhaven. Then again, the roads between here and there didn't experience a high volume of traffic, and many residents drove all-terrain vehicles.

My gaze snagged on Officer Leo Kilkenny at the opposite end of the bar. Officer Leo was even newer to Fairhaven than I was. He replaced a cop who'd been killed by a culebrón summoned by the overly ambitious Bridger witches. So far, he seemed friendly and sweet for a guy with a gun. He noticed me and lifted his pint in greeting. I frowned as I studied the woman next to him. It took me a second to place the tattooed woman from the Devil's Playground, the one who'd raised a glass of champagne to me during the fight. I wondered whether she was the same woman with whom he'd been spotted by Chief Garcia's friend.

Officer Leo motioned for me to join them. I pretended not

to notice, but a shrill whistle and the call of my name from across the bar made it impossible to ignore.

I carried my beer to the other end of the long counter, sipping it as I walked so as not to spill any. In a place like this, you spill a couple drops on the wrong pair of boots and you'd find yourself outside, facedown in the snow. I made it safely to my destination with three-quarters of my beer still in the cup.

"Good to see you again, Officer Leo."

"Lady Lorelei of the Castle." He performed a mock bow. "Staying warm, I hope."

"That's what the beer is for." I inclined my head. "Wasn't there a woman standing next to you a minute ago?"

"She went to the bathroom. Her name's Addy."

"She's pretty."

His smile broadened. "I know, right? I met her here last week. We've hung out a few times since then."

"Is she new in town?"

"Might be soon. She's been interviewing for jobs in the city and wants that small-town feel if she relocates to the area."

"In that case, she can't do better than Fairhaven."

"That's what I told her. I know I'm still new here, but this place already feels like home." He chugged his beer. "I'll introduce you when she comes back. I bet you two would hit it off."

I wasn't so sure. "What makes you think that?"

"She's got that worldly vibe like you."

I laughed. "I have a worldly vibe?"

He seemed concerned that I'd taken offense. "I don't mean you're a sophisticated snob or anything, far from it."

I'd always prided myself on being down to earth. That was all Pops. He'd made sure I didn't think too highly of myself given my identity. I was a reincarnated goddess, sure, but I still had to do my chores and finish my homework on time. Humble pie was a regular item on the menu, and he was willing to serve it all day every day.

The tattooed woman threaded her way through the tangle of bodies until she reached us. She tucked a loose strand of lustrous brown hair behind her ear.

"That was a more harrowing experience than I anticipated," she said. "I need another drink."

Officer Leo grinned. "That can be easily arranged. Addison Gray, this is my friend Lorelei Clay." He brightened. "Hey, your names rhyme."

"Must be fate," Addison said. She offered a hand, which I politely declined to shake.

"Sorry, my hands are sticky from the beer," I lied. "I don't want to gross you out."

"I just shared a bathroom with a woman who preferred to keep her stall door open," Addison said. "I can take it."

There was no way I was touching this mysterious woman, not when she set off my supernatural radar. She had to be the same woman Lance had seen. No human should have hair that glossy, he'd commented. Newsflash, Lance. They don't. It shouldn't come as a surprise. I'd first seen her at the Devil's Playground, which was a supernatural hotspot. I was usually better at identifying supernaturals, though. Strange that I didn't register her signature.

"Officer Leo says you're looking for a job in the city," I said.

Addison smiled. "You call him Officer Leo? That's adorable."

Officer Leo didn't seem amused. "Because I'm an officer of the law. It's respectful."

Addison nudged him with her shoulder. "Should I be more respectful the next time I borrow those handcuffs of yours, Leo?"

The blood rushed to his face. "Who needs another drink? This round's on me."

"How about shots?" Addison suggested. "The weak beer isn't doing it for me."

"Shots it is." Officer Leo turned to signal the bartender.

Even with his back turned, I made sure to keep the handsome cop between us to avoid any physical contact with Addison.

"Yo, we've got a Code Green," a voice yelled.

The bartender picked up a megaphone from behind the counter and repeated the message to someone by the jukebox.

"Dare I ask what a Code Green is?" Addison asked.

Officer Leo groaned. "If Chief Garcia is to be believed, it means someone drank enough to get their stomach pumped. Probably a college kid home for the holidays." He passed his shot glass to Addison. "I'd better go check. Be right back."

With Officer Leo gone, Addison looked at me with a strange mixture of curiosity and familiarity. "Alone at last."

"Excuse me?"

"I noticed you at the Devil's Playground the other night. Great name for a nightclub, isn't it? You subdued that big guy like he was a harmless kitten." Her gaze traveled down my body. "I admire a woman with that kind of strength and confidence."

"Thank you. Interesting tattoos," I said, eyeing the interlocking symbols on her arm.

"I have a few more you can't see with my clothes on, if you're interested in checking them out later."

Addison didn't know the meaning of the word 'subtle,' that much was clear. "I'm not really into tattoos. I was being polite."

Despite my admission, her smile remained intact. "If you can fight with that level of passion and skill when the stakes are low, I'd love to see what you can do when they're higher."

It was an odd compliment. Then again, Addison Gray struck me as an odd woman. It bothered me that I couldn't identify her species. Touching her would be the fastest way to get information, but I wasn't willing to give her any of my own. Gods willing, she wouldn't land a job, and Fairhaven would be spared her permanent presence.

"It was no big deal," I said. "I like the club, and I didn't want to see it get wrecked." *I thought the owner was out of town but turns out he was right there all along. And if he wasn't such a chicken shit, he could've stopped the fight himself.*

Officer Leo returned, looking grim. "Monk's doesn't tend to overserve, but that guy's vomiting like he's trying to turn himself inside out."

I cringed. "That description will haunt me. Did you call an ambulance?"

"His friend did. Should be here any minute."

"Do you need to stay with them?" Addison asked. "I wouldn't want to interfere with your civic duty, Officer Leo."

He grinned at her. "Aren't you sweet? I think they can handle it without me."

The wailing sound of a siren cut through the din of the bar and had the added bonus of interrupting the conversation, for which I was grateful. I didn't want Addison's rapt attention, not when anonymity was the key to my survival.

Emergency workers entered the bar, causing a stir. I took the opportunity to sneak out the door. The parking lot was covered in slush as I started toward the road. My boots would need a good scrub tomorrow. It was a hike from here to the Castle. With the cold air already biting my face and my fingers sure to freeze inside my gloves, I was beginning to regret my decision to walk.

As I considered an Uber, a small object ricocheted off the back of my head. "Ouch!" I rubbed the injured spot and turned around to identify my attacker. "Who did that?"

The only light was from Monk's.

I looked down to see a perfectly round rock. A second, smaller rock pelted my forehead.

"What the hell?" I yelled.

A shadow darted between cars. The movement was too fast to determine whether my attacker was human or supernatural, although the speed suggested the latter.

I waited to see whether another rock would come flying my way. Instead, I was greeted by a flying fist. My unseen assailant managed to throw a sucker punch from the shadows and promptly disappear again. There were many demons and monsters with the invisibility trait. I needed more information before I could identify this one and decide how to best defend myself. I couldn't risk the creature entering the bar. Most of the patrons were human; they'd be sitting ducks for someone like this.

I stood still and concentrated, listening for sounds of movement. If I could anticipate his next move, I might be able to catch him.

The door to Monk's opened, and Officer Leo stumbled outside. I swore under my breath. I didn't want the cop to get involved. He and Chief Garcia were fairly oblivious to the supernatural happenings in town, and it seemed best to keep it that way.

He stood awkwardly in the parking lot, scanning the area. I cringed when his glassy gaze landed on me. "Lorelei, is that you?"

"Hey," I said weakly. "What are you doing?"

"Looking for my car." A thick branch soared overhead. He looked up in confusion. "Who threw that?"

"Someone's having a good time assaulting me with elements of nature," I said. "I'm hanging around until I catch him."

"It's probably one of those college kids. They've been up to no good all night."

Unless those college kids had acquired an invisibility cloak from Hogwarts, I highly doubted they were responsible.

I put a finger to my lips. Officer Leo nodded. "Could you

help me find my car after I find your prankster?" he asked in a stage whisper.

I groaned. It seemed the officer was too tipsy to remain silent.

A car alarm sounded off. The silhouette was startled from his hiding spot and forced into the open. Officer Leo sprang into action, leaping over the hood of the car to tackle the assailant.

"I've got him!" the cop's voice rang out.

I ran over to see him wrestling with empty air. The shadow was gone.

The cop sat on the ground, baffled. "I had him, I swear."

I patted his shoulder. "I know you did."

"I think I drank too much." His hangdog gaze shifted to me. "Would you mind giving me a lift? My date already left."

I hadn't seen Addison leave, but he was in no state to argue with.

"I got dropped off," I said. "I was planning to walk or Uber."

"Drive my car. I'm not fit to drive anyway."

Those shots must've caught up with him quickly. "Come on, hero. I'll drop you at home."

"Thanks. I'm on a public servant's salary," he said, slurring his words. "The cost of a car service adds up fast."

I helped him into the passenger seat of the car. "I didn't realize you'd had that much to drink."

"Me neither. It didn't seem like a lot at the time." He rested his forehead against the side window. "I swear, the beer here is laced with regret."

I laughed as I reversed out of the spot. "That's one possible ingredient. What's your address?" I plugged it into the phone's GPS as he told me.

"I can't believe she left," he murmured. "We were getting along really well." He sighed loudly. "Story of my life."

"I'm sorry. I'm sure it wasn't personal. It's late. She probably got tired and didn't want you to feel obligated to leave too."

"I don't think she has those kinds of feelings." He yawned. "She was more into fun."

"Fun can be good." Not that I would know. I had neither fun nor feelings.

"I should never date someone I met during a traffic stop."

I squinted at the passing headlights. "Are you serious? That's how you met?"

"She was speeding. Seventy in a thirty zone." He shook his head. "I should've known."

"That she plays fast and loose with the rules?" I didn't need to give her a ticket to figure that out.

"I need to meet a nice young lady with a bright future." His voice was almost inaudible now. "But she's got to have a great ass."

"Everybody needs standards," I said, pulling into the driveway of an old brick townhouse. "Home sweet home."

He seemed to notice the townhouse for the first time. "Oh, I live here."

"You do. Need help getting inside?"

"I can do it. Thanks."

I turned off the car and handed him the keys. "I'll walk home from here so you have your car in the morning."

"Good thinking. I have to work." He grimaced. "I'm going to be so hungover."

I watched as he practically crawled to the front door. It took him a solid minute to master the key and the lock. "Don't forget to hydrate!"

He gave me a shaky thumbs-up as he stumbled inside. Once the door closed, I headed for home.

The walk was dark and cold, but I needed the outlet. I stomped to the point where my knees hurt, and my teeth rattled. I didn't care. I needed to work through the aggression I was feeling. Kane had waltzed into town like a Downton

Abbey gentleman, but did I have any messages or missed calls? No. No, I did not.

The angry part of me wanted to swing by the nightclub and give him a piece of my mind. I immediately felt guilty for using that turn of phrase, given Chutney's current state. I'd have to think of a better one that didn't invoke the werewolf's remains.

A cooler head prevailed, and I walked all the way home without embarrassing myself or injuring any princes of hell. Brownie points for me.

I marched through the gate and across the bridge. A lone figure sat on my front porch. My heart jumped. Maybe Kane hadn't called because he'd opted to show up in person. That was forgivable.

Except Kane didn't own a fuzzy purple coat that made him look like a giant Muppet.

CHAPTER 6

Gunther glanced up as I approached. His boots looked more appropriate for the runway than the walkway, but I'd come to expect that from Gun. The mage had more fashion than sense.

"Where have you been?" he demanded. "It's late, and I'm frozen solid. You're now speaking to an ice sculpture."

I did the mature thing and ignored him. He leaned to the side to give me room to pass.

I unlocked the front door and said, "I'm not speaking to you."

He moved to an upright position to stand behind me. "Really? Because you're saying words right now, and I'm the only one hearing them."

"I can hear them, too," Ray said, materializing out of thin air.

I shifted my glare to the ghost. "Rules, Ray."

He promptly disappeared.

"Can I come in before my mascara freezes to my lashes?" Gun asked. "My eyes are too sensitive to handle the fallout."

I entered the house but blocked the doorway to prevent Gun from following. "You lied to me."

He opened his mouth as if to object, then seemed to think better of it. "I had no choice. I was sworn to secrecy."

"Since when does that matter?"

"If you'd seen Kane's face when he told us to keep his presence confidential, you'd understand."

"So there *was* a guild meeting. I knew it!"

He nodded. "We got a mysterious text from Josie calling an emergency meeting."

"What was the emergency?"

"That Kane had returned and wanted us to know. It was straight back to business as usual, like he never left."

"Did he say why he left?"

He cocked an eyebrow. "What do you think? Kane doesn't share personal information with anybody."

But I'd shared with him. And I sorely regretted it.

"I'm more than happy for you to rake me over the coals right now," Gun said, dancing from side to side to stay warm. "Anything for a little heat."

"You won't find much in my house. Some of the radiators must be on the fritz." I stepped aside to let him pass.

"Anything's better than outside." He removed his coat and hung it on the rack. "I'm glad to see you're putting the coat rack I bought to good use. I'd murder for a hot drink right now."

"That isn't saying much when you murder for a living."

"A hot drink would be a major discount." He walked ahead of me into the kitchen. "Why not have these radiators ripped out and install a modern heating system?"

I stared at him. "You're already on my list. Do you want to dig yourself deeper?"

He looked blank. "What do you mean?"

"You had to buy me a coat rack. Do you think I have the kind of money that pays for a new heating system? This is an old house. A new system means new duct work."

"I see your point." He opened the cabinet. "Do you have

any decaf? I'm not sure I should be caffeinated at this hour."

I pushed past him to reach the cabinet and removed a bag of coffee. "Decaf is an abomination. I can make tea."

"No, coffee is better." He glanced at the bag. "Next time could you get a medium roast? The dark roast upsets my stomach." He offered a cheeky smile. "Happy to see it's organic, though."

"You're this close to getting booted." I held my index finger a hair from my thumb.

"Listen, I'm the one spitting nails at the moment."

"Are we talking literally or figuratively?" When it came to the mage assassin, one couldn't be too sure.

He let loose a dramatic sigh. "You haven't even asked me why I walked here."

"I wasn't aware that you did."

"Somebody stole my car," Gun complained. "Who steals a car from an assassin?"

"I'd say somebody who didn't know the owner of the vehicle."

"Fair, but my street is protected. It shouldn't have been able to happen."

"What do you mean by protected?"

Gun's eyelashes fluttered in dismay. "I mean we have a protection ward on the street that prevents property crimes. Nobody should've been able to bypass it with my car while it didn't contain me."

"Why not use a ward like that for the whole town? It would save Chief Garcia a lot of work."

Gun gave me a long look. "I'm a mage, not a miracle worker. And the real salt in the wound is I saw a snake disappear into the sewer."

"How is that related?"

"It isn't. It just made my day that much worse." He shuddered. "I'm like the Indiana Jones of the mage world. I hate snakes."

"Don't let your enemies know. They might use it against you."

"I have too many cards up my sleeve to worry."

"This time you do mean literally, right?"

He unbuttoned his cuff and rolled up a sleeve to reveal a stack of tarot cards fastened to his arm. "Always be prepared. Assassin's motto."

"And the Boy Scouts. I bet you both know how to start a fire, too. Who knew you had so much in common?"

"My fire is harder to put out. I usually add a little something extra to give it some staying power."

I held my hands over my ears. "I don't want to know any more." My blossoming friendship with Gun meant ignoring some of the more distasteful aspects of his profession.

"I don't kill without good cause, remember?" He adjusted his sleeve. "Or a good paycheck."

"You need to afford those designer shirts somehow."

His head bobbed with enthusiasm. "See? You get me, Lorelei. That's why I like you."

"Did you file a police report about the car?"

"No, I was thinking I'd go through private channels. More efficient."

"Chief Garcia is up to her eyeballs in cases right now, so you probably made a wise decision."

"You know who didn't make a wise decision?"

"The person who stole your car?"

He showed me a set of perfect teeth that only money or magic could procure. "Exactly, although I doubt a regular human would've been able to bypass the ward. It had to be someone supernatural, like your special friend…"

I shot him a warning glance. "Don't you dare say his name."

His brow furrowed. "Otto Visconti? Why, did you two have a fight?"

Oh, right. Otto. "No, but Otto has a fleet of cars. He'd never steal one."

"Interesting choice of collectibles for a blind vampire," Gun said.

"When you're as rich as Otto, you do as you please."

Gun scowled. "Same can be said for our mutual friend Magnarella. You haven't had any horse heads left on your welcome mat, have you?"

"My mat doesn't welcome anybody."

He chuckled. "Yet people keep turning up anyway. Why don't they get the hint?"

I watched the coffee percolate. "Seriously, though. Why don't they?"

"Because it's too subtle. That's the midwestern version of go away. You need one that's more New York City."

"A giant fist that punches them back outside the gate?"

He nodded. "That would send a strong message. Might be a problem when the chief pays you a visit, though."

My mind kept turning. "Is there any chance Magnarella could be responsible for the crime wave?"

"He threatened you specifically. I'm not sure how wreaking havoc in the town is a problem for you." Gun pursed his full lips, pondering the issue. "Then again, he knows you stepped in for my sister. Maybe he assumes you'll do the same for the town. Still, it doesn't seem to hurt you, and my impression is that he wants you to suffer."

"The crime wave could benefit him. Maybe he sent someone to steal your car."

His penciled eyebrows drew together. "That would violate the Gentleman's Agreement."

Magnarella and Kane had a Gentleman's Agreement in place to stay out of each other's respective businesses. Stealing the car of a guild assassin would definitely fall on the side of don't-do-that-or-else.

Gun gestured to the coffeepot. "Are you going to do the

honors or shall I?"

He wasn't kidding about his desperation for coffee. I withdrew a mug from the shelf.

"Oh, not that one," Gun said.

I glanced at the mug. "What's wrong with this one?"

"It has a weird stain in the bottom. Makes it look dirty."

"That's what tea and coffee do, Gun. They stain things."

"It wouldn't hurt to wash it in a little vinegar mix," he said meekly.

Mutely, I held my index finger close to my thumb again.

He swapped the mug for a different one. "This one is acceptable."

"And here I thought Cam was the neat freak."

"We're cousins, remember? I'm neat and she's a freak."

"I'll be sure to tell her you said that the next time I see her."

His eyes widened over the rim of his mug. "You wouldn't dare."

I filled the mug and gave it to him before he drank straight from the pot. Then I pulled myself into a seated position on the counter. "Did you ask in the group text if one of the other guild members borrowed your car?"

He took a long, grateful sip of coffee. "Do you seriously think that's a possibility? Just because we're in a guild together doesn't mean we borrow each other's clothes and cars. We're not high school cheerleaders." His eyebrow drew together. "Now that you've said it, though, I strongly covet Vaughn's new Prada loafers. I wonder if we're the same size."

"He won't get much wear out of them in this weather."

"You don't know Vaughn. He looks more like a thug than I do, but he's every bit as vain."

"That isn't saying much. I look more like a thug than you do."

"It's pretty late. Would you mind if this thug stays the night, unless you don't mind driving me home?"

I was ready to crash, and I preferred not to do it in my truck. Gary wasn't built for comfort. "You can stay. There's a sleeping bag in the closet. I'll get it for you."

He sighed. "Do I need to buy you a second bed, too?"

"If you want to have occasional sleepovers, then yes." A second bed was very low on my list of items to purchase. "I'll grab an extra blanket for you."

"No need. My coat will be warmer than anything you scrounge up."

I was relieved when Gun was situated, and I was finally able to crawl beneath the covers. It had been another long day. For someone without a job, I sure kept busy.

"Sweet dreams," Gun yelled from the neighboring bedroom.

I closed my eyes and imagined throttling Kane. Sweet dreams, indeed.

I awoke the next morning to a freezing house. I tested my theory by blowing out a breath. White puffs of air lingered in front of my face. I pulled the covers back over me.

"You've got to be kidding me."

I remained under the covers for a full minute, debating whether to stay in this position until spring. Ray and Nana Pratt were getting adept enough with moving objects to bring me food and water. It was feasible.

With an aggravated sigh, I pushed down the covers and reached for the fuzzy blanket folded at the base of the bed. My sweatpants and T-shirt wouldn't be warm enough on their own.

Wrapping the blanket around me, I crossed the bedroom and banged on the radiator a few times. The radiator resisted my attempts to bully it into submission.

"This is not what I need," I grumbled.

I padded downstairs to gauge the temperature of the rest

of the house. Some radiators were working. Naturally, not the ones in the most frequented rooms. Clay's Law.

Bracing myself for the cold air, I opened the front door in search of Ray. The ghost was a former carpenter. He'd have an idea where to start. My instinct was to tear the radiator off the wall, which seemed like the kind of thing that could result in greater problems. That I even considered that outcome was a sign of personal growth as far as I was concerned.

There was no sign of Ray or Nana Pratt. Typical. When I didn't want them around, they were hovering within six inches of me.

I closed the door and turned around to see Gun at the base of the staircase.

"You look like someone scared you out of bed this morning," he said.

Gun, on the other hand, looked exactly the same as the night before. Life was so unfair.

"Did you sleep okay?" I asked.

"Other than waking up in the tundra, yes. Is your house always this cold in the morning?"

"No, this is a new problem for Lorelei."

"It isn't as bad as someone stealing your car."

I eyed him. "This isn't a small violin competition, Gun."

"Why don't I make breakfast?"

I folded my arms. "Because you don't trust my cooking?"

"In return for letting me stay." He shook his head. "Someone's grumpy sunshine when she first wakes up. I'd ditch the attitude, or you'll lose the first guy you persuade to stay the night."

"I don't need to persuade anybody."

Gun offered a Mona Lisa smile as he sailed into the kitchen.

A prickling sensation alerted me to a visitor. After last night's attack, I wasn't taking any chances. Keeping my back flat against the wall, I maneuvered my way to the foyer. I peeked outside and was confronted by a cascading floral arrangement.

My pulse sped up. Maybe these were an offer of apology from Kane. I opened the door.

"Oh, what gorgeous flowers!" Nana Pratt enthused from the front porch.

The deliveryman peered around the side of the arrangement. "Lorelei Clay?"

"That's me."

"I heard somebody bought this old house." He looked past me into the foyer. "No furniture yet?"

I guess I could add 'flower delivery guy' to the list of people judging my choices. "It's a work in progress."

"Speaking of work, you should put more salt on the bridge. It's slippery."

"I used up my supply, and Hewitt's is sold out," I said, inhaling the floral scent. I wasn't big on sweet fragrances, and these flowers were the perfect combination of citrus and rosy.

"Yeah, nobody was expecting this weather. There was nothing in the forecast and then bam! Mother Nature's revenge."

Gunther's head poked into the foyer. "Are you almost finished flirting with the deliveryman? I have a crisis; in case you've forgotten."

"Sorry to keep you. Somebody must really like you. Do you have any idea how hard it is to get some of these flowers this time of year?" He thrust the delivery into my hands. "Enjoy."

"Thanks." I closed the door and carried the arrangement into the kitchen, setting it in the middle of the table.

"Aren't you going to read the card?" Gun asked.

"Where is it?"

He looked at me sideways. "You act like you've never been sent flowers before." He plucked the card from the little stick in the middle of the arrangement and handed it to me.

His eyes narrowed. "Dear gods. You've never been sent flowers before."

"I don't know. I can't remember."

"Of course you know. Everybody remembers the flowers they've received." His voice softened. "I'm not mocking you for it, Lorelei. I just wasn't expecting that to be the case."

I forced a smile that probably fell somewhere between pathetic and deranged. "Because I'm so friendly and outgoing?"

Gun patted my hand. "Sure, let's go with that."

My hand trembled as I opened the small envelope to read the card. An apology from Kane would make everything better. I'd stop complaining about the weather. I'd even stop torturing him in my dreams.

Hope you had a swift recovery. Thinking of you. Vincenzo

My heart plummeted straight to my feet.

"Well, don't keep me in suspense. Who's it from?" He snatched the note from my frozen fingers. "Recovery? What's he talking about?"

"He sent someone to attack me last night outside Monk's."

"Are you serious? Why didn't you tell me?"

"Because you were too busy talking about you."

Gun tossed the card on the table. "If this friendship is going to work, you should know a couple things about me. One, I am my favorite topic of conversation, but if I have a friend in need, that moves to the top of the list—temporarily, of course. Two, you can tell me anything, and I won't judge you." He paused. "Okay, that's not strictly true. I will judge you in my head for about two seconds, and then I will move past it to support you."

"I appreciate the transparency."

"On that note, is there anything I should know?" He looked at me expectantly.

"Someone or something attacked me in the parking lot at Monk's," I said.

He examined me. "You don't look too worse for wear, other than that bruise on your forehead."

I touched the spot where the rock had pelted me. "It bruised already?"

"You don't know who did it?"

I shook my head. "He was like a shadow. He threw things at me and then ran off."

"Sounds more like a ten-year-old than a monster." He paused. "Although they can often be one and the same."

"I don't think Magnarella is in the business of hiring children."

"No, but he clearly decided to make good on his threat."

"Chucking rocks at me seems kind of lame for one of his henchmen."

"You're right. Maybe he went with cheap labor." His gaze slid to the flowers. "I don't suppose you're planning to report this to Chief Garcia."

"No point. Magnarella is outside her domain." And worse, she didn't know it. The chief of police could easily get herself killed over a supernatural feud. I refused to allow it.

Gun gave me a hesitant look. "There's always a certain of prince of hell."

I shook my head. "Absolutely not. Don't breathe a word to him."

"Why not? He'd want to know."

"Trust me, Gun. Kane doesn't want to know as much as you think."

He shot me a curious look. "What's that supposed to mean? Kane Sullivan is the collector of secrets. He wants all the dirt on everyone."

I dropped the subject. "Are we sure the flowers aren't poisoned?"

Gun leaned over to sniff them. "I doubt it. The vampire is toying with you, but if it makes you feel better, I can give them a quick exam. Free of charge."

"Better safe than sorry."

He rolled up his sleeve and selected a tarot card. "This one should work." He held up The Sun card and proceeded to scan the flowers with it.

"How long did it take you to master a poison detection spell?" I asked.

"Not long. It's a fairly basic one. If there's poison to be revealed, this card will enlighten us."

La Fortuna mages like Gun and Cam were born with the ability to channel tarot cards, but not the specific skills. Those they had to earn by mastering each card and, from what I understood, sometimes the process was harrowing. Mages died in their pursuit of certain magic. The more cards a mage masters, the more powerful they are. There was also depth versus breadth. A mage could possess the ability to activate all the cards but only one simple spell per card. Another mage might only be able to activate two cards but multiple advanced spells per card. I got the impression that Gunther and Camryn were somewhere in the middle of the mage spectrum.

"I hereby give this arrangement the all clear."

"Thanks, Gun." As much as I didn't want to admit it, I felt better knowing the flowers were just flowers.

"Are you sure you want to keep them? If they serve as a reminder of your dangerous foe, I'd be more than happy to take them off your hands. After all, Dusty and I are the ones who put you in that situation in the first place."

"I chose to put myself in that situation. You and your sister are off the hook. Besides, it'll be nice to have a pop of color in this room, especially since I spend the most time in here."

Gun appeared vaguely disappointed by my willingness to keep the arrangement. "Can we get back to talking about me now? You have a tiny bruise, but my ego is sporting a rather big one."

CHAPTER 7

After breakfast I drove Gun home. The snow had taken a break overnight, but now it was back in full force. By the time I returned to the Castle, the roads were thick with snow. The fresh layer of salt I'd sprinkled had already disappeared beneath another coat of white powder.

Thunder boomed as I reached the front door. The unexpected sound made me jump.

"Thank goodness you're home," Nana Pratt said. "Can we come inside? Storms make me uncomfortable."

I gestured for them to enter ahead of me, not that they needed to use the door. We hunkered down inside, feeling the house shake every so often as thunder rattled the Castle to its core.

"Maybe we should work on the radiators while I'm stuck inside," I said. I was currently swaddled in multiple layers of clothing to keep myself at what should have been room temperature.

"I'd wait until the storm passes," Ray advised. "It's hard to concentrate."

Nana Pratt peered outside. "Seems like it's hard to do anything. I haven't seen a single snowplow go by today."

"It is highly unusual," Ray commented. "The township is typically on top of this sort of thing."

"I'll tell you what's highly unusual," Nana Pratt huffed. "I die and suddenly there are weather events that never existed before."

"Thundersnow is only a winter thunderstorm," Ray told her. "It's rare, but it isn't a new phenomenon. According to my research, there are on average 6.3 such events per year."

The elderly woman didn't seem too impressed. "I guess that makes you an expert on just about everything now that you're dead."

"I was pretty smart when I was alive, too. I have more time now to indulge my curiosity. That's the difference."

Nana Pratt shifted her attention back to the outside world. "I still say there's something not quite right about this. I don't care what your statistics tell you, it feels unnatural."

I didn't disagree. I felt a charge in the atmosphere, and it had nothing to do with lightning. "Come away from the window. You're stressing me out." Nana Pratt seemed obsessed with the condition of the road that she could see but not travel.

"She's stressing herself out," Ray said. "Come on, Ingrid. Let's find a good book to read."

I glanced at the time on my phone. "I'd better call Otto and tell him I won't make lunch today." I felt bad having to cancel yet again, but it seemed unwise to leave the house under the circumstances.

Nana Pratt swiveled to face me. "You should never use the phone during a storm, dear."

"It's a risk I'm willing to take." I called Otto's number and was surprised to hear it ring three times. Usually, his housekeeper snatched it up on the first ring. I was equally surprised to hear Otto's voice on the other end. He rarely answered himself, and that included both the door and the phone.

"Good morning, Lorelei."

"Where's Heidi?" I asked.

"Well, hello to you, too."

"Sorry. Good morning, Otto. I expected Heidi to answer."

"Clearly. As it happens, she's asleep in her quarters."

"What happened? Did you make her shovel your massive driveway?"

"I'm not sure. I wonder if she's coming down with something. It isn't like her to nap."

"Then it's probably good that I'm calling to cancel lunch." Otto wasn't responsible for making the impressive platters, only paying for them.

"If you hadn't called, I would've suggested it anyway. Apparently, the roads haven't been plowed yet this morning. People are calling the township to complain. It seems two of the drivers slept through their alarms and got a late start."

"How do you know all that?"

Otto was silent for a moment. "That's irrelevant."

"Not to me." Kane had once told me he collected secrets, but right now Otto could give the demon a run for his money.

"I have my sources," was all the vampire would admit.

"Is your source a municipal employee or a device?"

His chuckle reverberated in my ear. "You should have been a journalist, Lorelei. You always know how to cut right to the heart of the matter."

"And now you're trying to use flattery as a distraction."

"I'll tell you the next time you visit. How about that?"

"And you're hopeful I'll forget by then, and you won't bring it up." I sighed. "Fine, but you should realize I'm too nosy to forget."

"I regret you won't be able to join me for lunch, but I understand. This weather is quite unpredictable."

"Stay inside today." The vertically challenged vampire could easily disappear in a snowdrift, never to be seen again.

"That's the plan."

"You've been around the block a few thousand times. Have you experienced thundersnow in Fairhaven before?"

"Not that I recall. If it makes you uneasy, I'm sure there's a certain prince of hell who would be more than happy to comfort you."

I could practically hear him smiling. "That's highly unlikely considering he isn't speaking to me."

"And why is that? What did you do to him?"

I strangled a cry of indignation. "Why would you assume it's my fault? He's the one with 'hell' in his title."

"He's also the one quite besotted with you. If he's shut you out, I'd be looking in the mirror for an explanation."

I made a static sound in the phone. "I think the storm is affecting the line. Gotta go!" I hung up before he could insult me any further.

"Would you mind checking on Steven and Ashley?" Nana Pratt asked. "I want to make sure they have a working heater."

"Oh, and after that, call Renee and Alicia," Ray added.

I stared at them. "Do I look like your assistant?"

"You look like you're alive," Ray shot back. "It's a low bar."

Begrudgingly, I called Steven, then Renee.

"All good," I told the pestering ghosts. "Satisfied?"

"Did Steven say whether he shoveled the steps?" Nana Pratt asked.

"You didn't tell me to ask about the steps. I only asked about the heater, which you heard because you were breathing down my neck during the entire call."

Nana Pratt folded her arms and gave me a withering look. "I think you'll find I'm not breathing at all, dear."

"Renee stayed home from work, right?" Ray interrupted. "Tell me she didn't go into the city in this weather."

"Renee is home with Alicia today." Ray worried about the amount of time his teenage granddaughter was left on her own before and after school. Between Alicia's father on the west coast and Renee's high-powered job, there wasn't much of a choice.

"Small mercies," Ray said under his non-breath.

The phone rang in my hand. I stared at it like a foreign object.

"Hey, look. Someone is calling to check on you for a change," Nana Pratt helpfully pointed out.

I glanced at the name on the screen. Weston Davies. The werewolf would hardly be concerned with my welfare.

I clicked the screen. "Hey, West. I gather you're not calling to make sure my heater is working."

"I assumed you didn't have heat. Your radiators look older than I am."

"A correct assessment."

"Strange storm, don't you think?"

"I do think. Any ideas?"

"Hard to say. Could be anything. Fae with a grudge. Storm demon. Elemental mage. Who knows in this town?"

"Or it could be a natural but rare weather event that occurs 6.3 times per year on average," Ray interjected.

I ignored the elderly ghost. "How's the pack reacting to it?"

"Oddly enough, most of them are lounging around like it's a lazy Sunday. Bert's hosting a movie morning and invited half the Pack."

"What's the movie?"

He grunted. "Why? You interested?"

"Just wondering about his taste in cinema. My money's on *Weekend at Bernie's* or *Dumb and Dumber*."

"Close. *Talladega Nights*."

"That's a masterpiece."

"You're more than welcome to join them."

"In this weather? I'll stay inside, thanks. Anyway, I heard the roads haven't been plowed yet."

"Huh, that's not like them. Rick and Tommy are usually on the ball. They take road safety very seriously."

"You haven't noticed your street?" I asked.

"The road to the trailer park is private, so we handle it ourselves."

Typical pack attitude. "If you know the plow drivers, would you mind giving them a call later to find out what delayed them?"

"You think their delay might have something to do with the thundersnow?"

"Unusual storm. Unusual behavior. It's worth asking."

"I agree."

I listened to another roll of thunder that shook the Castle to its foundation. "Did you call to see if I knew the cause?"

"I know you like to stay on top of these things. Thought you might have a lead."

"Why aren't you lounging around with the rest of the Pack?"

"I'm not a Will Ferrell fan."

"I don't think we can be friends anymore." The joke fell flat, which didn't surprise me. West never bothered to pretend how he felt about me and my presence in his neighborhood.

"If you figure out what's causing this storm, will you let me know?"

"I'll send you a text. That way you don't need to compromise your morals and values by speaking to me." I hung up.

"If he doesn't like you, he should stop calling," Ray said.

"He can't help himself. He knows there's something off about this storm. The only other call he might make is to Kane, and we both know he draws the line there."

Another clap of thunder rattled the house. Nana Pratt jumped closer to Ray.

"You know it can't hurt you, right?" I asked. "You're already dead."

I opened the door and stepped onto the front porch as lightning brightened the dark sky. Snow covered the bridge, the steps, and half the porch. The hair on my arms stood on end, but it wasn't from the cold air.

Ray joined me on the porch. "Is that a donkey on the road?"

I nodded, watching the creature trot past the gate like it was on its way to be blessed on an island.

"Must've gotten loose from one of the farms," Ray said. "It'll find its way back once the storm's over."

I looked at Ray. "Is our internet working?" My internet service was spotty at the best of times. It wouldn't surprise me to lose service even if I didn't lose power.

"I believe so. Why?"

I retreated into the house. "I want to do a little research." I walked to the kitchen where the ancient computer occupied a quarter of the counter space.

"Anything I can do?" Ray asked.

"I doubt we have any relevant books in the house. The internet is my best bet." I booted up the computer and waited. It wasn't the fastest unit in the East, despite Steven Pratt's technological expertise. He'd fixed my computer in exchange for helping find his missing sister. Poor Ashley had been the victim of kidnapping and nearly sacrificed to a monster so that the Bridger witches could improve their financial situation. It didn't end well for the witches or the creature they'd summoned. That particular battle introduced me to Kane's flaming sword, which sounded like a hot euphemism but, sadly, wasn't.

Did I say sadly? I shook my head to clear the unwanted thoughts. The only thing sad was that I'd shared a piece of myself with him and lived to regret it.

I typed in a couple search terms and scanned the results. I only made it through the first two entries when I lost the internet connection.

"Typical," I grumbled.

"What did you want to look up?" Ray asked. "Maybe we can help you."

"Know anything about the Bible?" I asked.

"I can tell you all about the Good Book," Nana Pratt said. "That's the book I'm most familiar with. What do you need to know?"

"What does the Bible have to say about the donkey?"

Ray looked at me with interest. "You have a theory."

"I have a dozen theories, but I need more than that."

"Jesus rode into Jerusalem on a donkey to convey his humility and his desire for peace," Nana Pratt offered.

I mulled over the thundersnow and the donkey sighting. "What else?" I knew that donkeys were considered unclean under Jewish law, but that tidbit didn't seem helpful either.

"Donkeys are notoriously stubborn," Ray said.

My brain started firing on all cylinders. "What other traits do we associate with a donkey?"

"Wasn't Pinocchio turned into a donkey?" Ray asked.

"Yes, but why?" I struggled to remember the story.

"It was a punishment." Ray pressed his ghostly lips together, thinking.

Nana Pratt hovered next to the large picture window. "My father used to call my brother a donkey when he was being lazy. It didn't make sense to me because I thought donkeys were hardworking."

"That's it," I said, my excitement rising. "Pinocchio and the other boys in the story were punished for being lazy and mischievous."

"You think the loose donkey is a harbinger of laziness and mischief?" Ray appeared doubtful.

"The plow drivers are usually reliable, but they were late this morning because they overslept. Werewolves are disinterested in this weather phenomenon because they'd rather lay on the sofa and watch a comedy. Otto's housekeeper was napping. I don't think the woman's missed an opportunity to serve since she left the womb. I don't think all these instances are coincidental."

"But what does a donkey have to do with thundersnow?" Ray asked.

"Not sure yet. First, I need to find out if any farms are missing a donkey." I glanced at the ghosts. "You two know almost everybody in town. Can you give me a list of all the working farms?"

"That's easy," Nana Pratt said. "There aren't many left. The Bridger farm is one of the last."

That was an easy call to make. I already had Phaedra Bridger's number programmed into my phone. Too bad there was no phone service now either. I'd have to check with her later.

"What does it mean if you discover the donkey doesn't belong to anyone?" Nana Pratt asked. "I don't understand."

"It means…" I faltered. "I don't know yet."

But whatever it was, I knew it would be significant.

CHAPTER 8

The storm raged until the next morning. I was so relieved to look outside and see the roads had been cleared, I actually yelped for joy.

"For somebody desperate to hide behind a moat, you sure seem anxious to go out," Ray remarked.

"First, I am not hiding behind a moat. I simply enjoy it for entertainment purposes."

He made a noncommittal sound in response.

"Second, I'm anxious to go out because there's something supernatural going on in Fairhaven, and if experience has taught me anything, it's that Chief Garcia is focusing on the wrong elements."

"Because she's human."

"Exactly. She has no knowledge of the supernatural world. She thinks all the stories she knows are nothing more than folklore and myth. It's a hindrance."

"When did somebody pin a deputy badge to your chest? I must've missed the ceremony."

I glared at him. "I feel a sense of responsibility."

"The question is why? Did you personally bring these supernatural elements to Fairhaven?"

"No, at least I don't think so." There was always a chance though. I attracted ghosts and certain demons. Why not mystic donkeys?

"Are you still worried about the lost dog?" Nana Pratt asked. "Because I'm sure someone has taken it in by now. It's been days."

"It's about the fact that the supernatural circus seems to have arrived in Fairhaven, and nobody is doing anything about it."

Ray gave me a long look. "If that's your plan, I'd bring more than those throwing knives."

"How do you know I have my throwing knives?"

His gaze lowered to my legs. "You walk funny when you're packing them."

I straightened, indignant. "I do not."

"You do. Not that it matters. Your opponent won't know the way you usually walk. Anyway, if there's a chance you'll be fighting a magic donkey, I'd consider that long blade you keep in the trunk in your bedroom." He snapped his fingers, although there was no sound.

"The longsword?"

"Ooh, I'm partial to the one with the curved blade," Nana Pratt said. "Is it a scythe?"

"A scythe has a long handle," I told her. "Mine is a sickle."

"Steven dressed as the Grim Reaper one year, and he carried a scythe made of plastic," Nana Pratt reminisced. Pausing, she looked at me. "You're not the Grim Reaper, are you, dear?"

"No."

She didn't press the issue. "What if the donkey is a shifter, like your friend?"

"West isn't my friend. He's an acquaintance by necessity."

"Would you be upset if you killed someone because you thought they were a donkey harbinger of doom, but they were really a circus shifter?"

"There's no such thing as a circus shifter," I said. "Anyway, West doesn't think the mysterious dog is a shifter. The animal didn't have a smell."

"All animals have a smell, dear. Ask any farmer."

"We haven't seen any evidence that these animals take human form. If that were the case, people would be talking about the newcomers nonstop the way they talked about me." And right now, the only newcomer seemed to be Addison Gray, a fact which hadn't escaped me.

I left the kitchen and went upstairs to choose more weapons. Ray was right; a better range of weapons would come in handy if I crossed paths with anything fiercer than a donkey.

"Would you like a cup of hot cocoa when you get back?" Nana Pratt asked. "I noticed you bought some when you went to the store."

I zipped up my coat. "Are you going to make it?"

"I thought I might try, if you give me permission to stay in the house while you're gone."

I considered the idea. "Do you think your skills have progressed to lifting objects filled with boiling water?"

"It isn't a bathtub," she objected. "It's only a kettle."

"How about I fill it now with just enough water for the mug?" I suggested.

"An excellent compromise," Ray interjected.

I cut him a glance as I passed by on my way to the kitchen. "Are you the supervisor of this experiment?"

"Seems prudent."

I filled a quarter of the kettle with water and set it on the stovetop. "Please don't burn down my house while I'm gone."

"Are you sure?" Nana Pratt asked. "The insurance money might pay for those improvements you've been wanting."

I strode toward the front door. "What makes you think I have insurance?"

Half an hour later, I was shivering from the cold and cursing myself for choosing to wear my rainbow socks over the insulated ones. To be fair, they were my lucky socks, and I wanted to manifest a good outcome with whatever tools I had at my disposal.

Thanks to the fresh coat of snow, any recent tracks were crisp and clear. If the donkey had walked into the forest, I'd find it.

As I stooped to examine a set of tracks, an arrow whizzed over my head. I turned to see the point embedded in a tree trunk. I dove to the right as another arrow shot past me.

"Hold your fire!" I yelled.

"No can do. Sorry, sweetheart," a voice replied.

Sweetheart? Somebody was cruising for a bruising.

I belly crawled to the side of an oak tree for a better view of my assailant. He was dressed in a dark green jumpsuit that reminded me of the Riddler from the old Batman television show, minus the question marks. Pops and I used to watch it together on the occasional lazy Saturday. There weren't many of those. Weekends were my training time. Pops had been adamant about school, but he'd been more adamant about my supernatural education. I was grateful for his dedication, especially in a town like Fairhaven.

"Are you the one who attacked me at Monk's?" I demanded.

"'Twas I."

Laughter bubbled up in my throat. "Twas I? What are you—a Shakespeare demon?"

"Not a demon at all, little miss."

"Stop using terms of endearment. I don't even know you. Why did you throw rocks at my head outside the bar?"

"I was testing to see whether you were warded. Then your friend appeared and caught me off guard."

"What do you want?"

"To kill you."

Great. "Shouldn't it be 'to kill ye?'"

"Are you mocking me, young lady? Bold choice for a woman about to die."

"I hate to break the news, but you've got your work cut out for you."

"Magnarella warned me you might be a formidable opponent, although I didn't see much evidence of it in the parking lot. Regardless, I welcome the challenge."

Another arrow skimmed my left shoulder. "Close but no cigar. Why don't you tell Magnarella to fight his own battles? He's a vampire. He can handle it."

"I'd tell you to ask him yourself, but I'm afraid you won't get the chance."

Whizz. Another arrow shot past me, taking a few strands of my hair along with it.

"How can you turn invisible? Is it a potion?"

"'T'isn't a potion. T'isn't truly invisibility either. Only an illusion."

"So would you classify yourself as more of a magician than a mage?"

"My father was a mage, and my mother was one of the Hidden People. I inherited the skills of both, which comes in quite handy in my profession, as I'm sure you can imagine."

"You know assassins are forbidden from operating within the borders of Fairhaven, right? The guild won't take kindly to someone breaking their rules."

"Ah, yes. I'm aware of the infamous Assassins Guild in this town. As it happens, I'm not an assassin."

I heard a swishing sound as another arrow brushed the top of my head. "Okay, that one was too close for comfort."

"I told you I intend to kill you, not give you a haircut."

"If you kill me, you'll be hunted by every assassin in the guild until you're found."

"How many members of the guild are there?"

"Membership is closed if you're thinking about joining."

"No, I'm wondering how many I'll have to kill after you. Could be fun."

Leave it to me to be hunted by a lunatic with an adventurous streak. "I can't get a read on you. Are you some sort of shadow demon?"

He spat into the snow. "I already told you I'm no demon. Blasphemy."

"Well, you're not a wizard either, Harry."

"The name's not Harry, and I'm no wizard. No cloaks or spells. My magic is innate."

"Isn't all magic innate to some degree?"

"Certainly not. I'm a nature mage. Mine comes as easily as breathing."

What was happening in mage families that so many ended up as killers? It was a topic worthy of research.

I peered around the tree trunk. "I take it you don't channel your magic through tarot cards."

"Ah, you've met a La Fortuna mage. Very powerful. My magic doesn't rely on card tricks. I use the tools Mother Nature provides." To demonstrate, he broke a branch off a nearby tree and ran his hand along the bark to reveal another arrow. "No whittling required."

"Okay, that explains the endless supply of arrows. What else can you do?"

He regarded me. "You're trying to appeal to my vanity to get me to reveal my abilities."

"Is it working?"

"A little. I do like to show off. It's so rare that someone appreciates my talents in real time."

"I've never seen anyone do that before. Can you make any weapons aside from arrows?"

Grinning, he broke a larger branch and slid his hand along the bark. He fashioned a broadsword in fewer than five seconds.

"That's honestly one of the coolest things I've ever seen.

What are your limitations?" I was genuinely curious now.

"It has to be a natural substance. I can't turn a plastic milk bottle into a dagger, for instance."

"Good thing, or the grocery store would be a dangerous place when you're around. I'm guessing the crossroads amplify your magic, too."

He inclined his head in the general direction of the gateway. "Quite an impressive show of power, your crossroads. I feel like I've taken magical steroids when I'm here."

"Without the 'roid rage, it seems. What's your name?"

"I don't think my name is important, Lorelei Clay."

"You know mine, and I'd like to know the name of the mage about to kill me. Seems only fair."

The sound of his sigh ricocheted off the trees. "Brody."

"Brody," I repeated. "No, I don't think so."

"I beg your pardon?"

"I don't think I can be killed by someone named Brody. Maybe if your name was Mason."

He scoffed. "Mason? Surely you jest. Mason isn't a warrior. Mason is someone who works as a snotty maître d' at the upscale steak house."

"Be that as it may, I still see Mason as more likely to kill me than Brody." I watched and waited. If that taunt didn't bring him closer, I wasn't sure what would.

Brody brandished his newly made broadsword and broke into a run. Good thing Ray encouraged me to bring my own. I jumped out from behind the tree with my sword at the ready. Our blades clashed, and the sound of steel on steel rang through the quiet forest. Birds that had been lurking on branches scattered into the sky.

"You've had training," he said, with a note of admiration. "And here I thought the old skills were lost to the younger generations."

"How old are you anyway?" With his relatively smooth skin and reddish-blond hair, he didn't look a day over forty.

"Old enough to know I can disarm you in two more moves."

Which the bastard did.

The sword twirled through the air and landed five feet away in a snow-covered thorny bush. Terrific.

Before I could move to retrieve it, leaves snapped off the surrounding branches. I glanced up, unimpressed. "Too bad it's winter. You'd have a lot more foliage to work with."

Brody maintained his confident air. "I'll make do."

More leaves, along with sticks and stones, hurtled toward me in large clumps and began to move together in a circular motion until I found myself in the center of a woodland tornado. A delightful combination of dirt and snow blew into my eyes and mouth. I made the mistake of using my hands to smack away the twisting debris. With the amount of bandages I'd need later, I'd look like a mummy.

"You know what they say about sticks and stones," I shouted to be heard over the noisy tornado.

"They break your bones?" he offered.

I crouched down in a squat position, careful not to get hit by the flying debris. It would be all too easy to lose an eye to a sharp stick in this chaotic mess. I wasn't sure what Brody's next move would be, but at least I knew mine.

I withdrew one of the throwing knives from my boot and braced myself. Ducking my head to protect my face, I crashed through the tornado wall and somersaulted to a standing position.

"I should've tightened the twister," Brody said. "I misjudged your size." He pointed to a spot on his cheek. "You've got scratches and a dab of blood here. Any other injuries?"

I made a show of examining my limbs. "I think they're fully functional. Let me test that theory." I whipped the knife at my assailant. The blade lodged itself in Brody's chest, just above his heart.

His head tilted to observe the knife. "Nice shot. I wasn't expecting it." He wrenched the blade from his body and tossed it back to me.

"Very sporting of you," I said.

His grin was almost infectious. "You're going to need it, love."

Vines slithered down from the trees and coiled around me as roots broke through the earth to attach themselves to my boots. They entangled me, preventing me from moving. The more I strained against them, the tighter they became. The knife fell from my hand. So much for that idea.

"Would you mind picking that up for me?" I asked.

Brody chuckled. "I like your style."

"And I like this trick, except the vines are digging into my skin. It's uncomfortable. Show me something else you can do."

Brody ambled toward me with the dull side of his sword resting casually on his shoulder. "So you can run away? I don't think so."

"You insult me, Brody. Do I seem like the kind of person who runs from a fight?"

His grin faded. "No. You don't, as a matter of fact."

He was close enough to reach. I gathered my strength and snapped the vines wrapped around my left arm. Before he could react, I lunged, punching the wound in his chest. His blue eyes widened at the shock of my touch. Taking advantage of his momentary pain, I forced my way into his head and let the darkness seep into his skull. I quickly released my hold on him, not wanting to overdo it. For someone who wanted to kill me, he didn't seem half bad.

Groaning, he fell to his knees. "The stars," he muttered. "They're too bright." He stared blankly at the cloudy sky. "No stars."

"That's because it's daytime. They're still there. We just can't see them."

Now that he was momentarily inert, I took the opportunity to retrieve my discarded weapons.

"What did you do to me?" he asked in a hoarse whisper.

"Nothing a warm bath, ibuprofen, and a cold beer won't cure."

His mouth twitched. "I prefer brandy."

I tucked my throwing knife into my boot. "I'll be honest. I don't think your heart is in this, Brody. Might want to consider a career change. You should look at balloon animals. You've got the skills for it."

Brody struggled to his feet and dusted off the snow. "I'm enjoying the company. Seems a shame to kill you too quickly."

"Sounds like you need to socialize more. Maybe hanging out with asshats like Magnarella doesn't suit you."

"No," Brody said. "It doesn't."

His tone prompted me to dig a little deeper. "It's totally normal to dislike your boss. I'm sure I'd dislike mine if I had one."

"Magnarella isn't my boss."

A heavy branch struck the side of my head. Brody was back in play. I had to hand it to the mage, he recovered more quickly than I anticipated. This was my first fight with a nature mage, though. I was bound to make a few errors in judgment.

As I brought my sword around, it was met with a hard object that wasn't there a second ago. I looked down to see that Brody had managed to fashion a shield out of moss and pinecones.

"I'm starting to feel envious of your abilities," I admitted. "That rarely happens."

"I'm feeling the same," he said. "I still have no idea what you did to me."

I wasn't about to tell him that I'd inflicted him with

temporary insanity. It revealed too much. "And if you kill me now, you'll never know."

My response seemed to intrigue him. "Magnarella only said you were dangerous. He didn't say why."

"Magnarella only cares that I ruined his game. This is petty revenge."

"Yeah, I got that impression when he referred to you as 'that thorn in my side.'" Brody rolled his shoulders. "Still, a debt is a debt."

As the mage raised his hand, I heard a low growl from behind the bushes and caught sight of blurred movement out of the corner of my eye. Whatever it was, it was fast and headed straight for Brody.

Acting on instinct, I tackled the mage and pushed him to the ground. The creature sailed over us and landed gracefully on four massive paws. A giant white she-wolf turned her head to regard us. The glint in her eye was filled with such venom and hostility that I actually stopped breathing for a heartbeat, waiting to see what she would do next.

Brody remained motionless beside me.

Finally, the wolf seemed to decide that we were beneath her and continued her journey through the forest.

Brody and I sat side by side in a mound of snow. My butt was numb, but I was too mesmerized to move.

The nature mage was first to break the silence. "You could've let that thing kill me."

"Yes. Lucky for you, I chose not to."

He stared at me with a mixture of awe and disbelief. "I told you I intended to kill you. Did you forget that part?"

I tapped the side of my head. "Lodged that intel right here."

"I don't understand."

"I'm not an assassin, Brody."

"Maybe not, but you want to live, don't you?"

I did. Very much. "Truce?"

He studied me. "For now." He glanced in the direction the wolf had gone. "Did you recognize it?"

I shook my head. "The only wolf close to that size is the local alpha, West. That wolf is female." Which meant it wasn't Kane either, although I'd already determined that because the prince of hell's enormous wolf form included a pair of griffin wings.

"Wore a collar, too," Brody said. "Know anybody daft enough in this town to claim ownership of a wild wolf?"

No, but I was beginning to think Noah himself had moored his ark right on the riverbanks of Fairhaven.

CHAPTER 9

Every muscle in my body ached as I dragged myself into the house. In this moment, I felt like I'd be sore for the rest of my life. My number one priority was a hot bath and a nap, which had nothing to do with a mystic donkey and everything to do with a nature mage called Brody. We'd parted amicably with the promise that he'd kill me the next time we met.

I added it to my list of Things to Look Forward to.

I crossed the threshold and immediately noticed the increase in temperature, which was odd given the state of my radiators. Ray was a competent ghost, but there was no way he could've fixed them without me. For a hot second I worried I'd started early menopause, until I turned the corner and saw a fire crackling in the hearth of the room I'd dubbed Fat Cheek City due to the carved cherubs all over the ceiling.

"Ray?" I crept into the room. There was a wingback chair upholstered in crushed purple velvet where one hadn't been before, along with a familiar pair of Gucci shoes resting on the floor.

Every sore muscle in my body grew tense. "How did you get in?"

Kane remained seated. "It wasn't difficult. I thought you intended to upgrade your ward."

"I do, but last time I checked, magic isn't free." I was tempted to leave the room, but the warmth of the fire kept me rooted in place. At least that's what I told myself.

"Nice flowers in the kitchen," he said. "New admirer?"

"I'm not sure 'admirer' is the right word. More like psychopath."

"What do you think of your new chair?" He patted the upholstery.

"It looks expensive."

"It's from an estate sale of a house built during the same time period as this one. I thought it would work well in this room." He rose to his feet, and I was ashamed to admit that the sight of all six-foot-four of him took my breath away. The mature part of me wanted to kick him in the balls, run upstairs, and slam the door closed. I didn't want to admit what the immature part of me wanted to do.

"I'd like you to leave now."

"I only just arrived."

"If you'd arrived two days ago—hell, even ten days ago, this conversation might have a different outcome."

"You're angry with me."

"Congratulations, Detective. You solved the case."

"There's no need to be hostile, Lorelei."

"Because you brought me a peace offering?" I motioned to the chair. "You think one decent piece of furniture will negate the fact that you ran away the moment I opened up to you?"

"I appreciated your honesty."

"Doesn't seem like it."

He rubbed his temples. "There are things you don't know."

"There are things *you* don't know. Do you think I tell everybody the truth?"

"It's very clear that you've taken great pains to hide your identity, and I respect your decision."

"And what? I'm supposed to throw you a parade because you haven't told anyone? Congratulations, Kane. You're a half decent demon."

He smirked. "A compliment? I'll remember this moment always."

I curled my fingers around the handle of my sword. "I told you to leave. If I have to tell you again, it won't be with words." I glanced at the guilt gift. "Leave the chair, though. It looks good in here."

He nodded. "And you'll look good seated in it. The color suits you."

I withdrew my sword. "Leave. Now."

"No need to threaten bodily harm. Your wish is my command."

I averted my gaze as he walked past me. I heard his footsteps fade and then the sound of the front door opening and closing.

My shoulders sagged. "He left," I whispered. The fact that I'd demanded his departure didn't matter. He left without an explanation, and I let him. All the weeks of waiting and wondering, and I ordered him to leave when he finally showed up ready to talk.

Filled with self-loathing, I practically crawled upstairs to run the bath. It didn't take long to realize there was a problem with the water. I ran downstairs calling Ray's name. The ghost appeared by the basement door.

"Ray, the water isn't working. Can you help me figure out why?"

Looking at the floor, the ghost scratched the nape of his neck. "I already know why."

"Is it the township again? Somebody fell asleep at the water wheel?"

"Not quite. The pipes burst."

"Burst? Why did they do that?"

"They can freeze if they're not kept warm enough, and then they burst."

I tried not to calculate the number of dollars this fix would require.

"You're the expert. Why didn't you warn me that could happen?"

"Hey!" Ray's voice was indignant. "I do what I can around here."

"This is the last thing I need right now."

He looked at the basement door. "You're not going to want to go down there, but unfortunately you have to."

I closed my eyes and counted to ten in my head. "Please tell me the basement isn't flooded."

"Okay, I won't tell you. You can see for yourself, although I'd bring a flashlight. I already turned off the main water supply and disconnected the electricity so you don't electrocute yourself. The excess water will need to be removed quickly to avoid further damage."

"Thanks, Ray."

"You've got a flashlight app on your phone, don't you? Use that."

I tapped the flashlight icon and crept down the steps. Sure enough, the basement floor was covered in an inch of water. Hell was freezing over right in my own basement.

I retreated upstairs to sit on the floor and cry. Leaning against the basement door, I looked at Ray, feeling utterly defeated. "Who do I call?"

"It'll be cheaper to fix it yourself."

I didn't have the strength to offer a snarky reply. "Do I seem like I'm in any shape to fix my own pipes at the moment?"

"You keep telling us how poor you are. A professional's gonna cost you."

I had to find someone with whom I could barter. If only I

possessed the kind of skills that could be written on a business card. Pops taught me a multitude of skills, but I couldn't exactly hire myself out as sellsword in Fairhaven. I pictured people ripping off those little tabs off a flyer stuck to a telephone pole when they were angry with their neighbor for getting too aggressive with the leaf blower.

I pulled myself to my feet. "I'll handle it." I bet Kane knew someone who could deal with the pipes on short notice. Too bad I sent him away.

I tapped my phone screen and prayed the line was working. I nearly burst into tears when I saw that it was. I made a few calls, starting with Otto. The vampire gave me the number of his plumber and a water restoration specialist. Then I grabbed a bucket and headed downstairs in a pair of rain boots to start scooping out the water.

Ray trailed behind me. "Let Ingrid and I handle this part, Lorelei. Why don't you go upstairs and rest until the plumber arrives?"

I whirled around to face him. "How can I possibly rest? The pipes are broken. The radiators are broken. I'm broke-n. This house is one big, never-ending project, and I rue the day I ever clicked on that stupid website." Pops would drop dead all over again if he knew I'd bought this pile of stones sight unseen. It wasn't the kind of practical decision he'd instilled in me.

Ray leveled me with a look. "Did you ever stop to consider that maybe you're focusing on the wrong project? Maybe the project you ought to be focused on is *you*. This drafty house is nothing more than a distraction that gives you a reason to avoid yourself."

My mouth opened, nothing came out, and my jaw clicked shut. I didn't have a response to that. I marched upstairs, leaving a trail of wet footprints behind me.

Ray intercepted me. "I'm sorry, Lorelei. I didn't mean to upset you."

"I don't want to talk to you right now. I'm invoking the rules."

"You want me to go outside? But the water…"

"You're dead, remember? The state of this house doesn't concern you." I slammed the door to the basement behind me.

"I shouldn't have said that," Ray pressed.

I pivoted to face him. "The more you push your apology, the more I dig in my heels. Go outside before I force you out."

Nana Pratt glanced up from her book. "Me, too?"

"You can stay." I strode into the kitchen without a backward glance. Nothing would bug Ray more than being singled out.

I opened the cabinet and pulled out a mug. When I closed the door, Nana Pratt's face was inches from mine.

I yelped. "Don't sneak up on me like that!"

"I wasn't. What happened between you and Ray?"

"None of your business."

"It is if I want to make sure I don't repeat his mistake."

Fair point. "Ray wanted to play armchair psychologist when he should've been playing armchair plumber."

"Did you clog the toilet again? You really ought to consider fiber supplements."

I narrowed my eyes. "The pipes burst in the basement. It's flooded."

She puckered her lips. "Ooh, I can see why you'd want Ray's help with that."

"He was too busy psychoanalyzing me to make himself useful." I went to add more water to the kettle and remembered that I couldn't. I couldn't do anything. I was ready to hurl myself from the second-floor balcony into my frozen moat.

"Now, now, dear. I think Ray makes himself plenty useful in this house. You may not have liked whatever he had to say, but that doesn't negate the good he's done."

"No, of course not. I wasn't suggesting that." I watched the kettle, wishing I had the kind of magic that would make it boil.

"Would you like me to help get rid of the water in the basement?" Nana Pratt asked. "I think I can manage that."

"I don't want to ask you to do that."

"You're not asking, Lorelei. I'm offering."

I hesitated. "Okay. Thank you."

The ghost disappeared. By the time the plumber arrived, the water had been reduced to half an inch. I left him to deal with the rest and went upstairs to my bedroom to shut out the world. Right now, it was the only way to survive it.

The next day was better. I had working water. Electricity. All the modern conveniences—except working radiators. I soaked in the bath and felt a rush of gratitude for the help I received.

Once I was rested and clean, I went outside in search of Ray. I hadn't seen the ghost since our argument, and I felt the need to apologize.

The sky was swathed in a gray blanket, but the only sign of snow was on the ground. I observed the frost-covered bridge with a sigh. As pretty as it looked, it still meant more work. I pushed the thought aside and continued my search for Ray. I found him in the cemetery, lurking near his headstone.

"The snow manages to make this place look picturesque," I said.

The ghost glanced at me before returning his gaze to his headstone.

"I'm sorry I snapped at you, Ray. I know you meant well."

"Of course I did. I always mean well."

"Why are you here?"

"Just reflecting on my life. Seems like an appropriate place to do it."

"Come up with any revelations?"

"A few. Don't feel like sharing them though." He angled his head toward the house. "I saw the plumber was here. Everything good?"

"As good as it can be for now."

"How'd you pay the bill?"

"I didn't. Otto did."

"That was kind of him."

"He said it's the least he can do for introducing him to Scrabble. He thinks he might prefer it to chess." I knew the vampire was full of shit, but I appreciated the sentiment.

"I'm glad you're in a better mood," Ray said. "Testy Lorelei isn't fun."

"If you want to know the truth, I don't enjoy her much either."

"You're under a lot of stress."

"Tends to happen when somebody wants to kill you."

"Want to talk about it?" Ray had a way of looking at me that made me feel seen, which struck me as ironic, given that I was the only one who could see him.

"I'd rather learn about it. Might keep me alive longer. My stalker is a nature mage."

"What's a nature mage?"

"A guy who can do cool stuff with an acorn, apparently. Ever hear of the Hidden People?"

"I can't say that I have. Want me to look online?"

"The internet's down again."

"Of course it is. Why not give the library a call? Doesn't seem like the kind of research that ought to wait."

I agreed. The more I knew about Brody, the faster I could defeat him, hopefully without killing him.

I made good use of my working cell service and called the

library. Librarian Hailey Jones was a fan of mythology. The Hidden People sounded right up her alley.

"Fairhaven Public Library."

"Hi, Hailey. This is Lorelei Clay."

"Lorelei! Great to hear from you," she shouted. The background noise matched her volume.

I raised my voice. "I was hoping you could tell me whether you have any books that reference the Hidden People. I'd check online, but my internet is down."

"Yours isn't the only one. It's down for half the town because of the weather. One minute it's working, and the next minute it's offline again."

That explained the excessive noise. "It's busy there, huh?"

"It's a madhouse. I want to pull the fire alarm." She hesitated. "Not that I would ever do such a thing. I would never waste the precious resources of our town to avoid helping kids remove their grape gum from the board books."

"Sounds like a job for their parents."

"Tell you what, I'll take a look during a quiet moment and call you back if I find anything. Sound good?"

"Thank you. I appreciate it." The phone rang in my hand. Gun's name lit up my screen. "Good morning, sunshine."

"It certainly is," Gun replied. "I found out who stole my car. You'll never guess who it was."

"Do I know this person?"

"Not well, but you'll still be surprised." He waited a beat before delivering the news. "It was Alfonso."

That was a surprise. "He's in the guild with you."

"I know, right? He had the audacity to park it in his driveway. When I confronted him, he said he's wanted that car since the day I brought it home."

I snorted. "So he just decided to take it? Does that make sense to you?"

"Not at all. The stranger part is that I asked him how he bypassed the ward, and he said he didn't. He was coming over to discuss a business proposition with me, and when he saw the car, he got overtaken by feelings. He used magic to unlock the car and drove away."

"But the ward should have stopped him?"

"Theoretically. That's why I'm calling. Would you mind coming over to help me test it?"

"Not if you're going to make me steal something."

"We'll discuss the details when you get here. I'll even sweeten the deal with the offer of lunch. Save you from those sandwiches you call food."

I wasn't one to turn down a meal. "Okay, I'll see you soon."

Gun's neighborhood was unlike most of Fairhaven. The houses were more modern and spaced a respectful distance apart. Nobody's tree branches hung over anyone else's property line. Everything was neat and tidy with no gray areas. Each driveway boasted at least one luxury vehicle. It was obvious why he'd want a protective ward. If I were a thief, this is the neighborhood I'd target. Then again, Alfonso earned a respectable income. Why he'd been overtaken by the desire to steal from one of his fellow assassins was a mystery.

Gun met me outside. He seemed reluctant to stray too far from his beloved vehicle.

I gestured to the visible pavement. "How did you get somebody to clear the driveways and walkways so quickly?"

"We pay for a private service. It's rolled into the HOA fees."

Money might not buy happiness, but it sure made life easier. "How did you handle the situation with Alfonso?" I asked.

He patted the roof of the car. "Kane made him return it."

"Made him how?" I almost didn't want to know.

"I didn't ask."

"What about consequences? Will he be kicked out of the guild?"

"Kane seems to think he was under some sort of spell at the time. He's looking into it."

"Imagine if every defendant claimed to be under a spell when they committed their crime." I shook my head. "It's a mitigating factor, but at the end of the day, he still stole your car."

"We're assassins, Lorelei. We're hardly trustworthy individuals. We just don't typically stab each other in the back. We stab someone we don't know." Gunther fell back against the car. "Mother of Giant Shitballs! Is that a lion?"

I spun around to see a large lion padding down the sidewalk across the street like he didn't have a care in the world. Hakuna matata, indeed.

The lion took no notice of us as he continued along the pavement. The spikes of his collar glistened in the winter sunlight. He suddenly slowed his pace.

Gun huddled closer to me. "Dear gods, I think he's hunting."

"Why are you so nervous? You kill for a living."

"I know, but that's a lion. It's different," he whispered.

"How?"

"For starters, there's no banter. If I can't banter with my target before I kill him, does it even count?"

"I think the fact that he dies is what makes it count."

"Fair."

The lion stopped and lowered himself into a crouched position. He seemed to have locked on his prey. I followed the beast's gaze to a man walking from his house to his car.

"That's Kevin Swarthmore. Human. Works in financial services."

That explained the Mercedes and the Porsche in the driveway. Kevin was currently unlocking the Mercedes.

Gunther crouched behind his car. "This is where years of

training comes into its own." He pulled my shoulder so that I was beside him. "Observe."

The man didn't seem aware of the approaching lion. He was too busy checking out his reflection in the side mirror. He seemed pleased with what he saw.

"I wouldn't be so satisfied with that hairline," Gun whispered.

"What's he supposed to do about it?"

"It's called magic—or hair plugs."

The lion crept around the back of the Mercedes. I felt my boot for my throwing knives and swore under my breath when I realized I didn't have them.

"We can't observe if it means letting the lion eat him," I said in a harsh whisper.

Gun looked at me with a deadpan expression. "Did I mention he works in financial services?"

My phone rang in my pocket.

Gun shushed me. "This is the twenty-first century. How have you not learned to silence your phone by now?"

I fished the phone out of my pocket. "Look, the lion kept walking. Your neighbor is safe." I tapped the screen. "Hey, Hailey. What did you find?"

"Not much, but there's a reference to them in one book in the section on Icelandic mythology. I've set it aside for you to pick up."

"You're a saint. Thank you." I hung up and tucked the phone away. A popping noise startled me. It sounded like a muffled gunshot, except one look across the street told me it wasn't.

Kevin Swarthmore was no longer standing beside his Mercedes. He was now in pieces on the driveway.

Gun clamped a hand over his mouth. I'd never seen him speechless before. I couldn't decide which view was more unsettling.

Gun slowly removed his hand from his mouth. "He blew up. You saw that, right?"

I nodded. "Should I call Chief Garcia?"

"And tell her what? A lion stalked past him and then he exploded from fear? You and I will find ourselves in a holding cell getting drug tested."

"We can't leave him like that for someone else to find."

Gun sighed. "I have experience with this sort of clean up, but I don't like the idea of a lion on the loose. At least call animal control."

I pulled out my phone to make the call and remembered Hailey. "Shit. I need to go to the library."

Gun gaped at me. "We're kind of in the middle of something here."

"Oh, I know. I mean after this."

"There's a deadly lion on the loose, Lorelei. There might not be an 'after this.'"

I turned to look at him. "How many times have you been at death's door?"

"More than I can count."

"Exactly. Do you really think a lion will be the way you leave this world?"

He seemed to mull it over. "I guess not. On the other hand, we're not dealing with an ordinary lion. You saw what happened to Morgan Stanley."

"I don't think that's his name."

"Fine. Chase Manhattan."

"You really dislike the financial services profession, don't you?"

"They're the scourge of humanity."

"Says the assassin."

"Exactly. That's how you know it's bad."

"Your feelings on capitalism aside, I don't know that your neighbor deserved to explode in his driveway."

"Do you think it should've happened on his front step for easier cleanup?"

I glared at him. "We'll have to test your ward another time."

"Yeah, no kidding." He gazed down the street. "Maybe one of us should go after the lion."

"Not without somewhere to keep it." Even if I managed to subdue it, I had nowhere to store a potentially magical lion.

Gun pulled a tarot card from his pocket. "Let's get this over with."

I emerged from behind the car and hurried to my truck in case the lion decided to walk this way. "I'll talk to you later, Gun."

"Give me a couple days," he warned. "After cleaning up this mess, I'll be too traumatized to talk."

CHAPTER 10

Hailey wasn't kidding about the library. The place was a war zone. I ducked under a wayward paper airplane as I made my way to the counter where a frazzled Hailey was scanning books into the system.

"Remind me never to come here on a snow day again," I remarked.

Hailey's eyes bulged. "I wish I had the option. This is insanity. Have they forgotten how to stay home and enjoy each other's company?"

"It's the lack of internet, I think. They don't know how to occupy their kids."

She turned toward the masses and growled, "Play a board game, people."

"I'm a big fan of Scrabble."

Hailey passed me the book. "I already checked it out for you." She rubbed her neck as a spitball made contact. "Go now. Save yourself."

I took the book and hurried to the exit. "I owe you one, Hailey!"

I nearly slipped in the parking lot in my rush to escape. If I got to the point where I needed to seek traditional employment, I made a mental note to avoid the library. No matter how much I loved books, Fairhaven's public library wasn't worth the price.

My truck rattled as I tried to start the engine and, for a brief second of horror, I thought I'd have to return to the library to stay warm until a tow truck arrived. Thankfully, Gary didn't let me down. It was clear the cold was affecting the ancient truck, though. Too much more of winter's wrath and I'd have to switch to my motorcycle, which wasn't the ideal mode of transportation right now.

On the drive home, I replayed the scene from Gun's neighborhood over and over again in my mind. The lion simply walked by Kevin without touching him and the man exploded. It could have been a coincidence, except people didn't go around blowing up for no reason. A heart attack, maybe, but bursting into a million pieces? No.

I carried the book into the house and made myself a sandwich since Gun and I didn't make it to the promised lunch stage of the afternoon. I didn't see a problem with a sandwich as a meal. I'd long ago given up on my five a day. In the warmer months, I added lettuce to my sandwich. Ta da. Vegetable.

I settled in my new wingback chair in front of the roaring fire and cracked open the book to the page with a green tab. Hailey was worth her weight in gold.

It didn't take me long to learn a new fact about my opponent.

"Brody is part elf," I told the fire.

I brought the book into the kitchen and set it aside to access the computer. I was relieved to see the internet was once again functional albeit slow. I typed a few keywords into the search bar and scanned the results. I clicked on a few links and read the limited information the search engine turned up. There wasn't much, but it was enough.

Like me, my new friend Brody was an actual freak of nature.

"The inter-webs are up and running?" Nana Pratt asked, startling me.

I twisted to glower at her. "Rules, Nana Pratt."

"Blame Ray. He saw flames through the window and thought the house was on fire."

The responsible ghost appeared behind her, wearing a guilty expression. "We were only looking out for your welfare."

I sighed. "Were you looking out for my welfare when you let Kane in the house when I wasn't home?"

The ghosts exchanged glances. "The demon was here?" Ray asked. "When?"

"While you two were outside waxing poetic about Christmas during the days of yore, clearly."

"Did you two make up?" Nana Pratt asked.

"We were never fighting. Kane has intimacy issues and no interest in resolving them."

They were both silent.

I narrowed my eyes. "What?"

"Nothing," Ray said quickly.

"You said Kane, right?" Nana Pratt asked.

"Yes, who else?"

"Obviously him," she replied, in a tone that suggested otherwise.

I turned back to the computer screen. "I'm studying up on the mage who's trying to kill me."

"Someone's still trying to kill you?" Ray now hovered beside me.

"The important part is figuring out his weaknesses, which I believe I have."

He read over my shoulder. "Hidden People."

"Brody is half mage, half elf. His mother was one of the Hidden People, which is why he's so good at camouflage.

They were known for breaking into houses and hosting wild parties."

"Sounds more like a teenager," Nana Pratt said.

"They're an Icelandic group. The Hidden People would show up in the winter around the holidays. On New Year's Eve, the people would've had enough of their merriment and lit candles to show them the way out of town."

"So you think if you light a few candles, this mage will leave you alone?" Nana Pratt asked.

"Fat chance," I said. "He's working for Magnarella. Besides, he's only half huldufólk. His father was a mage. Between their two skill sets, his parents ended up producing a nature mage."

"He's one of a kind?" Ray asked.

"It's possible."

"In that case, he must be very expensive," Nana Pratt said.

I had no doubt.

"You should be flattered," Ray said. "That means Magnarella thinks you're worth the cost."

"Are you sure his name is Brody?" Nana Pratt asked. "It doesn't sound like a very dangerous name. I'm sure I embroidered the name Brody on custom underpants for at least one baby in my lifetime."

"I can confirm the name, but you're more than welcome to call him the elf mage if that sounds more sinister."

"No, if anything that makes him sound like the star of an animated Christmas movie, the kind I used to watch with Steven and Ashley where the characters looked like they were made of clay."

"Stop-motion animation," I said. My grandparents and I used to watch those movies, too. Rudolph was my favorite. A shiny nose that he tried to hide. Those who didn't understand him. A new family that consisted of an outcast elf, an adventurer, and a doe. I related to Rudolph more than I'd like.

"Should we be keeping a lookout for this Brody?" Ray

asked. "If you need us to stand sentry outside, Ingrid and I can rotate schedules."

"I don't think he'll come to the house."

"Why not?" Nana Pratt asked. "It sounds like the elves were very good at breaking into houses."

"It doesn't seem like his style." Brody excelled in the woods, surrounded by natural objects he could wield as weapons. It was the forest I'd have to avoid.

"It's always something with you," Nana Pratt muttered. "Would it kill you to try making friends instead of enemies?"

"The whole reason she got involved with Magnarella was because of her friends," Ray pointed out.

"Then choose better friends," the elderly lady said. "I remember when Ashley started hanging around with this particular girl in middle school. It was clear the child was a troublemaker, but nobody could tell Ashley, or it would only push them closer together."

"I'm not in middle school," I said.

"No, but you're stubborn like Ashley was. If I tell you to stop hanging around with those assassins of yours, you'll tell me I'm being ridiculous."

"Because you're being ridiculous," I shot back. "Gunther and Camryn aren't troublemakers. If anything, they're professional problem solvers."

"Can they professionally solve the problem of your broken radiators?" Nana Pratt asked.

I looked at her. "That's not the kind of problem they solve." The skin on my arms prickled. "I have a visitor. Can you see who it is? If it's a salesperson, feel free to haunt them."

Ray rushed straight through the walls and back again. "It's Alicia and two friends."

I got up from the table to look out the foyer window. "Are you sure those are friends?" Two boys were pulling her in a sled across the bridge. They didn't look a day older than eleven.

"Look at that girl," Nana Pratt said. "She's as regal as a queen."

Alicia hopped off the sled and waved at the boys, who turned and left.

I opened the door and met her on the front porch. "Leave your boots outside. I don't need the snow melting and leaving water marks on my hardwood floors."

Alicia sat on the step and dutifully removed her boots.

"Your friends didn't want to come in with you?" I asked.

She tipped her back to peer at me. "Would you have let them?"

"No, but it seems rude to make them pull you all the way here and then force them to leave."

"It's cool. I paid them to pull me." She climbed to her feet and skipped over the threshold into the house. "Today's a good day for hot cocoa. Do you have any of those little marshmallows?" She paused halfway through the foyer. "Is Grampa here? Tell him I said hi."

"He says hi." I held out my hand. "Let's hang up your coat."

She shrugged out of her coat and hung it on the rack. "Somebody's in a bossy mood today. What's wrong? Your boyfriend still out of town?"

I shot Ray a menacing look. Of course, there was no way Ray was responsible for spreading gossip, not when Nana Pratt and I were the only ones who could hear him.

"I don't have a boyfriend."

"Maybe that's your problem then. You should get out more. Live a little." She continued into the kitchen.

"In case you haven't noticed, it's a little difficult to get out these days. Not all of us have access to a sled team."

"I'll give you their number. They're brothers. Twenty bucks will get you all the way to the river. Cost me twenty-five because you're uphill." She opened the cupboard and scanned the contents. "Where's the cocoa?"

I stood behind her and pointed to the lower shelf.

"I don't like that brand. What happened to the other kind?"

"I drank it. The store didn't have any in stock the last time I went shopping."

Begrudgingly, she stood on her tiptoes and pulled the tin off the shelf. "Can you make it with milk? Tastes better."

"Ask her if the milk is going to aggravate her IBS," Ray said.

I glared at the ghost. I was not about to interrogate the teenager about her gastrointestinal issues. That was her mother's job.

Alicia made herself at home at the table while I prepared the hot cocoa.

"I heard a lion tore a guy to pieces right in his own driveway." She gave her head a sad shake. "What's this world coming to?"

News traveled fast in Fairhaven. I opened the bag of marshmallows. "Where did you hear that?"

"One of the kids that pulled the sled told me. Tim's best friend's uncle lives over on Hedge Row, and he found the guy's pinky finger on his front step."

Hedge Row was Gun's street. I debated whether to tell Alicia the truth. The teenager had nursed her mother through a supernatural-inflicted coma. She took care of herself while her father lived across the country and her mother worked insane hours in the city. Alicia was young, but she was wise beyond her years.

"I was there when it happened," I said.

Ray groaned.

Alicia spun to face me. "Are you for real?"

I walked her mug to the table and set it in front of her with a spoon.

She gave the mug a cursory glance. "You forgot the whipped cream."

"My mistake, Your Highness." I hurried to the refrigerator to retrieve the can of whipped cream. Winter was the only time of year I kept such a luxury item on hand. Hot cocoa without whipped cream was like sex without an orgasm.

"What was the guy doing?" Alicia asked, as I passed her the can. "Did he try to hurt the lion, and the lion attacked him?"

"Honestly, I don't know what happened. One minute the guy was checking out his reflection in the car's side mirror, and the next minute he was dead."

She added a small mountain of cream to her hot cocoa. "Sounds like he was bursting with pride. Get it?" She laughed at her own joke. "Ooh, and the collective noun for lions is a pride. Did you know that?"

I stirred two spoonfuls of cocoa powder into my own mug of warm milk. "I did know that."

"There's also rainbow flag pride, but that has nothing to do with being boastful. The other kind is when somebody's ego goes off the rails. Right, Grampa?" She searched the air as though she might catch a glimpse of her grandfather.

"She's smart as a whip," Ray said.

"Now that's boasting," Nana Pratt pointed out.

My hand stilled, and I let the spoon fall to the side. "Shit."

Alicia twisted to look at me. "That'll be one dollar for the swear jar, please."

"I don't have a swear jar."

"I have one at home. I'll add it to that one."

Ray chuckled. "My girl can hustle with the best of them."

I dug through my purse until I located a dollar bill and placed it on the table in front of Alicia. "Let's not make a habit of this," I said.

"That's what I keep telling my mom, but she keeps swearing all the same." She folded the dollar in half and tucked it into her pocket. "Why'd you say that anyway? Did you burn your tongue?"

"Yes," I lied. I didn't want to burden her with my thoughts. It was one thing to correct her version of events; it was quite another thing to give the girl nightmares based on nothing but a theory.

Ray eyed me carefully. "You just lied to her. Why did you cuss?"

I shook my head and mouthed, "Not now."

The witness to Chutney's death said that the werewolf was particularly proud of his hunting skills that night. If the lion was some sort of pride demon at large, Chutney literally could've burst with pride. Bert had described an animal that sounded more like a lion than a dog. Spontaneous combustion suddenly wasn't as ridiculous as I'd originally believed. But how on earth would I track the creature's movements? Ask around to see whether anyone was floating their own boat more than usual lately? I was better off trying to hunt the animal than the behavior. Animals left tracks, except the inconsistent snowfall would make that difficult, and the wolves hadn't picked up a scent. I'd have to find another way.

It was hard to focus on my conversation with Alicia when my brain was firing and wiring in all directions. I gave it my best though. The kid paid twenty-five bucks to be dragged uphill in the snow. The least I could do was give her my undivided attention for half an hour.

Alicia shivered. "Your house is cold."

"Some of the radiators are busted."

She hopped off her chair. "I'm going home where it's warm. Thanks for the cocoa."

"Alicia, I want you to promise me you'll go straight home and stay inside, except to go to school."

"School's closed."

"Good. Then stay inside."

"I can't do that. I'll get bored to death."

Better than being mauled to death, I wanted to say but refrained. "That lion is still on the loose. It isn't safe outside until it's been caught."

"But you said it didn't really attack that guy."

"That doesn't mean it won't attack you. Maybe the man saw the lion and had a heart attack."

"A heart attack doesn't break you into a gazillion pieces."

No, that was the grief that followed the loss of a loved one. Ask me how I know.

"Tell her I said she's to stay indoors until further notice," Ray intervened.

"Your grandfather is backing me up," I told her.

She scowled. "Fine. Can I at least take home that can of whipped cream to keep me busy?"

I didn't have the strength to argue. "Take it. Try not to eat it all in one sitting."

"Thanks, Ghost Lady. You're the best."

"No, I'm easily manipulated. There's a difference."

Alicia sucked down the remainder of her hot cocoa. "This stuff wasn't as bad as I expected. I approve of this brand."

"I'll make a note of it." I followed her to the door where she slipped on her coat. "Will the boys come back to pull you home?"

"No, it's mostly downhill. I can do it without them."

I didn't relish the idea of sending Alicia home by herself. Given the current situation, anything could happen between here and her house.

"You know what? I need to drive out to Bridger Farm. Why don't I drop you off on the way?"

Alicia's eyes turned hopeful. "Are you sure?"

"It's no trouble."

"The roads are kind of messy."

"Good thing I excel in messy."

"You can say that again," Nana Pratt said. "One look at your kitchen sink and it's obvious."

I glared at the ghost. "I wasn't talking about the state of my house."

Ray aimed a finger at Nana Pratt. "No harping on Lorelei for the rest of the day, not when she's taking care of my grandbaby."

Nana Pratt seemed to take it under advisement. "Would you mind checking on Steven and Ashley while you're out? As handy as Steven is with computers, he's not that great when it comes to work of a more practical nature. I bet he hasn't even shoveled the driveway yet."

I had no doubt Steven and Ashley were fine. Nana Pratt's grandchildren were older than Alicia and had proven themselves more than capable of taking care of themselves, unless you counted Ashley getting kidnapped, of course.

"I'll check," I promised.

CHAPTER 11

I dropped off Alicia and then drove straight to Steven and Ashley's house. The walkway and driveway had been cleared. Judging from the clean roof, the Pratt grandchildren had been ticking off jobs on a winter maintenance checklist. Nana Pratt would be proud—but hopefully not so proud that she exploded. Good thing she was already a ghost.

After my brief visit, I continued to the Bridger farm. I stayed alert as I parked my truck and entered the part of the forest where the Bridger Farm was located. This would be the ideal time for Brody to stage another attack. I'd intended to avoid the woods for the time being, but I needed Phaedra's help. Facing off again with the nature mage was a risk I was willing to take.

To my left, a flock of birds circled above the trees, and I briefly wondered whether one of the mystery animals failed to survive the night.

Leaves rustled, and a shiver ran down my spine. "I'm a little busy right now, Brody," I called. "Come back later when killing me is more convenient."

A familiar figure cut through the shadows, but it wasn't the nature mage. "Who wants to kill you?" West asked.

Relief surged through my body. "Nothing for you to worry about. What are you doing out here?"

"Hunting one of your supernatural animals. A pig."

"In human form?"

"I don't want to get mistaken for the wolf. I told the pack to stay human until we've sorted this out."

"What makes you think this pig is supernatural?" I asked.

"Because I can't smell it. It isn't normal."

"Interesting use of magic. Why not let him reek?"

"To hide him, I imagine." West waved a hand. "Although his owner isn't doing such a hot job of keeping him hidden if he's gallivanting around Wild Acres."

"Maybe he escaped."

"There are a lot of maybes right now and not enough certainties."

I shrugged. "That's called life, West."

His eyes widened. "There it is!" He bolted for the pig, and I ran after him.

West tackled the pig to the ground. "Quick, Lorelei. Where's your knife?"

I stared at the writhing animal. "I can't kill a pig."

West struggled to maintain his hold on the slippery animal. "Are you kidding me? I've never seen anybody devour bacon the way you do."

Gods above, I really did love bacon. But still. "This pig has a collar. He's loved."

"Or he's owned. Either way, he's some kind of mystic pig that's causing problems. I say we kill him and cook him."

"If you're so sure, why don't you kill it?"

The pig slipped out of his grasp and fled. Shit.

Mystical or not, I was faster than any pig on earth. I sprinted after the swine and grabbed it by the tail. It squealed and pulled away.

"The tail's too slippery," I said.

West caught up to me. "What's your plan if you catch it, since you're so against killing it?"

"To lock it up until I have more information."

"You have quite the bleeding heart."

"It isn't compassion. It's the smart play. I have no idea what's going on, and this pig might have the answers."

We rushed after the pig.

I vaulted into the air and landed on the pig. Instead of feeling the hard earth beneath us, I felt the sensation of falling into nothingness. My stomach rolled, and I choked down the rising puke.

Light returned. I squinted until my eyes adjusted. The snowy forest floor was gone. In its place was a flat ground of dirt and patches of green grass. The cold air was now warm and arid.

I turned to find my target, except the pig was no longer a pig.

He was a man.

Was the pig's nightmare that he would become human? I mean, I guess I couldn't blame him. The human race had a lot to answer for, but at least the man wasn't in danger of ending up on my breakfast plate.

At well over six and a half feet tall, the man towered over me. His dark hair was worn in two thin braids and topped by a headdress made of metal and black feathers. His shoulders and chest were covered by a half-cape of turquoise and other colorful gems, and rectangular metals.

He was either unaware of me or unconcerned. His head tipped back and looked upward. I followed his gaze to see a cloudless blue sky. Circling above us were five vultures.

Terrific. His nightmare involved getting eaten alive, or maybe it was a Prometheus nightmare, where the vultures would gnaw on his organs only to have them reappear the next day and the whole torturous sequence would start again.

I didn't want to bear witness to any of it. It was time to put on my Melinoe crown.

I cleared my throat. "Excuse me, sir." I stopped short of tugging on his loincloth. It looked a little on the flimsy side.

His gaze shifted from the sky to me.

"Can you speak?" I asked. If this towering inferno of a man oinked, I couldn't be held responsible for my reaction.

He spoke. Unfortunately, it was in a language I didn't understand, and I knew more than a few.

"I'm so sorry. Would you mind repeating that? My pig Latin is a little rusty."

Fierce dark eyes stared at me as he repeated his answer. "¡Xinechpalēhuia!"

I still had no idea. Whatever it was, he was passionate about it, or so said the multiple bulging veins in his neck. "My name is Lorelei. I'd like to…"

He grabbed me by the neck and squeezed. Not the introduction I was hoping for. There was no time for delicacy. I reached inside his head and yanked.

The blue sky disappeared, replaced by the forest canopy. Most of the branches were bare, leaving a direct line of vision to the dismal sky above. No vultures. Only a bright spot of red where a cardinal flew overhead.

"Go to sleep," I commanded.

Beneath me the pig grew still, bringing me back to earth.

"Neat trick," West said. "Where do you plan to lock him up?"

"You have a containment cell at the trailer park, don't you?" I knew the Arrowhead pack kept special cages for werewolves that were a little too excitable during their time of the month.

West stared at the pig. "What if it uses its magic on us?"

"I'm working on that now."

I couldn't tell West about the nightmare, so I came at it from another angle. "I think he's possessed by a spirit."

"What makes you say that?"

"I think he tried to show me how he died." I tried to recreate the word spoken by the pig man, but none of the letters I put together seemed to mean anything. I even spoke it into the phone to see whether technology could identify it but no dice.

"And came back as a pig?" He looked at me. "Do you believe in reincarnation?"

"Yes," I said. There was no harm in admitting that much. "I wonder what the vultures meant."

"Obviously, that he was dead meat."

"I don't know. They didn't seem to be waiting for him to die." I thought about the vision a little more. "It felt like they were there to serve him."

"On a platter," West said. It was the closest thing to a joke I'd ever heard him make.

"It seemed like more of a symbol." And I was determined to find out what they meant. It seemed the pig might have answers after all.

In the wintry conditions, Bridger Farm looked like a picture postcard. Seeing the snow-covered rooftop and white-washed land, you'd never guess that a coven of witches died here after a brutal attack by a culebrón, and a little help from Kane and me. The only remaining Bridger witch was Phaedra, and only because she'd tried to stop her family from sacrificing Ashley Pratt. Her reward was life—and sole ownership of the farm. Luckily for me, she was a talented witch who didn't hold my involvement in the death of her family against me. I wasn't a fan of witches in general, thanks to a few bad experiences, but Phaedra was well on her way to restoring my faith in their kind.

I shook the snow from my boots and knocked on the screen door.

"Come in, Lorelei," Phaedra's voice said, although I saw no sign of her.

The door swung open toward me, and I backed out of the way to avoid being hit. The interior door creaked open inward.

I stepped across the threshold. "Phaedra?"

"In the kitchen," her voice rang out.

I walked to the back of the farmhouse. Phaedra stood at the open hearth, stirring the contents of a black cauldron. Her hair was pulled back in a messy bun. Over her plaid shirt and jeans, she wore a green apron adorned with black cat faces.

"You installed a new ward," I said.

"Yes, sorry about the screen door. I'm still working out a few kinks," Phaedra said apologetically.

I gestured to the cauldron. "You're going old school."

"I found it in one of the outbuildings when I was clearing out all the junk. I decided it was time to get back to basics."

I scented the air. "It smells good."

"It should. It's got enough cinnamon and vanilla to compete with Starbucks."

"Is this for you or a client?"

"A client. Business has been steady, even with the extreme weather." She glanced at me. "How's the Castle holding up with all the snow?"

"Still standing." Phaedra didn't need to hear my tales of woe.

"That's encouraging."

"I've been considering getting those fake Santa legs that stick out of the chimney to make it look like he's stuck upside down."

"I'd be more concerned with getting a grate to keep squirrels from climbing down the flue."

"That's because you're more pragmatic than I am."

She smiled. "Bullshit."

I laughed. "You do remember I bought Bluebeard's Castle,

right? Does that strike you as the type of purchase a pragmatic person would make?"

"Maybe not, but everything you've done since then suggests so. You've tackled one project at a time, very methodical."

"Only because I'm limited by funds. If I had an infinite pool of money, I'd be making decisions willy-nilly."

Phaedra let go of the large wooden spoon and regarded me. "If you say so." She wiped her hands on her apron. "I don't think you need me to remind you not to summon any demons to help you replenish your bank account."

"Definitely not." Phaedra's family of witches had been so desperate for wealth that they'd summoned a variety of monsters to help fund their desired lifestyle of champagne witches and caviar dreams. As was often the case with summoning demons for personal gain, it didn't end well for them.

"On that note, I found more evidence of my family's failed efforts. They were committed to the cause; I'll say that for them."

"Dare I ask what?"

She shook her head. "You really don't want to know. The only thing I'll say is that I'm glad I didn't live here at the time."

I decided to cut to the chase. "Did you happen to find any cages for fattening up children during your purge?"

She offered a wry smile. "Not that kind of witch."

"I'm kidding, but I'm serious about the cage."

"Are you getting a dog or something? I don't blame you in that big house of yours. I've been thinking about adopting one or two for the farm. Even with magic, I feel a little too isolated sometimes."

"I'd be a terrible pet owner." I was barely capable of handling the two ghosts in my house, and they didn't require any care at all.

"I think many of us underestimate our capacity to love and care for another living being," Phaedra said. "My family wasn't exactly thriving in that department."

I didn't want to discuss the subject of families. I had no interest in disclosing anything too personal about mine. "I need a warded containment cell," I said.

Her eyebrows inched up. "Not the request I expected. Mind if I ask what you intend to keep in it?"

An ethical witch. Phaedra was a rare find. "There are animals terrorizing the town, and if I get my hands on one or more of them, I'm going to need a place to keep them."

She opened the lid of a jar and tossed a handful of herbs into the cauldron. The pungent smell of rosemary filled the air. "Why not kill them if they're holy terrors?"

"Because I don't know what I'm dealing with yet."

Phaedra smiled. "See? Pragmatic."

True, I wasn't reckless, not usually. Pops had taught me better than that. Survival meant thought and careful consideration when the situation allowed for it.

She nodded. "I've got something that will work."

"How much and how long will it take?"

She quoted me a price.

"That's too low," I said. "You should be charging more."

She arched an eyebrow. "You're my boss now?"

"No, but I don't want to see you undervaluing your work."

"Fine. How about ten percent more?"

"Done." Inwardly I cursed myself for putting Phaedra's needs ahead of my own. I was hardly swimming in a moat of money.

She sealed the jar and placed it back on the shelf. "What are the specs?"

I considered the range of animals. "Big enough and strong enough to house a large lion and contain his powers."

Her eyebrows inched up her forehead. "A magical lion? Are you sure?"

"It's a lion, but I don't know anything about the magic, other than he seems able to make people combust."

She grimaced. "Not a circus I'd want to attend. One zoo enclosure coming right up. I'm guessing this is urgent." She regarded me for a moment.

"Fine. I'll pay a rush fee."

She broke into a wide smile. "I'm a quick learner."

"It's fair. You'll have to put other work aside to do this. Those clients won't be happy with you." Depending on the client's temperament, she may lose their business altogether.

"Were you a lawyer in another life?" she asked.

"I've spent time with Big Boss. Picked up a few tactics."

Phaedra snorted. "Sure. I believe that."

"You have my number. Give me a call when it's done."

"Never mind that. It's an emergency. I'll deliver it to your door."

"Even better. Thanks."

She eyed me closely. "You don't act like someone tight on funds."

I shrugged. "I'll shift around a few priorities." Who needed heat in the winter anyway? I had blankets. I was fine.

"You mentioned animals, plural. What else is out there? I've got chickens to protect."

"I don't get the sense they're behaving like typical wild animals. There was a wild boar in a nightclub."

"Who blew up there?"

"Nobody, but there was a mighty brawl. And when the nature mage tried to kill me in the woods, we saw an enormous she-wolf, bigger than any of the local wolves. I ended up saving my would-be assassin from her."

Phaedra laughed. "I don't even know how to respond to that."

"The wolf had one strange characteristic. Her eye." I shuddered. "The way she looked at me was intense and not in a good way. I felt like she had a grudge against me." Probably because I snatched Brody from her jaws of death.

Phaedra grew pale. "You saw the evil eye, Lorelei. You said the wolf was in the woods?"

"Wild Acres. She could've come through the crossroads."

"That would be my guess, but why would Invidia come here?"

"Invidia? The Roman goddess of envy?"

Phaedra blinked. "Yes. I'm surprised you knew that."

"I could say the same to you."

Her lips compressed in a smile. "Witches are well acquainted with envy. It's probably our number one vice."

"Something you struggle with?" I asked.

"Not personally. Mine falls into the eating too much junk food before bed category. Better for humanity, but worse for my waistline."

I considered her theory. "I don't recall Invidia being associated with a wolf, though."

"Maybe not that goddess specifically, but a wolf is known as the animal aspect of envy."

"I thought it was a dog, like two dogs fighting over a bone."

Phaedra shrugged. "Depends on the source."

An idea slid front and center in my mind. "Envy makes perfect sense. Theft and burglary crimes have increased dramatically in town." And Kane had mentioned that Alfonso seemed like he was under a spell when he coveted Gun's car. It could've been the wolf's influence.

Phaedra stirred the spoon around in her tea. "Is that unusual for the holiday season? Seems like it might be a normal uptick."

"Chief Garcia says otherwise." I debated whether to divulge the related information. Phaedra had proven herself trustworthy so far, and it seemed only fair to share details that allowed her to protect herself. "There have been other incidents in town recently."

Her gaze flicked to me. "Like what?"

"A murder-suicide that doesn't make sense. Two victims that burst with pride. Then there's thundersnow…"

She let go of the spoon and it continued to slide around the interior of the cup. "What about the murder-suicide? Do you think that was envy?"

"It depends. If all seven deadly sins are at play, then it could be wrath and lust working in tandem. Maybe envy too. It's hard to know at this point." It certainly explained the random animals on the loose. They were spreading their sins through town like the plague.

Phaedra wrapped her hands around her cup. "I'm not sure I want to know the rest."

"You might want to take precautions for more than your chickens." Phaedra lived alone at the farm, which was fairly isolated from the rest of town.

"I appreciate your concern, Lorelei. I'll strengthen the wards around the property before bed."

I cleared my throat. "Speaking of wards, I was hoping I might be able to upgrade mine soon."

She cocked her head. "What kind of upgrade are you thinking?"

"Something stronger than an alert. I had an intruder recently, and I'd like to make sure that never happens again."

Phaedra recoiled. "I'm so sorry to hear that. Were you hurt?"

Only emotionally. "No, but I don't want to take any more chances. I know the magic is pricey, though, and you've got a full client list." I wasn't sure how to proceed. I couldn't quite bring myself to ask for a favor, no matter how desperate I was. Maybe I was about to burst from a different sort of pride.

Phaedra reached for my hand but withdrew it midway when she noticed me flinch. "I'd be happy to conjure a stronger ward for you, although it'll take longer than the pen. Why don't I lump together the cell and the ward, and you can pay me in installments? We'll set up a reasonable timeframe. Interest rates are fairly high at the moment, but I'm willing to waive that because I want you to continue looking out for me." She smiled. "Do we have a deal?"

"We do." I hesitated. "But just so you know, I'd warn you regardless if there was danger headed your way."

Her face softened. "I know you would, Lorelei."

CHAPTER 12

If these animals were deadly demons in disguise running rampant through town, there was one source that could confirm or deny.

"Why are you applying mascara?" Nana Pratt asked.

I stepped back from the mirror and looked at her. "Is that a problem?"

"Not for me, but the last time you used it, you ended up with those black rings under your eyes. I worried you might be shifting into a raccoon."

Ever since Nana Pratt learned about the existence of shapeshifters, she thought she saw them everywhere. The pumpkin in the patch was sprouting legs. The squirrel on the tree branch was chittering in English. The blackbird on the finial was … okay, that one was Kane.

I shook off the thought. I didn't want to think about Kane in bird form or any other capacity.

"I'm making a little effort with my appearance today," I said. "Gun told me my eyes looked tired."

"Probably because you had mascara smudged under your eyes. I've never seen you wear that shirt before. Is it new?"

I glanced down at the cobalt blue top with a deep V neckline. "No, but I haven't worn it since I left London." I was relieved to find it still fit. New clothes were very low on the list of priorities. I'd make do with what I already owned.

"It's a pretty color for you."

Something in her voice gave me pause. "But?"

"I just wish it weren't so low-cut is all. It's showing more skin than is good and proper."

I bit back a smile. Good. Let the demon prince see what he'd walked away from.

"I think you look very pretty, Lorelei," Ray interjected.

"And you'll look even better once you run a brush through your hair," Nana Pratt added.

"I already brushed my hair." I pivoted to face the phantasmal duo. "My bathroom suddenly feels very crowded. I don't think it was designed to accommodate one person and two judges at the same time."

They took the hint and evaporated. I gave myself a final glance in the mirror. *Not too shabby, Lorelei. You clean up nice when you're invested.*

I quickly averted my gaze. I meant invested in the situation, not the someone I wanted to talk to about the situation. There was no reason to invest in someone who learned your deepest, darkest secret and then disappeared without an explanation. Kane was not a safe bet; then again, there were no safe bets when it came to my secret. Pops had warned me time and time again, yet I'd let myself believe otherwise for a fleeting moment.

Hard lesson learned. The hardest, in fact.

I exited the bathroom and slipped on my take-no-shit boots. My footwear would back me up if my mouth failed me. To be fair, my mouth never failed me. It was as reliable as a Roman aqueduct.

"Be careful," Ray said, as I put on my coat. "There'll be black ice on the roads."

Black ice was the least of my concerns. I was about to stick my head voluntarily on a chopping block and test the sharpness of the blade.

I had issues.

I tugged on a pair of warm gloves as I walked to my truck and noticed the snow had been cleared from the walkway. Ray's handiwork no doubt. His poltergeist skills were really coming into their own. The heels of my boots crushed the remaining chunks of icy snow, and I relished the satisfying crunching sound. I may or may not have imagined someone's body parts in its place.

It took a solid five minutes to warm up the truck—the downside of buying a vehicle that was on the road when Nixon was president.

I heeded Ray's advice and exercised caution as I drove. Although the roads had been cleared and salted, there was no reason to take a chance. I couldn't afford to fix any damage the truck might incur in an accident, especially without insurance.

I didn't pass a single vehicle on my way to the Devil's Playground. It seemed nobody wanted to risk the unsafe conditions today. If everybody stayed home, maybe that would help cut down on the number of incidents today, although it wouldn't have helped Connie and her lover, John.

I pulled into the empty parking lot and listened to the engine rattle as it idled. The truck didn't function well in the cold. I patted the dashboard. "Me neither, buddy."

I exited the truck, ignoring the churning of my stomach. I pretended the discomfort was due to hunger, but I knew the real reason—and he was just on the other side of this door.

There was no bouncer or lock to keep out the riffraff. Seemed like a bad idea, but what did I know about running a supernatural nightclub?

I entered the main room and saw Josephine behind the counter with her head and shoulders bent over a book. The vampire looked up at me and exposed her fangs with a half-hearted snarl.

"Hello to you, too, Josephine." I kept my voice nice and pleasant. It seemed to irritate her more when I was friendly.

Dantalion emerged from the stock room, carrying a stack of empty crates. "Lorelei. I didn't know you were here."

"Just arrived."

"We're not open," Josephine said flatly. "Come back later. Or better yet never."

"I'm not here for a drink." I crossed the room to stand at the bar. "I'd like to brainstorm with you."

Josephine closed the book on the counter and straightened. "Me, specifically?"

"All of you. I need ideas."

Dantalion set the stack of crates on the floor at the end of the counter. "I would be happy to oblige."

Josie rolled her eyes. "Of course you would. I liked you better when you weren't so agreeable."

Dan chuckled and gave her arm a light punch. "I never realized how funny you are, Josephine. I can see why Kane enjoys having you around."

The vampire maintained her deadpan expression. "Yes, it's my sparkling wit."

Dan looked at me expectantly. "What are we brainstorming? I've been trying to persuade Kane to host a singular species night, but he dislikes the notion of segregation."

I was momentarily distracted by the idea. "Like a werewolves-only night?"

Dan's bright blue eyes shone with enthusiasm. "Yes, exactly! An opportunity for members of the same species to meet each other."

"This is Fairhaven, Dantalion." Josie sounded bored. "They all know each other already."

"Not true," Dan said. "I've been studying the clientele, and the club reaches far beyond Fairhaven's borders. It wouldn't have to be a weekly event. Perhaps once a month, we could host a different species."

"I don't personally love the idea of a club full of wolves," Josie said. "They like to brawl, which means more work for me."

The demon duke nudged her. "But I bet you'd enjoy a vampires-only night. We could schedule that one first. Test the waters."

"I believe I'm the one in charge of the schedule." The prince of hell strode into the room, looking impossibly handsome. If I ever wanted proof there was no justice in the world, the evidence was right in front of me in a perfectly tailored pinstriped suit.

The temperature seemed to drop a good ten degrees when he spotted me. "Miss Clay, I didn't expect to see you."

"No, you've made that pretty clear."

Dan and Josephine looked at us, then looked at each other before inventing excuses to make themselves scarce.

Kane and I locked eyes in mutual silence. It was a battle of wills, and I had no idea who was winning, mainly because it felt like we were both losing.

I broke first. "You left."

"Very observant."

"Why?"

He refused to make eye contact with me. "I believe that's my business."

"I told you something deeply personal, information I rarely share. I bared my soul, and you took off."

He grunted. "If that's the extent of your soul, I'd be concerned with your lack of bargaining power."

I stared at him in disbelief. How was this the same demon that held up a phone during the god fight and played music he knew would rouse me into action?

"Why did you come back if you're so unhappy to be here?"

He finally looked at me. "I'm not unhappy to be here."

"Gee, you sound ecstatic."

His face remained impassive. "Why are you here?"

"To torture myself, apparently." I pushed away from the counter. "I was hoping to talk about the current situation in town."

"I understand there've been a few incidents. These things happen when you live near a crossroads as powerful as ours." He sounded blasé, as though I'd mentioned the milk spoiling because it was left out overnight.

"People have died, Kane. Multiple deaths within a week. Crime is way up. This is a serious problem for Fairhaven. I assumed you'd care. My mistake."

The prince of hell seemed to absorb the information. "I didn't realize. I've been … preoccupied."

"Unpacking your suitcase takes all your mental effort, I guess."

With the snap of his fingers, he summoned Dan and Josie back to the room and explained the purpose of my visit.

"How many deaths did you say?" Josie asked. Mark this moment down in the history books. She actually sounded concerned.

"At least three."

She glanced uneasily at her boss. "I didn't realize the situation was so dire."

"Your job is at the nightclub," Kane reminded her. "You're not responsible for what happens outside these four walls."

"Neither is she," Josie pointed out.

Kane pulled out a chair and motioned for me to sit. Gallant as ever. The immature part of me wanted to sit elsewhere, but I wanted his help, so I played nice.

We sat around a table wearing matching grim expressions.

Kane slotted his fingers together and rested them on the table. "The team is assembled. Tell us what you know."

His tone ruffled my feathers. Then again, the fact that he

was breathing ruffled my feathers right now. "I'm the one gathering intelligence."

Josephine grunted. "Intelligence. More like incompetence."

"Says the vampire who was nowhere to be found during the recent nightclub brawl," I snapped. "When you're in charge of a life-threatening situation that impacts an entire town, then feel free to talk to me about incompetence."

The vampire glowered at me from beneath a set of thick, dark eyebrows that matched her luxurious hair. "And why is that?"

"Why is what?"

"Why is it that a relative newcomer to town has assumed control of this life-threatening situation?"

"You mean what's in it for me?"

Josephine angled her head toward Kane. "He pays me to act as his director of security. Who's paying you to act as defender of the realm?"

Kane patted her hand. "I appreciate the comparison, Josephine, but we both know you'd work for nothing if the situation required it."

Josie snatched her hand out from under his. "Okay, but she doesn't know that."

I smirked. I would've guessed as much anyway. Josephine appeared blindly devoted to the prince of hell, although I didn't sense any romantic feelings between them. It was more of a big brother and bratty younger sister vibe.

"I work for nothing," Dantalion interrupted. "But now that I know you pay Josephine, I might need to remedy that."

"Your money's no good in hell," Kane said.

"Yes, but I'm here right now."

"Can you settle your labor dispute later?" I interrupted. I was here for more pressing reasons. "There are dangerous creatures roaming the streets of Fairhaven. This impacts all of us, no matter how long we've lived here."

Josephine leaned back against her chair and assessed me. "How do we know your theory is right? Maybe it's a rash of bad luck for people. Crime waves aren't unheard of, especially close to the holidays."

"A lion, a wolf, and a wild boar..." I began.

"Walk into a bar?" Dantalion interjected, chuckling to himself. "Well, the wild boar did."

Oh, boy. I was beginning to regret my decision to come here, for multiple reasons.

"Where's the closest zoo?" Josephine asked. "Has anybody checked with them about missing animals? It's possible they kept it out of the news on purpose."

"These aren't zoo animals," I said firmly. They didn't behave like regular animals in any sense of the word, and most zoo animals didn't have supernatural abilities. The number was low, of course, but never zero. "Phaedra Bridger thinks the she-wolf is the spirit of the Roman goddess of envy."

"Why envy?" Kane asked.

"She has an evil eye."

Josephine snorted. "Does that make me a Roman goddess, too?"

"Not a stink eye," I countered. "An actual evil eye. I saw it up close. It definitely made me feel like I was being hexed."

"But you weren't affected?" Kane asked.

"Don't seem to be." I glanced at Dantalion. "The wild boar was in the club when the fight broke out. I don't think that was a coincidence."

Kane was the first to catch on. "Wrath?"

I nodded. "And the lion is pride, I think. The animals might be acting in concert with each other. The murder-suicide suggests both envy and anger influenced John Landisville."

"And possibly lust," Kane added, "assuming your theory is correct."

Just hearing the word 'lust' spill from his full lips made me shift in my seat.

"And there's a donkey roaming around that could be sloth," I added. Sloth was far less sexy than lust.

Dantalion looked at Kane. "It could be," the great duke said vaguely.

Kane remained stoic with his arms crossed. "It isn't."

"It's worth a conversation," Dan insisted.

Kane looked ready to throw the demon into whatever circle of hell tortured annoying friends. "None of them has an evil eye like she-wolf."

"Because all their body parts are evil," Dan shot back.

"Just spit it out, Dan," I said. "If Mr. Grumpy Pants doesn't want to participate, he's free to take his scowl elsewhere."

Wordlessly Kane rose to his pricey loafers and left the table.

Josie watched him leave, appearing uncertain whether to stay and hear whatever Dan had to say. "I need to prep for tonight," she finally said, and abandoned the table.

Dan sighed. "I was hopeful you and Kane made up earlier."

"There's nothing to make up. He's a tool, and tools are for stabbing people in the eye."

"They're also for fixing things," Dan said in a gentle voice.

I placed my hands on the table. "Can we get on with this? I have a town to save from whatever is plaguing it."

Dan glanced over his shoulder at the bar. "I believe this discussion warrants a drink. Bourbon?"

"Sure. With Coke." Because I was a lady, but mainly because I craved sugar like Gunther craved attention.

Dan returned a minute later with two glasses filled to the rim. "I know where Kane keeps the good stuff."

I smiled as I accepted the glass. "You've already annoyed him. Might as well double down."

Dantalion took a drink and rested the glass on his thigh. "What do you know about the seven princes of hell?"

My gaze instinctively shifted to the door that separated Kane's private quarters from the nightclub. "I know one of them has a real chip on his shoulder and hasn't told me why."

"But you hadn't heard of Kane Sullivan before you moved here, I take it."

"No. The princes of hell I remember from books had names like Beelzebub and Satan."

Dan nodded. "Lucifer, Belphegor, Mammon, Livyatan, Asmodeus, Satan, and Beelzebub."

"Quite the boy band. All friends of yours?"

He ignored the smart remark. "Do you know what those princes are associated with?"

"Torture? Fiery pits?"

"And the seven deadly sins."

Right. I straightened in my chair. "Lucifer is pride."

"Belphegor is sloth. Mammon, greed."

"Beelzebub is gluttony." I drummed my fingers on the table, trying to remember the lesson Pops had taught me. "Satan is wrath."

"Livyatan is envy and Asmodeus is lust." Dan watched me expectantly. "You see where I'm going with this."

The idea took my breath away. It made sense. Fairhaven sat at a powerful crossroads. If the princes of hell decided to hand out sins the way environmental activists handed out fliers, it was no wonder the town was in chaos.

"It's a solid theory. Why is Kane so sure you're wrong?"

"Because he's a prince of hell and thinks his finger is on the pulse of all the circles."

"Are they here because of him?" If that were true, Kane's response was understandable. The demon couldn't bear the weight of that guilt.

"It's the only reason I can think of. The animals are strange forms for them to take, though. That part doesn't make sense. If they wanted to hide from Kane, they'd be less obvious about spreading their influence."

I stared at the bottom of my empty glass, thinking. "So where does Kane fit in?"

Dan glanced up. "Pardon?"

"You named seven princes of hell and Kane wasn't one of them. So, where does he fit in?"

"You won't find him in any stories, and that's how he likes it." He drank. "Kane worked his way up to duke, doing everything Lucifer wanted."

I didn't want to contemplate that job description.

"Over time, he developed a conscience. He refused to torture souls and suggested alternative measures. You can imagine how that was received. Anyway, he eventually got wind that Lucifer planned to appoint himself the supreme king of all the circles."

"And Kane tried to stop him?"

Dan blew out a breath, as though remembering it in detail. "He launched a revolution. Fought Lucifer on full display for all the legions to witness. Claimed the title of prince and banished Lucifer from the circles of hell."

"Kane took control of Lucifer's circle so that Lucifer couldn't control all the circles?"

Dan nodded. "He knew firsthand what Lucifer was capable of, and he didn't want to inflict that on the other circles."

"He's kind of soft for a demon."

A smile touched Dan's lips. "I won't tell him you said that."

I swirled the liquid in my glass. "What happened next?" Kane's presence in Fairhaven made it clear his victory was short-lived.

"The short version is that Kane was betrayed. Lucifer returned to hell and reclaimed his circle. The pain and suffering were beyond anything hell had ever seen."

"Lucifer sounds like a lot of fun at parties."

Dan snorted. "He used Kane's newfound enlightenment against him, threatening to extend his cruel warfare beyond the circles of hell unless Kane surrendered."

I closed my eyes. "And don't tell me the idiot surrendered."

"He didn't feel that he had a choice. Lucifer intended to torture him for eternity, but a band of demons that had supported the revolution helped him escape."

"And Kane chose to flee to Fairhaven."

"It's not the kind of place Lucifer would ever think to look. Lucifer vowed to track Kane to the end of time, which is one of the reasons Kane keeps a low profile."

"You call those custom suits and fancy car keeping a low profile?" I laughed. "Okay."

"You should see his true demon form."

"I've seen his blackbird, his flaming sword, and his monster form. What else is there?"

Dan grimaced and shook his head. I didn't want to know. Got it.

"And he hasn't tried to stage another coup since then?"

Dan lowered his gaze to his empty glass. "I don't think it's a job he wanted unless he could save lost souls, which required a change in Hell's entire infrastructure. The betrayal cut deep. Kane felt that all his efforts had been in vain."

"And where were you during all this, Dantalion, Great Duke of Hell?"

Dan met my gaze. "I'm the one who orchestrated his escape."

The great duke just blew my mind. "I thought you were still in the business of torment."

"A necessary lie. Kane and I are no longer welcome in Hell."

Naturally, Kane chose this moment to emerge from his

quarters. His gaze briefly met mine, and he continued to the counter as though I wasn't here.

"I need to prep for opening," he said.

"Josie can do that," Dan said.

"Josephine is my head of security. She has different matters to attend to."

Dan slid back his chair. "Then I'll do it."

My work here was done. I wasn't going to get anything else from Dantalion now, and the sight of Kane was wreaking havoc on my interior world. I had to save myself if I intended to save Fairhaven.

"Thanks for your help, Dan. I appreciate your input—on everything."

Dan shot a reluctant glance at Kane. "Anytime."

I got up and left without a backward glance.

CHAPTER 13

My stronger ward couldn't come too soon. I arrived at the Castle to find a tattooed woman on my front porch with her face pressed against the window.

I cleared my throat, causing her to jump. "Looking for something?"

She spun to face me. "You, of course. And here you are."

"Here I am. What brings you here, Addison?"

"Leo told me about your amazing house. I was hoping for a peek inside."

I walked past her and unlocked the door. "Sorry. My radiators are on the fritz. Not the best time to entertain company."

"I won't be any trouble. I'll wear my coat."

Addison seemed a little too eager to enter my sanctuary. "I'm afraid the answer is still no."

She leaned against a column. "You're a young, single woman like me. What made you decide to hide away in your own personal Fortress of Solitude?"

"I like a house with history."

She smiled in the direction of the cemetery. "And plenty of dead people, apparently."

"Cemeteries bring down house prices, which worked in my favor." I refused to open the door while she stood on my porch. I didn't like her, and I certainly didn't trust her.

"Leo also told me there's a lion at large. Isn't that crazy? A lion in a small town like this?"

Something in her tone of voice triggered me. I pivoted to face her. "Let's cut to the chase. We both know you're not human, so you can drop the act."

Addison flashed a wicked smile. "Neither are you. Are you sure this is a game you want to play?"

I tried to stay calm. Just because she identified me as supernatural didn't mean she knew any more than that. "Why wouldn't I?"

"Because if someone has to win, that means someone has to lose." She made a frowny face in the air with her fingers.

"What are you?"

She wagged a finger. "Nah-ah-ah. That's not how this game works. I've given you all the information you need to figure it out. If you're as clever as I think you are, you'll reach the right conclusion soon enough."

"You haven't given me squat," I retorted. "I know your name and that you like to canoodle with Officer Leo, which is understandable. The guy is hot, in a sweet Labrador puppy kind of way."

She fanned herself. "And that tongue isn't just for wagging."

"TMI, stranger." I didn't want to know the details of anyone else's sexual exploits, especially not when it had been so long since I had any of my own.

"If you're in the mood for a little loving, the goat might be able to help you with that."

There was a goat? "I've been in close contact with the wild boar, the wolf, the donkey, and the lion, but they had no impact on me. Why not?"

She offered a nonchalant shrug. "You tell me."

"I'd say supernaturals aren't affected, but I know that isn't true because of the fight at Devil's Playground."

"I'll give a little hint. Only weaker minds are affected. Looks like yours is strong enough to withstand their influence. Congrats."

"How do you know all this?"

"I'm highly educated. Can I come in now?"

My jaw tensed. I didn't want this woman anywhere near me, let alone on my property. "No. I'd like you to leave."

She clasped her hands together. "But we have so much to discuss!"

"Like what?"

"You'll see. Toodles." Addison blew me a kiss and disappeared.

I stared at the spot where she'd been standing, wondering if I'd just conversed with a ghost without realizing it.

No, that wasn't possible. I had control over ghosts, and I had *no* control over Addison Gray.

"What's the matter, Lorelei?" Ray asked. "You look like you've seen a ghost."

"She wasn't," I said, "yet she disappeared right before my eyes."

He glanced at the empty air. "What do you mean she disappeared?"

"Disappeared as in standing right in front of me and then poof! Gone."

"Is she a ghost like me?" Ray asked.

"Definitely not, but she isn't human. She said I had all the information to figure out her identity."

Nana Pratt joined us on the porch. "I'm stumped. Then again, I don't even know what you are, so I don't see how I'd figure out someone I haven't even met."

My gaze flicked to her. "Does that bother you?"

"Not as much as my arthritis used to bother me."

"I have no idea how to gauge that response."

Nana Pratt floated closer to me. "I don't have to know what you are to know *who* you are."

"I agree with Ingrid," Ray chimed in. "I know Lorelei Clay, whoever and whatever she is, and I give her my stamp of approval."

"You have to trust me," I said. "If it weren't for me, you'd both be yammering at people on the Other Side."

"I suppose that's true," Ray said, "but I've watched you, Lorelei."

"Not in a creepy way," Nana Pratt added quickly.

"I've watched you," he continued, "and I've seen you put yourself in harm's way for the sake of others. I've seen you step in when the fight wasn't yours. You didn't just earn my trust; you earned my admiration."

I felt a puddle of warmth stream from my center all the way to my outer extremities. In that moment, I realized Ray's stamp of approval meant more to me than I ever would've guessed. "Thank you."

"If you have any theories about this disappearing tattoo lady, I'd be happy to do a little research," Ray offered.

"And I can read over his shoulder," Nana Pratt said.

"You can do more than that," I told her. "I've seen you turning pages."

"Oh, I know, but it takes a lot out of me. I haven't gotten to Ray's level yet."

Both ghosts had enthusiastically embraced their poltergeist abilities, mainly due to a desire to read in the afterlife. Ray had started first and, therefore, had progressed faster than the elderly woman.

"I wouldn't object to assistance," I told them. "If you can figure out which books you need from the library, I can pick them up for you."

"I've been doing well typing on the computer keyboard," Ray said. "Some of the letters are a little more resistant to my touch, but I feel good about it, if only the internet were more reliable."

I was mildly afraid of what my search history would include once Ray was able to use the computer without any issues, but that was a problem for Future Lorelei.

I gave them a rundown of everything I knew about Addison to date.

"Can you describe the tattoos?" Ray asked. "Are they the normal ones?"

"What are the normal ones?" I asked.

"Well, you said she's a white woman in her late twenties. I'm thinking a rose, Chinese letters that she doesn't know the meaning of, or a dolphin."

I let loose an inelegant snort-laugh. "Addison isn't your standard twenty-something white woman, remember? Her tattoos are symbols." I opened the front door. "Come inside, and I'll draw them for you."

I did my best to recreate as many of Addison's tattoos as I could and left the drawings with Ray, who was already immersed in his efforts to find matches online.

Once Phaedra dropped off the specialized containment cell, I filled a sling with weapons and prepared to hunt game both big and small.

Nana Pratt didn't seem too enthusiastic about my plan. "Why not call for backup? Don't you agree, Ray?"

Ray's face was currently buried in the computer. "I don't want to stop what I'm doing in case we lose service again."

I answered for Ray. "Because it's unclear whether someone will be affected. I don't want to end up fighting the person I asked to help me." As usual, it was safer to be alone.

"Have fun and be careful," Ray called over his shoulder. He seemed to hear his own words because he turned to look at me. "Sorry, old habits die hard. Just be careful."

I saluted him with a throwing knife.

The truck sputtered as I drove toward the forest. Wild Acres was the perfect hiding spot for the coterie of animals. It was large enough to hide them, and mystical enough to amplify whatever power they possessed. For the hundredth time since I moved here, I regretted my failure to thoroughly research Fairhaven before I decided to put down roots. All I wanted was solitude. All I got was … whatever the opposite of solitude was.

I parked the truck and headed into the woods. There was no plan. I figured whichever animal I found first would be the prize.

The she-wolf's tracks were easiest to spot. They were fresh, large, and directly in front of me. Achievement unlocked.

A bush rustled, and I paused to listen, slowly withdrawing my longsword. Although I only intended to subdue the animal, I had to be able to defend myself. My skin crawled as I sensed something watching me. I turned my head a fraction, and I caught a glimpse of white fur. My palms began to sweat, and I tightened my grip on the handle.

The wolf charged.

She leapt over a neighboring bush and knocked me backward. I avoided eye contact as she towered over me. Each paw was the size of my head.

I slid back and kicked the wolf's snout. As her head jerked to the side, I seized the opportunity to scramble out from under her.

"I don't want to hurt you," I said. "I only want to keep you from hurting others." I had no idea how deep Addison's involvement ran. Right now, my only goal was to round them up and neutralize them until I knew more.

The wolf didn't seem to care. Growling, she displayed a sharp set of fangs.

"What big teeth you have," I said. "I'd consider a new

toothbrush. You've got a little tartar buildup right here." I touched the same spot on my tooth, which only made the wolf's growl deepen.

If I could get my hands on her without getting bitten, I could take a peek inside her head and see whether Phaedra's theory was correct. Although if this wolf was Invidia, she didn't seem to have an interest in changing forms.

The wolf snapped her jaws, forcing me to step backward. She was calling my bluff. I had a sword, but I wasn't willing to use it, and now she knew it.

My back smacked against the trunk of a tree. I studied the wolf, debating the best place to land a nonfatal thrust.

The wolf lunged.

I jumped aside and slipped on the snow, losing my grip on the sword. I braced myself for the wolf's body weight and watched in confusion as she seemed to be carried away in midair, as though a strong wind had overtaken her. She eventually landed on her feet and ran off.

I grabbed my sword and stood. "Who's there?"

A shadow moved closer, becoming a solid form.

"Brody?"

The nature mage bowed. "'Tis I."

I was too shocked to mock him. "What just happened?"

"That beast tried to slay you."

"Let me guess. You stole her thunder because you have to prove you did the honors or you don't get paid."

"I don't get paid either way. I owe a debt to Magnarella. This is supposed to be how I pay it."

"Supposed to be?"

Brody bent down on one knee and dropped his sword. "I cannot do it. You, Lorelei Clay, are a warrior with a heart and integrity, like me. There are too few of us in this world to justify removing you from it."

My fingers tightened on the handle of my blade. "Is this a trick?"

He shook his head. "You could have slain that she-wolf ten times over, but you wanted to spare her, the way you spared me." He bowed his head. "I hereby pledge my allegiance to thee, Lorelei Clay."

"Thee but no ye?" I spread my arms wide. "Make it make sense!"

Frowning, the mage looked up at me. "You have strange triggers."

"What about Magnarella? Aren't you worried about your debt?"

"That's for me to handle."

"He won't stop, you know. If you refuse to kill me, he'll find someone who's willing to try, and he'll punish you for your failure."

The hint of a smile emerged. "Let them try. I have a feeling they'll be regretting their choices by the end of it."

Steeling my mind, I offered my hand to help him to his feet. "Are you?"

He grabbed ahold and resumed an upright position. "Not in the slightest. In fact, I'd say 'tis the best decision I've made in a long time. You've restored my faith in humanity."

"I'm flattered. What will you do now?"

"You seem to have a magical infestation on your hands. I thought I might offer my assistance, if you're willing."

Brody and I had been near the wolf twice without consequences. He would be the ideal assistant. "I am."

"Then tell me what we're hunting. I'm a nature mage. This forest is my armory."

"Not hunting, remember? This is a capture-don't-kill mission."

The bleating of a goat brought the conversation to a quick close. The animal came within view and stopped between two trees to bleat again. I crept forward, holding my breath.

Brody caught my eye and gestured to the goat. I nodded.

A goat would be far easier to cart off as evidence than the wolf.

Quickly and quietly, he gathered a pile of loose branches from the ground and waited. The goat trotted forward, away from the trees. With incredible precision, he threw each branch like a spear until the animal was trapped in a makeshift cage.

"Nonviolent and efficient," I said. "Good work."

"What do you intend to do with it?" he asked.

"I have an enclosure for it at my house."

"Enchanted, I hope."

I nodded. "Only the best for my mystical animal farm."

The goat's bleating seemed to have attracted a friend. The donkey I'd spotted outside the Castle gates was now standing in a nearby glade.

Brody reached for a branch, but I stayed his hand. If my theory was correct, the donkey wouldn't be hard to catch.

I approached the animal slowly, with both hands raised. When I was less than a foot away, the donkey started to bray.

"Good grief," Brody said, clamping his hands over his ears.

The donkey was sounding a warning to her friends. I lunged for her, wrapping my arms around her neck. The spiked collar snagged on the sleeves of my coat, but I'd worry about that later. I had to prevent the donkey from further communication. I slipped into her head and injected a lullaby to subdue her. The creature grew limp and dropped to the ground. I released my hold on her and took a step backward.

"That's quite the headlock you've perfected," Brody said. "In another life, I might've asked you to teach it to me."

"You've got enough weapons of your own to keep you busy for two lifetimes."

"Why don't I help you carry it to your truck and accompany you home?"

"To the truck, yes, but I can take it from there. You

wouldn't want to be spotted at my house helping me. You want to control the flow of information to Magnarella."

"True. That bastard would have a guillotine ready to behead me the second I crossed the threshold. Let me know when you're ready to track the rest of them. 'Tis a fun game."

"'Tis," I agreed.

At least I had the containment cell ready and waiting in the Castle. The goat and donkey could chill in there until I gathered more information.

CHAPTER 14

With a donkey and a goat secured in the enchanted enclosure in the dining room and the pig safe with the pack, I settled in front of a crackling fire in the parlor room and delved into my favorite tome on the town—*The Complete History of Fairhaven*. The local crossroads were unlike other gateways. The one in Wild Acres provided access to multiple realms, which made it highly likely these animals came through there from one or more of those realms. Maybe there was a record of other wild animals invading the town that would provide a solid lead. Addison's claim of responsibility could be a red herring to throw me off the trail. For all I knew, this was Magnarella's real revenge, and Brody was an unwitting decoy. The vampire knew I was willing to go to bat for others and that a situation like this would torture me.

I made myself cozy under a blanket in the wingback chair delivered by the prince of hell himself. I hated to admit how comfortable it was. I considered putting it out for the next garbage collection, but my desire for spite was overridden by my desire to sit in a comfy chair. We all had our price, and apparently mine was free furniture.

I scanned the index for references to lions, wolves, and other seemingly ordinary mammals. At some point, Hailey was going to deny my request to renew this book. I should probably check with Jessie Talbot to see whether the elderly owner of the local bookstore had a copy for purchase. Her collection of books reflected the uniqueness of the town. She was far more likely to have a local history book than *War and Peace*.

"You sure seem to love that book," Ray remarked.

I glanced up, midyawn.

"Okay, I retract that statement," he said.

All this reading was making me tired—or maybe it was my lack of sleep. I needed to pay better attention to my body.

"I was hoping for a blinking neon sign that pointed to the answers I'm looking for, but I haven't even found a dog-eared page."

Ray gave me a wry smile. "Life rarely works that way."

"So I'm learning." I closed the book and set it on the floor. A side table would be my next acquisition. Once the winter weather cleared, I'd hit the road for dumpster diving. Pops had been an expert. I'd been remiss in not utilizing the lessons he'd taught me in relation to cheaply furnishing a house.

"Where's Nana Pratt?" I asked.

"Outside. She doesn't like seeing the animals indoors. Thinks it's unnatural."

"She can just avoid the dining room for now," I said.

"Are you sure you'll be able to fit the other animals in there?"

"The pen is enchanted. It will expand to fit whatever I put in there."

"Won't it be dangerous to have them all in the same pen together?"

"If they were normal animals, sure."

"Do you really think they're the root of the chaos in town?"

I rose to my feet and stretched my arms overhead. "They're the root of two-sevenths of the chaos."

My skin hummed. Company.

"Ray, would you mind seeing who's here?"

The ghost returned a moment later. "Don't kill the messenger."

"You can't kill a ghost, Ray."

"It's His Royal Highness, Prince of Hell."

"You might want to join Nana Pratt outside," I warned.

I marched to the door, propelled by the healthy combination of anger and frustration. I flung open the door as he arrived on the front porch.

"What are you doing here?" I demanded.

Kane appeared unperturbed. "I'm surprised I was able to pass through the gate. I thought for sure you would've put up a special ward."

"Just for you? Don't flatter yourself. I figured you do a good enough job of keeping yourself out. No need to waste magic."

"May I come in?"

"No."

He brushed past me and stepped inside. "Your house is freezing."

I swiveled to face him. "I'm surprised you can tell."

His mouth twitched. "Is that a reference to my cold demeanor?"

"You tell me, Mr. Ice King."

"That's His Majesty, the Ice King to you." He slipped off his coat and hung it on the rack. "Nice rack."

"Thanks. Gun bought it for me as a thank-you present."

"I wasn't talking about the furniture."

I glanced down at my cleavage. I was still wearing the same cobalt blue top with the plunging neckline. "You can't smarm your way out of this, Sullivan." I folded my arms, which only served to enhance my chest. My arms quickly moved to my sides. "Why are you here?"

"I came to apologize for not being more hospitable when you were at my club. I'm the consummate host. I should've behaved better."

I leveled him with a look. "That's it? That's what you came to apologize for?"

"Is there something else?"

I resisted the urge to shove him backward, right down the steps of the front porch. "Are you serious right now?"

"I'm a prince of hell. Serious is my stock in trade."

It was like talking to a brick wall. "You've made your apology. Now you can go."

A bleating sound drew his attention to the adjoining room. "What's that?"

"If you must know, I've apprehended three of the suspects, and I'm keeping two of them secure here until I have more information."

"Suspects? It sounds like a goat."

"I told you at the club they were animals."

"What else do you have?"

"A donkey."

He burst into laughter. "Saving the best for last, are we? Or are you too afraid to go after the one you really want?"

I stared at him. "I could say the same to you."

He blew past me and headed for the dining room.

"Hey! You can't go in there."

"I'd like to see these vicious beasts and determine whether Dantalion's theory has any merit."

"This is my house. You do not have…"

The bastard made a run for it.

I gave chase. He made it halfway to the dining room before I reached him. I chopped the back of his knee, and he went crashing down on the other knee. I tried to grab him in a headlock, but he jerked to the side just in time. I fell forward and narrowly missed faceplanting on the hardwood floor. He scrambled to his feet, and I launched myself onto his back like a spider monkey. We both went tumbling to the floor. My elbow hit the wooden board with such force that I bit my tongue.

He took advantage of my brief moment of pain and rolled on top of me, pinning me beneath his muscular frame.

"You're touching me," he said.

"I think you'll find you're touching me." I steeled my mind. If he didn't want me in there, I'd do my damndest to stay out. Still, I was curious. "Why did you leave when you found out who I am?"

"I had to." Damn his whisky-colored eyes. They seemed to see straight through to my soul.

"What are you afraid of?"

"You," he said quietly.

I made no move to escape. "I won't hurt you, Kane. I'm not sure I could even if I wanted to."

"You can hurt me in ways you don't understand." He paused. "And I could hurt you."

Our faces were no more than an inch apart. I'd insulated myself from his mind, but at this range, there was no escaping his emotions. His fear was now being overtaken by something far more powerful.

Desire.

He threaded his fingers through mine. "How well can you control your powers?"

"Fairly well." I wasn't sure I trusted myself with Kane though. Not with so many emotions of my own pushing their way to the surface. It was hard to focus on anything except the features of his face. The commanding jawline. The broad shoulders. The timbre of his voice.

His hand traveled along my waist. "Try."

May Day! Alert! Somebody throw me a life preserver because I was in danger of drowning in a sea of desire.

"What will you give me if I do?"

Dammit. That was not supposed to be my response.

His mouth claimed mine. One touch of his soft lips and I was undone. My lips parted, inviting him in. I tasted a hint of whisky and savored the flavor.

This was the goat's influence. It had to be. Despite my conviction, I couldn't bring myself to put a stop to what we were doing. Lust was in the driver's seat now, and Kane and I were its hormonal passengers.

Addison had been wrong about me. Apparently, I was weak enough to succumb to one of the sins after all.

The kiss deepened. Strong, pliant hands found my bare skin, and I shuddered.

"Cold?" he asked.

"Hot," I said, in a voice I barely recognized. "Very hot."

His lips grazed the curve of my neck. Every nerve in my body pulsed with anticipation.

"This is a bad idea," he murmured.

"Bad ideas happen to be my specialty." I rolled us over so that I was on top, straddling him.

"Where was this move when you were in the fighting ring?" he teased.

"My opponent didn't have your abs." A thrumming vibration spread through my chest as his fingers tightened on my hips.

"Any more moves you'd like to show me?" he asked.

"Depends. How expensive is this shirt?"

"It's custom. Why?"

"Because I'm about to ruin it, and you know I can't afford to replace it." I gripped the shirt by the seams and pulled. Buttons flew in all directions, clattering on the hardwood floor.

"What did that shirt ever do to you?" he asked.

"It was an obstacle, so I removed it." I explored his chest, feeling the strength of his heartbeat beneath the muscles. Its rapid pace matched my own. Warmth radiated through my body as his hands migrated to my backside.

"Your eyes are like storm clouds," he said, gazing at me with uncharacteristic tenderness.

My mouth sank into his, breathing in his scent of pine and sandalwood. Kane was a force of nature—compelling, yet somehow comforting. My mind went black. I was falling straight into his soul, and I had no interest in stopping. Only when the darkness cleared did I realize I wasn't in his soul.

I was in his head.

Kane was naked against a wall. Blood seemed to seep from every pore. It took me a moment to realize that his body was tacked to the wall with hundreds of nails. A winged demon with red scales hovered in front of him clutching a hammer. With a gleeful shout, the little bastard drove another long nail through Kane's arm. The prince of hell didn't make a sound; he simply observed the motion with apparent detachment.

Only I knew better. I could feel everything he felt in that moment. It was beyond any pain I'd ever endured. Agony didn't do the feeling justice.

The scene shattered into pieces. I was back on the floor of the Castle, my limbs entangled with Kane's.

"Quite the mood killer, isn't it?" he said.

I covered my mouth and stifled a cry. "Gods above, Kane. That was a horrific nightmare."

He removed himself from my grasp. "It wasn't a nightmare."

I wanted to throw up. "Someone did that to you?"

His eyes locked on mine. "Yes."

I felt guilty for glimpsing what he'd intended to keep hidden. "I'm sorry, Kane. I didn't look on purpose. I can't control it as easily when there are…" I nearly said "feelings" but settled on, "heightened emotions."

He glanced in the direction of the animals. "The magic circus?"

I nodded. "I think the donkey is sloth, and the goat is lust."

"So we're two lazy whores, which probably explains why we can't seem to get off the floor." He shrugged. "Could be worse. Could be wrathful whores."

I didn't want to imagine what that would've entailed. I was relieved we stopped before going too far. I didn't want to have sex under the influence of anything except good, old-fashioned hormones.

I sat up and wrapped my arms around my knees. "I won't touch you again. I would never want to invade your privacy like that."

He pulled himself into a seated position and tried to adjust his buttonless shirt. "Which is the reason I left. I didn't want to risk getting close to you." He paused. "Any closer than I already had." He lowered his voice. "I'm sorry you had to witness that."

Except it wasn't just witnessing. I experienced all of it. His agony. His despair. But I didn't want to make him feel worse than he already did.

He gazed straight ahead at nothing in particular. "Now that we're being a little more forthright, I have questions."

"After that vision, so do I."

"Me first, then it's your turn." He shifted his gaze to me, revealing eyes now a shade of rich amber. If I wasn't careful, they'd trap me like a butterfly.

"Go ahead," I said, sounding far more relaxed than I felt.

"What's your connection to music? I'm not aware that the goddess Melinoe had any special connection to it."

"It isn't a goddess thing," I said. "That one is all Lorelei."

"But…?"

I wagged a finger. "That was your question, and I answered. My turn. Why were you tortured in hell? At least, I assume that was hell." I was curious whether he would share the same story as Dantalion.

His face fell into shadow. "That's complicated."

"I'm a reborn goddess born to a human family and hiding from anyone who'd want to use me as a weapon. I'm equipped to handle complicated."

He inhaled softly. "Knowledge is power."

"Which is why you collect secrets."

"It was part of my job once upon a time. Old habits." He shrugged.

The realization hit me. "You used people's secrets to torture them?"

"I wouldn't do that now."

I believed him. "Are you afraid I'll learn your weaknesses and use them against you? Because I would never. I'm not vindictive, Kane."

He offered a vague smile. "You weren't exactly thrilled with me."

"Because you left."

"What you saw in my head ... there's so much more than that."

He feared vulnerability. I understood that well. I reached for him and ran my fingers through the hair at the nape of his neck. It felt like touching a cloud.

He didn't move away.

"I have spent centuries building up my walls," he said. "You've got a moat and a castle out here." He patted his chest. "I've built mine in here."

"What else are you worried I'll see? That you love puppies? That you're not the big, bad prince of hell you pretend to be?"

"I'm concerned that what you witness will change what

you think of me. I'm not proud of the demon I once was, Lorelei."

"How do you know what I think of you now?"

He glanced pointedly at his exposed chest.

"That was the goat," I reminded him. "Lazy whores, remember?"

His mouth formed the hint of a smile. "I told you when we first met that I'd retired here."

"I remember."

"That wasn't strictly true. It was more of a forced retirement. I ended up in Fairhaven by chance. I needed a place to put down roots and this seemed like a quiet place with a powerful energy. I found it a pleasant combination."

"Why did you leave hell?"

"You seem to have forgotten my building-a-wall analogy."

"Look at this house, Kane. I'm a demolition expert." I finally asked the question I'd been dying to know. "Where were you these past few weeks?" I'd assumed it was Hell, but Dantalion's version of events seemed to rule out his old stomping grounds.

"A story for another time." Kane dragged his fingers along my bare arm, sending pleasant shivers down my spine. "What's your favorite drink?"

"Talk about a non sequitur."

"I'd like to discuss lighter topics."

"Fine. A gin called Puck's Pleasure. It's a fairy-made brand you can only get in certain supernatural circles in London. It isn't even for sale."

"Aren't you going to ask mine?"

"I know yours. It's Yamazaki." I'd seen him drink the Japanese whisky enough times to identify it as a favorite.

His smile suggested he was pleased by my knowledge. "And now I'd like a more extensive answer to my music question."

It seemed only fair, given how much he'd divulged. I

knew it couldn't have been easy for him to loosen some of those emotional bricks.

"My love of music came from my human family. It was something I excelled at that had nothing to do with being a goddess."

"But your family knew what you are."

"My parents didn't. They died when I was a baby, before I showed any signs."

"How did your grandparents discover the truth about you?"

"I displayed strange abilities from an early age. I walked and talked before I should have, which wasn't so crazy, but then I started talking to ghosts and discovered I could make them do whatever I wanted. I'd make a game of it. Order them to dance a jig, silly things like that."

"Dance a jig?"

"I was a little kid. What do you expect? My grandfather was the one to figure it out. He trained me to protect myself, and to learn everything I could about my goddess self and the not-so-mythological world. It was hard for him. The most fighting he'd ever done was in the bunk of a submarine over comic books." Pops had served in the Navy before I was born. He'd grown up hunting and fishing, though. When it came to survival skills, he'd been a topnotch teacher. What he didn't know, he learned for my sake.

"What happened to your parents?"

"Car accident."

"I'm sorry."

"It's okay. I was only a baby. I have no real memories of them."

He stroked my arm with long, slow movements that revived those lustful feelings that had dissipated with my trip down Kane's memory lane. I did my best to ignore them.

"Do you think things would have turned out differently for you if they'd lived?" he asked.

"I think that's inevitable. Whether better or worse, though, I have no idea."

"Worse than foster care?"

"I try not to give it much thought. Can't change the past, so I don't see the point."

"Your family was musical, and when you hear it, you can't help but remember them."

I nodded. "Both my parents and my grandparents loved music. After Pops died, it pained me to listen and remember what my life had been like when I had people I loved and with whom I felt safe. I knew I'd never have that feeling again."

"You assumed," Kane corrected me.

"No. It's a fact."

"When you were fighting in the ring, music seemed to give you strength."

During the god elixir experiment, I'd been knocked down by my opponent. Kane had remembered my fondness for Debussy and played a song to help me rally. His idea worked, and I won.

"Music taps into my emotions in a way that I would prefer it didn't."

His mouth quirked. "Now who's afraid to be vulnerable?"

"It isn't safe for me to access strong emotions. Look what happened between us just now. I violated your boundaries."

His mouth twitched. "I believe I was very much in favor of being violated by you."

A flush of warmth flooded my body. "I wouldn't want to lose control and go full goddess on anyone."

"So you lock up your emotions and tuck away the key?"

"Safer for everyone that way."

"That's no way to live, Lorelei."

"Better than other people dying because of me."

"You don't give yourself enough credit. You've shown

incredible restraint since you've been here. If you hadn't, your identity wouldn't be a secret anymore."

"I don't think I showed incredible restraint twenty minutes ago."

A smile touched his lips. "I didn't hear any music playing, or was it the drumbeat of my heart that did you in?"

Groaning, I buried my face in my hands. "Don't make me regret this."

"Do you think you will?"

My gaze swung to his. "No." If anything, it left me wanting more, although I'd have to see how I felt once the goat was no longer under my roof.

"You should know there's another reason I left." He drew a deep breath, which put me on edge.

"I'm listening."

"I've spent many years trying to outrun my former self. I have no desire to be drawn back into that darkness."

I recoiled slightly. "And you worry *I* would do that to you?"

"You're the goddess of nightmares and ghosts. Darkness is where you dwell." Despite his words, his tone was gentle, almost apologetic. Still, his response threw me.

"I didn't choose this life. I didn't raise my hand in identity class and beg to play the role of Melinoe. I would've gladly traded it for the role of average human girl."

"Either way, it's who you are at your core, and I've worked too hard to get to this place to let myself sink again."

"Sink?" I couldn't quite wrap my head around what he was telling me. "Do you seriously think I'm going to drag you into the depths of darkness and despair? Have you seen my inflatable swan?"

"I have. I noticed you chose a black one."

I smacked his arm. "Kane, you're being ridiculous."

"Am I? You keep yourself hidden from the world because you're afraid of losing control and hurting people or attracting the wrong kind of attention. If that happens, I'll want to help you, Lorelei. I won't be able to stand idly by, but instead of me being your buoy, you'll be my albatross. We'll end up drowning together in a sea of darkness."

"That's bullshit, Kane. That's your fear talking."

"Yes, it is," he admitted. "Now you know another one of my nightmares without needing to see it for yourself."

CHAPTER 15

I spent the next morning in the dining room looking after the goat, the donkey, and the pig that had been delivered by West soon after I woke up. The alpha seemed thrilled to remove the pig from the trailer park. I explained my theory that the pig spread gluttony, which West seemed to accept without question.

"That explains the empty larder," was all he said before he departed.

I brought the animals food and water and was pleased to note that the enchantment included waste disposal. I'd been worried how I'd let them outside to relieve themselves.

As I left the room, I inadvertently glanced at the spot on the floor where Kane and I had exposed ourselves—in more ways than one.

I turned to shake a finger at the goat. "This was all your fault."

Before he left last night, Kane promised to help me recover the remaining animals. I told him I wasn't sure that was a good idea. If the prince of hell could be influenced, I didn't want him crossing paths with the lion or wild boar. It was too dangerous. I told him about Brody, my would-be assassin. He wasn't happy to hear that I'd been stalked by Magnarella's hired killer, but I warned him not to get involved. Thugs like Magnarella always ended up hoisted by their own petard.

"I need to find Brody," I said aloud as I wandered into the kitchen to cook breakfast.

Nana Pratt materialized by the stove. "The one who tried to kill you? Why on earth would you want to find him?" She gasped. "Unless it's to kill him first."

"He's not trying to kill me anymore. He's going to help me collect the rest of the magical animals."

"They're not Pokémon cards, Lorelei. They're dangerous beasts."

I looked at her, amused. "I'm guessing Steven was the Pokémon fan."

Her head bobbed. "Oh, yes. He adored that little yellow Pikachu."

"I assume if you're inside, Ray is lurking around here, too."

Ray emerged from the wall with a sheepish grin. "We saw West arrive with the pig earlier and wanted to see it."

"Good, I'm glad you're here because I need your expertise."

"I'm still researching the symbols on that tattooed woman."

"Set that aside for now. I'd like to know if there's anything special about five vultures."

"Sounds more like a roadkill issue than a research one," he grumbled.

"No, this was a vision I had when I jumped the pig."

"You jumped the pig?"

"It was the only way to catch it."

"People pay good money to watch that sort of thing," Nana Pratt interjected.

"Next time I'll make sure we're both encased in mud first." I pointed to the computer. "Is the internet working?"

"Last time I checked it was," Ray said.

I waltzed past the ghosts and stood at the counter.

"I thought you wanted Ray to look it up," Nana Pratt said.

I started typing. "Sorry, I came up with an idea and wanted to look it up before I lost it."

"You're far too young to worry about memory loss," the elderly woman said. "That doesn't really kick in until menopause."

"Something to look forward to," I muttered. Did goddesses even go through menopause? It wasn't as though I had anyone to ask.

I directed my attention back to the screen. "What does a pig represent to you?"

Nana Pratt answered first. "Filth."

"Except pigs are actually clean animals," Ray told her. "They get a bad rap." He peered over my shoulder. "Gluttony. That would've been my guess too."

"We have the seven deadly sins, right? And we have animals running amok in Fairhaven that represent those sins." I scrolled through my search results. "The pig's nightmare gave me a valuable clue." Phaedra's theory was starting to look like a winner.

"The vultures are a clue?" Nana Pratt asked.

Excitement rose as I clicked a link. "I believe the pig in my possession is none other than Macuilcozcacuauhtli." I stood upright and waited for a response. The ghosts simply looked blankly at each other.

"Was that a word or did you sneeze?" Nana Pratt asked.

"It's a name," I said. "He's the Aztec god of gluttony."

Ray blinked. "You're telling me we have the Aztec god of gluttony locked in a cell in this house?"

Nana Pratt didn't wait for an answer. "Why is a god from Mexico running around Fairhaven?"

"The Aztecs were the greatest empire known to Mesoamerica," Ray interrupted.

"Not the point, Ray," the elderly lady said.

"I don't know," I told them. "What I do know is we have to keep the pig locked up before someone else suffers the ill effects of gluttonous behavior."

"I think that ship has sailed," Nana Pratt said. "Have you seen this country?"

I ignored her.

"Who are the donkey and the goat?" Nana Pratt asked.

"I'm still working on those."

"Maybe you could try that magic spell to get the animals to talk the way you did with Gunther's sister," Ray suggested.

"Not a bad idea," I said. "I'll text Gun now." When Dusty drank the god elixir, she'd turned into a swan instead of embodying the full powers of Zeus. Most of the time she honked, but Gun was able to communicate with her via the use of one of his tarot cards.

One quick call revealed that Gun was out of town on a job, which left me with Camryn Sable.

"Can your magic make an animal speak?" I knew not all La Fortuna mages had the same abilities. Their magic was dependent on which tarot cards they'd mastered.

"That depends," Cam said. "Are we talking about your garden-variety animal in the woods, or the lion that makes people explode?"

"Somewhere in between."

"Hmm. I'm happy to try, but no promises."

"How fast can you get here?"

"Sounds serious."

"I may or may not have an Aztec god trapped in a cage in my house."

I heard a small gasp on the other end of the line. "He sounds hot. I'll be right there."

"Did she miss the part where you said there was an animal in the cage?" Ray asked, amused.

"I think she misunderstood the details," I replied. She'd find out soon enough.

Ten minutes later, my skin tingled, alerting me to Camryn's arrival. The petite mage assassin was color coordinated in a beige beret, coat, and high-heeled boots. She ripped open a fresh box of Nerds and tipped the candies into her glossy mouth. Then she held out the box to me.

I waved her off. "No thanks."

"I tried to switch to sugar free gum last week." She sucked in a breath and shuddered. "Never again."

"Would you like to see my petting zoo?"

She sniffed the air. "I expected to smell them before I could see them. Are you using an air freshener?"

"These animals don't have a scent." I walked into the dining room with Camryn right behind me. "Meet Lust, Gluttony, and Sloth."

The animals looked at us with matching soulful expressions.

"Oh, look at those big brown eyes." She edged closer to the pen.

"I'd describe them more beady than big."

Camryn removed a tarot card from her Chanel handbag. "This one should do the trick."

"Why doesn't she use a wand?" Nana Pratt asked.

"Because she's a La Fortuna mage," I explained. "They channel their magic through tarot cards, not magic wands."

Camryn examined her perfect French manicure. "Tell your Casper that a card is different from a wand. We can't pick up any old card and channel it. We have to master it first and claim it as our own. Some of those cards can take years off your life if they don't kill you first."

Nana Pratt shrank back into the wall.

Cam stepped forward and contemplated the pig. "If he turns out to be a hottie, this could be a real meet cute moment."

"I like your positive attitude." I glanced at the animal, still dirty from the cage at the trailer park. "Do you need him to be cleansed first?" Camryn took clearing the air to another level. Her visit to the Castle involved two shamans and more herbs than a garden center.

"I'll worry about that once I get a good look at him." She held up the card in front of the pig and focused. "Can you talk?"

The pig grunted.

Cam sighed. "This is disappointing. I was sure he was going to have muscles that defied nature. Did you try removing the collar? Maybe it's blocking my magic."

"It won't come off."

"That's odd."

"Everything about this is odd."

She shrugged. "Welcome to Fairhaven. A weird pig god just means it's Tuesday." She fished through her purse for a different card. "Let me give the Eight of Wands a whirl. It's more potent."

I watched as she channeled the card's magic.

Exasperated, she resumed an upright position. "There's a block all right. A very powerful one."

"Then you think I'm right?"

"I don't know about the Aztec god part, but this is definitely not a normal pig. I'm sorry I couldn't be more helpful."

"You've been plenty helpful, Cam. Thanks." Unfortunately, there was no way to prove my theory if I couldn't communicate with the animals. "Do you think another mage might be able to break through the block?"

Cam glared at me beneath heavily mascaraed eyelids. "Are you suggesting my work is subpar?"

"Of course not, but I know you don't all have the same exact magic skills."

She tucked her card in her purse and snapped it closed.

"That's right, we don't. And you should know that my work is highly regarded."

"I do know that, Cam, and I appreciate you coming over on such short notice."

"I charge a pretty penny for my services."

I nodded. "As you should."

"What about the goat?" she asked. "Maybe the magic is weaker on that one."

"Why not the donkey?"

"Donkeys are stubborn. The goat is my best bet."

I motioned to the goat with a flourish. "Give it a try."

She studied the bleating animal. "And which god do you think this one is?"

"Not sure about the god, but the vice is lust."

Her smile widened. "You don't say? And how did you figure that one out?"

I struggled to give an answer that didn't give me away. "Reports of certain activities in town. The goat seems to work in tandem with some of the other animals, like wrath. There was even a murder-suicide."

"Makes sense." Camryn approached the goat from outside the cell. "Hey, did you notice this collar is slightly different?"

I leaned over her. "How?"

"It's missing the silver spikes that the pig and donkey have." She retrieved the Eight of Wands and tried again. "Will you look at that? No block on this one."

"How do you know if this one isn't talking either?"

She stood upright. "Because it can't. This is a normal goat."

I balked. "What? No, it can't be."

"If you're right and there's a lust goat ripping its way through town, this guy isn't it."

I stared at the goat. "You're one hundred percent certain?"

"I'd bet my shamans on it."

Shit. That meant…

Nope. I refused to think about what that meant.

Camryn gave the pig a longing look. "This blows. I really wanted this to have a happy ending."

I steered her toward the door. "There's still a chance." I had no intention of holding these animals indefinitely. Maybe Camryn and the pig could be reunited once I determined whether my theory was wrong.

"I guess you'd better get hunting," Camryn said. "We don't want a population boom in nine months. This town doesn't have the infrastructure."

"Bye, Cam." I waved as she sauntered outside, adjusting her beret to a jaunty angle as she left.

Ray intercepted me on my return to the kitchen. "I did a little research while you were busy with the Nerds lady."

"You're a treasure. Find out anything good?"

"That all depends on how you define 'good.'"

"Not a promising start, Ray."

"I worked on the assumption that your theory is right, and the man you saw was an Aztec god. The language spoken by ancient Aztecs is Nahuatl."

"Just my luck. A dead language."

"Except it isn't. Nahuatl is still spoken by approximately a million and a half Mexicans."

"Okay, now I'm embarrassed. Does that make me racist?"

"No, just ignorant," Ray replied, "but when you know better, you do better. Anyway, the word you heard in the pig's dream is ¡Xinechpalēhuia!"

"Great. What does it mean?"

His ghostly face turned grim. "This is the part that isn't good."

"Don't keep me in suspense, Ray. I've got enough stress at the moment."

"Help," Ray said. "It means help."

CHAPTER 16

I was ready to kick off my plan, but I needed all claws and cards on deck if I expected to round up the remaining animals in one night. The snake would be difficult to find, and the rest would be difficult to catch. I would have loved help from the nature mage, but I had no clue how to contact him. For all I knew, Brody was long gone by now.

My first call was to the prince of hell. I launched straight into my request so he didn't think I was calling to discuss personal issues. We'd done quite enough of that already.

"I have the guild at my disposal," the demon said, "plus Dantalion and Josephine. Tell me what you need, and it's yours."

"I'll need the mages to ward everyone against the animals' influence." The last thing we needed was to end up fighting each other in the middle of Wild Acres.

"Simple enough. I'd offer my club, but I doubt Davies would agree to meet there."

"It's fine. The Castle is neutral territory. Be here in an hour."

"You've met the guild members. Make it ninety minutes."

"Oh, you're having company," Nana Pratt exclaimed. "Why don't I make cookies?"

I eyed her closely. "Cookies for the assassins?"

The ghost looked at me blankly. "Do they not eat?"

Okay then. "Do you think you can manage that without burning down the house with me in it?"

The ghost lifted her chin a fraction. "Yes. Yes, I do."

"Then the kitchen is yours. Call me if you need help."

West was my second call and the first to arrive. I asked him to come solo so that I could present him with my findings before I requested the help of the pack. There was a chance he'd say no, and I didn't want a dozen wolves standing awkwardly around my house while they figured out how to politely leave.

West sniffed the air. "Why does your house smell so sweet?"

The oven timer pinged.

"Help!" Nana Pratt's voice called.

"Follow me," I said. "I need to take cookies out of the oven."

He inhaled the fresh scent. "What kind of cookies?"

"I'll tell you when I see them." As I removed the baking trays from the oven, I updated West on the situation.

"You've got an Aztec god in the form of a pig locked up in a cage in your house, and he asked for help?"

"It sounds crazy when you say it like that." I held up a finger. "And he did try to strangle me in the dream, when he had hands."

"How did you end up in his dream and, more importantly, how did you get out again before he killed you?"

I beat a hasty retreat from that part of the conversation. "Must have something to do with his powers."

"Didn't you say he's the god of gluttony?"

"You know these ancient gods. They're never limited to one ability, and the connection between them is rarely logical.

Hermes is known as the Greek messenger god, but he's also the deity of sleep." I shrugged. "The gods don't always make sense."

He glanced at the fridge. "Got any milk?"

"Depends on how you feel about almond milk."

"Other than it destroys the environment, no strong feelings whatsoever."

I smiled. "You're welcome to dunk your cookie in a glass of water."

He seemed to ponder the option. In the end, he reached for a cookie without a drink. "I assume we still don't know who turned this god into a pig and why."

"You assume correctly."

He chuckled to himself. "I've got to hand it to you, Lorelei. You've got a real knack for getting yourself into interesting situations."

"I appreciate your polite take. Most people would say I was a trouble magnet and steer clear of me."

"The thought has crossed my mind once or twice." He took a generous bite. "So, if the pig is an Aztec god of gluttony, what are the other animals?"

"A large snake has been spotted in a few upscale neighborhoods where burglaries happened."

"Okay, that's greed and wealth. Who's the greedy god? Odin?"

"Similar but think more Slavic."

West chewed the cookie. "I'm afraid my deity knowledge doesn't extend that far."

"I think it's Veles," I said. "That would explain the thundersnow."

"There's a god of thundersnow?"

"There is when he wants to make a statement. I think he's the snake."

"The god of thundersnow takes the form of a reptile? That doesn't seem to fit."

"Because he typically doesn't. The animal form is associated with greed but not necessarily the god. It's another clue that the animals haven't voluntarily chosen this path. If they had, they'd be in their usual forms."

"So Veles would be what?"

"A cow."

West gave me an appraising look. "How do you know so much about this stuff?"

"My grandfather taught me. He was obsessed with mythology." Or at least he became obsessed once he realized his granddaughter was a natural born goddess. Pops was self-educated and refused to rest until he'd passed all his knowledge on to me. He knew he wouldn't live to accompany me through adulthood, so he did everything in his power to prepare me for life on my own.

"Why is an Aztec god, or any god for that matter, skulking around Fairhaven trapped in the form of animals?"

"I'm not sure, but I think it has something to do with Addison Gray."

"Who's Addison Gray?"

"She's new to the area. I saw her at Devil's Playground, and she was cozying up to Officer Leo at Monk's the next night. Claims to be up for a job in the city and is considering a move to Fairhaven if she gets it."

West regarded me. "But you don't believe her?"

"She's got a vibe."

"That's pretty vague."

I didn't want to share my strange encounter with her. It felt like opening a door too wide. "You know the vibe you get from me, the one that tells you that you don't want me here? That's the vibe I get from her."

The werewolf alpha seemed to take my description on board. "Okay, let's say you're right, and she's shady."

I stiffened. "I'm not shady."

"You're hiding something that I sense could endanger my pack. That makes you shady."

"For someone who thinks I'm dangerous, you're sure willing to invest time and energy into me."

He shrugged. "Keep your friends close and your enemies closer."

"Is that what we are to you? Enemies?"

West sighed. "Honestly, Lorelei. I don't know anymore. You've confused me."

"One of my specialties."

"So, if this Addison is somehow connected to Veles and the seven deadly sins…"

"They're not a band."

He glowered at me.

"Sorry," I said. "Please continue."

"If she's connected to all this chaos," West said, "what do you propose we do about it?"

"I have Ray researching Addison's tattoos. I think the symbols are significant. They might tell us who we're dealing with."

"Have you asked the chief to run a background check on her?"

"I don't think the chief and I have that kind of relationship."

"She was willing to run a background check on you. Why not Addison?"

"She ran a check on me because I bought the Castle. She wanted to make sure I wasn't the lunatic I appeared to be."

"The jury's still out on that one," he mumbled. Then more clearly, he said, "You mentioned Addison was hanging out with the new cop. That could be enough to encourage her."

"Why me? You've known Chief Garcia much longer. Can't you ask for a favor?" I wasn't enthusiastic about requesting favors; in my experience, they ended up more trouble than they're worth. Even my moat came at a steep cost.

West rubbed his stubbled jawline. "I guess I could."

"Call her now. Maybe she's in her office."

He shot me a quizzical look. "Are you giving me an order?"

"Don't get your alpha fur in a ball. I'm simply making a suggestion. That's what happens during a collaboration. Sheesh, and here I thought you were supposed to be the democratic leader of the pack."

"I am."

"Is it because I'm a woman?"

He frowned. "You assume misogyny goes hand in hand with full furry? It's because you're not a member of the pack, Lorelei."

"Fine. You're not sexist." I waved a hand at him. "Just get on with it."

West pulled out his phone. "Just to be clear, I'm not doing this because you told me to. I'm doing it because I want to."

I bit back a smile. "Duly noted."

He asked for the chief and paced the length of the floor while he waited. "Hey, it's West," he finally said. "Got a favor." He asked her to run a background check on Addison Gray. "That's the one. Did he introduce you?"

I continued to listen to the one-sided conversation. I wished I'd asked him to put her on speaker, but I had a feeling he would've refused. West had trust issues, that much was obvious.

"Great," he said. "Thanks. I owe you a beer." He smiled at the phone. "Okay, two. I can't make Tuesday. How about Thursday?"

He almost seemed like a different person talking to Chief Garcia. He certainly didn't seem that cheerful when he spoke to me. I was a chore, whereas the chief was an absolute delight.

He hung up and tucked his phone in the back pocket of his jeans. "No criminal record. Weirdly minimal information. The chief said it's almost as if she were born yesterday."

"Born yesterday or born before computers existed. Could go either way."

"Or the name Addison Gray was only recently invented. That seems more logical."

It did, except I knew that logic didn't always factor into situations like this. My existence made no sense. I was a complete anomaly, yet here I was.

"You two sounded chummy," I commented. "I didn't realize you were that close."

"We have a close working relationship."

"You don't work for the police department, and she doesn't know about the pack."

"Maybe not, but we interact regularly in connection with community matters. She's devoted to this town, as am I."

Somebody seemed overly fond of the chief. "You know you're not her type, right?"

He shook his head. "Didn't you ever learn that men and women can be friends?"

"I'm well aware. I assumed you were on the hunt for a mate. You're a burly male with an acceptable face. She-wolves should be lining up outside your trailer for a chance with the alpha bachelor."

He scratched behind his ear. "An acceptable face? Now don't you start gushing over me."

"Don't let it go to your acceptable head."

"If you really want to know, there are complications attached to choosing a mate."

"Let me guess." I ticked the reasons off on my fingers. "You snore. You don't share food. You hog the covers."

"I absolutely share food. I wouldn't be a good alpha if I didn't."

Which means the other two guesses were likely accurate.

"Seriously, West. You seem like a popular guy. What could be so complicated that it hinders your marital prospects?"

He observed me, as though contemplating whether I was worthy of this conversation. Finally he said, "I wasn't born into the Arrowhead Pack. I joined later, and then I took over as alpha."

I remembered. "Why?"

"Doesn't matter. The fact is that I was born somewhere else. Sure, I've got werewolf blood, but it isn't Arrowhead blood. This pack has been here for centuries."

I had a feeling the 'why' mattered more than he was willing to admit. "And you've been leading this ancient pack for years. They've clearly accepted you. Why would they not accept whichever mate you choose?"

He dragged a hand through his envious head of hair. "Because I don't want to choose one from the current pack."

Ah, now the picture was becoming clear. "You'd be asking them to accept two interlopers as the future of the pack."

"I'm not an interloper," he snapped. "I belong here. Nobody questions that."

Oops. I touched a nerve there. "My mistake." I examined his words. "You already have someone in mind."

He glanced away. "It doesn't matter. I don't see a future in it."

"I'm sure if you broached the subject with the pack, they'd understand."

He blew out a breath. "It isn't that simple, Lorelei. It isn't just that she's not from the pack. She isn't even a werewolf."

The plot thickened. I thought he wanted to import a mail-order werewolf from another pack. I agreed; a non-wolf was worse. "Is she at least a supernatural?"

"She is, and that's all I'm willing to say on the matter. I can't risk this information leaking to the pack."

I pretended to zip my lip. "You can trust me, West, even if you think you can't." Although what did it matter if he had no plans to introduce her into pack life anyway? "Maybe you should give your pack the benefit of the doubt and tell them the truth. They may surprise you."

His jaw set. "Too risky. If they don't like it, they might make life difficult for her."

"What's the alternative? Marry a wolf from the pack and make each other miserable for the rest of your lives for the sake of appearances? America has enough marriages like that."

"I appreciate the counseling session, but the conversation ends now. In fact, let's forget we ever had it."

"Had what?"

He nodded in approval. "Exactly."

My thoughts returned to the mystery woman that wasn't the object of his desire. "The nonexistent background supports my theory that Addison is the one pulling the puppet strings." And the fact that she basically admitted as much.

"I agree. Let me know what Ray finds out about the tattoos. In the meantime, why don't we track down the rest of the animals before they kill anyone else?"

I raised an eyebrow. "Are you sure you want to?"

"One of them killed Chutney. We're in this until the end."

I nodded. "I'm happy to have as many wolves as you can spare, but they've already shown they can't track the animals."

"That's when we thought we were dealing with ordinary animals. Now we know better. That information will help."

I tried to understand his reasoning. "How?"

"We've got a town full of magic users. Let's make use of them."

"Magic is expensive. Maybe we could start a Go Fund Me for Fairhaven.

He grunted his amusement. "I don't know about the Bridger girl, but Sage's fae magic is particularly handy in a forest. And we've got your card-flicking friends in the guild."

"Already called them."

He offered a small smile. "Feels good to be on the same page, doesn't it?"

"I think we're on the same page more often than not. You're the one who wants me in a different book."

He gave me an appraising look. "I'm beginning to think I was wrong about you."

I chose my next words carefully. "As much as I hate to admit it, you aren't wrong, West. There's a solid possibility I unwittingly brought the circus to town."

"Don't blame yourself. Fairhaven's been a magnet for supernatural trouble since the dawn of civilization here. Whatever it is, we'll handle it like we always do." His hand froze on my shoulder. "I smell patchouli."

My skin itched. "It's sandalwood," I corrected him. "Kane is here."

I excused myself to let him in.

The prince of hell noticed West behind me. "Good to see you, Davies."

The alpha snarled.

"I'll see you later," West said to me.

Kane flashed his teeth. "Don't leave on my account."

"Just heading out to round up reinforcements. I'll be back." He slapped Kane on the back. "Her cookies are delicious, by the way. You should try them sometime."

The demon waited until the front door clicked closed to address me. "He tasted your cookies?"

"When you say it like that, it sounds dirty." I returned to the kitchen. "Technically Nana Pratt baked him cookies. He showed up when they were in the oven. What was I supposed to do? Eat one in front of him?"

"You could've waited until he left."

"They taste best straight from the oven." I popped a lid off a bottle of beer and drank. "What does it matter to you anyway? I'm a free agent. If I want to feed every wolf in the pack, that's up to me."

"As long as you're only feeding them. Is there a bottle for me, or do only werewolves get food and drink privileges?"

"One exchange of bodily fluids and now you're the boss of me? I don't think so." I pulled another bottle from the fridge and handed it to him. "Wouldn't want you to feel left out."

He flicked off the lid with his thumb. "We should talk about this once the current situation is under control."

"Talk about what?" I drained the beer from my bottle.

"You know what." His voice sounded weary enough that I felt my defenses soften.

"I think you said everything you needed to say. Let's focus on these sinful animals. For all we know, they're the cause of all recent behavior."

His brow inched up. "Is there other behavior I should know about? Perhaps something brewing between you and Davies? You do have certain things in common."

"A love of chocolate chip cookies?" I selected a gooey one from the cooling tray and bit into it.

"You recall that I collect secrets, yes?"

"I do."

"Are you aware that Davies isn't an original member of the local pack?"

"He and I were just discussing that, in fact." Sort of.

"Did he tell you why?"

I savored the taste of the cookies. A-plus, Nana Pratt. "Not really my business."

"Davies was cast out of his pack as a pup when a rival killed his family to take over. The wolf tried to wipe out the whole line. West was the only one to escape. He ended up here and became the alpha of Arrowhead."

"I'm surprised he managed it. Packs tend to be insular."

"There was a power vacuum at the time. He seized the opportunity. Nobody's challenged him since then."

"I'm not surprised. He's grown into a strapping alpha."

Kane cocked an eyebrow. "Strapping's your type, is it?"

"Strapping is everybody's type." I smiled sweetly. "How about it, Kane? Would you like to nibble one of my cookies?"

He gave the tray a cursory look. "My tastes are a bit more refined, most of the time. West is more of a homemade cookie guy, as you seem to have discovered."

Kane Sullivan, master of mixed messages. It was as though our intimate conversation never happened, which was probably for the best. Getting involved with anyone, let alone a demon prince of hell, was a recipe for disaster.

He brought the beer bottle to those soft lips, and my body tingled, remembering with disappointingly vivid clarity how they felt on my skin. It took me a moment to realize that the tingle was actually in response to the activated ward.

Nana Pratt's imitation of a doorbell broke through my lust-filled haze, and I shoved the memory to the back of my mind.

Saved by the bell.

CHAPTER 17

Bluebeard's Castle hadn't hosted this many visitors since its last party during the Gilded Age. It felt uncomfortable and overwhelming to open my home to them, but it was all for a good cause.

I ended up deactivating the ward temporarily when my skin started itching like crazy. I now sported red streaks on my arms from where I couldn't stop scratching.

Kane, Dantalion, and Josephine were currently gathered in front of the fireplace in the living room. Ray had the foresight to light a fire, which meant the room was now a comfortable temperature for guests. Nana Pratt busied herself in the kitchen, somehow producing dozens more freshly baked cookies. I wasn't even aware that I had the ingredients.

West was next to arrive—again, along with six pack members and Sage—short for Savage according to the blond fae.

Gunther, Camryn, and Vaughn arrived together. I wasn't sure whether Kane had issued a demand or a request to members of the guild, nor did I want to ask. I didn't want to give the impression that I wasn't grateful for the number of participants he managed to rally.

Upon entry, Gun motioned to the coat rack, now covered in the outer layers of the visitors. "Good thing I bought that for you, or all these coats would be dusting the floor."

"It was a timely purchase," I agreed.

He peered into the living room. "Interesting cast of characters. Where's your cursed friend?"

"Otto didn't feel comfortable running around in the snowy woods in search of animals he can't see."

"That's fair."

"I'm glad you got back to town in time for all the fun."

"I did, but most guild members are out of town on assignments," Gun replied. "I'm afraid it's only the three amigos."

I tried not to dwell on the number of murders happening as we spoke. Not my assassination circus, not my guild monkeys. "We've got plenty of help. Between all of us, we should be able to capture the rest of the animals."

Now that we were all assembled, I called the meeting to order.

"We're looking for a lion, a wolf, a serpent, a wild boar, a goat, and a large snake."

Kane frowned. "Not the goat. You have the goat."

I swallowed hard. "About that… It seems this one is a regular goat. The godly goat is still out there."

Kane stared at me with a look I couldn't pinpoint. "I see," was all he said.

"And where are we keeping this cirque du so-freaks once we catch them?" Josie asked.

"Right here in my house with the others," I said. "These animals can affect supernaturals. Chutney is evidence of that, which is why the mages will use protective magic on each of us."

"What about capturing the animal?" West asked. "If you don't want us to kill them, how do we subdue them without injury?"

"By pairing you with a magic user." As expected, I heard a few audible groans.

West piped up. "Listen, unless you want the rest of us picking pieces of you out of the branches of evergreen trees, you'll follow Lorelei's orders. We can't afford to be dicks about this."

Cam looked at him with sharp interest. "I never knew you could be so succinct, West." She leaned over and whispered to Gun, "It's pretty hot."

"I can be succinct," Vaughn said.

Oh, how the tides had turned. It seemed Cam and her crush might've swapped places.

Cam sidled up to the alpha and linked her arm through his. "I'm with the wolf."

Bert sighed. "We're all wolves on this side of the room."

"If Brody pops up once we're out there, consider him part of this operation. I don't care how long your magic wand is, you don't go macho man on the nature mage, understood?"

Gun scowled. "Nobody here uses a magic wand. We're not book characters."

"It was a metaphor," Vaughn said, "for our male members."

Camryn rolled her eyes. "That's just using a metaphor to describe another metaphor."

I ignored her. "Josie, you can team up with Gun." At least they knew each other from Assassins Guild meetings. I wasn't convinced Josie would work well with a complete stranger—and I included myself in that category.

The vampire glowered at Gun from beneath a set of naturally thick lashes. The vampire should at least have the decency to possess anemic eyelashes. It didn't seem fair that she was blessed with both immortality and gorgeous genes. "I work alone," she said in a low voice.

Gun smiled. "I expected nothing less from you, Josephine."

"Remember, we're there to capture, not kill," I said, once the groups had been formed.

Vaughn scratched his head. "Remind me why that is again?"

"Because they're not operating under their own steam. We think they're being controlled by their collars."

"What happens if you remove the collar?" Vaughn asked.

"We haven't managed to do that yet," I replied. "They're enchanted."

"I tried to break the enchantment," Cam chimed in. "It was like banging my head against a brick wall."

"Which I've seen her do," Gun added, "so she knows firsthand what that feels like."

"How do you know they're not behaving willfully?" Sage asked. "They could be trapped in animal hides but still acting of their own free will."

"Because the pig asked for help," I said.

"I thought Cam's magic didn't work," Vaughn said.

"The details don't matter and we're wasting time," I insisted. I started to feel flushed under the glare of the artificial lights.

"How about those cookies before we go?" Josie interrupted. "Hunting is hungry work."

On cue, Nana Pratt entered the room carrying a large plate of cookies. Josie snatched one and gobbled it down like she hadn't tasted sugar in a century.

Vaughn regarded the floating plate as he bit down on a cookie. "What kind of magic is that?"

"Her name is Nana Pratt," I said. "She's a ghost here."

Vaughn stopped chewing and swallowed. "For real?"

Gun burst into laughter. "You kill for a living. What's so scary about a ghost?"

"They can watch you when you're asleep," Vaughn replied.

"I do that, and I'm not a ghost," Cam said.

Gun patted her back. "You probably shouldn't admit that out loud, sweetie."

The cookies were gone in under ten seconds. Nana Pratt seemed pleased by this outcome. "It feels good to be useful again," she said with a contented sigh.

I hurried upstairs to my bedroom to gather my weapons and zip on my boots. When I turned to leave, Kane stood in the doorway.

"When this is all over, I'd like to talk."

"We already did."

"The goat…"

I held up a hand. "The goat doesn't change anything. You told me that getting involved was a bad idea. I accept that."

"Lorelei." He reached for my hand, but I pulled away.

"We have work to do, Kane. Let's focus on that." I ran downstairs ahead of him.

"We'll hold down the fort," Ray said.

I made sure to activate the ward on my way out. There was no point in taking any chances.

"Follow the yellow brick road," Gun's voice rang out.

"If we encounter flying monkeys, I'm out," Anna said.

"If we encounter flying monkeys," Josie said, "I'm adopting one."

Our vehicles formed a procession as we drove to the nearest access point for Wild Acres. The teams spilled out of the doors, and we arranged to regroup in an hour.

It was go time.

We marched into the forest like an army preparing for battle. I was the only one with obvious weapons. Everyone else had the advantage of magic or claws.

As I walked at the end of the line, I felt a familiar burning sensation on my back. Someone was watching us.

I stopped and turned around. "Brody, where are you?"

The nature mage peeled away from the tall shadow of an evergreen. "I heard there was a party, and I wasn't invited."

"You were. I just had no idea where to send the invitation."

He puffed out his chest. "Well, I'm here now. Might as well make good use of me."

I caught up to the group with Brody in tow. "Everyone, this is Brody. Brody, this is everyone."

Kane was the first to shake his hand. "You're the nature mage."

"'Tis I."

Gun frowned. "'Tis? What accent even is that?"

"A special blend," Brody replied.

"Like my coffee," Cam said.

Brody turned to face Kane. "You must be the prince of hell I've heard so much about."

"Not from me," I said quickly.

"Perish the thought," Kane murmured.

We divided Wild Acres into sections and separated into our groups.

"What if they're not all in the forest?" Vaughn asked. "Should we start combing the streets?"

"We'll cross that tightrope when we come to it," I said.

Kane glanced at me. "Ready to channel your inner Artemis?"

"We're not hunting," I emphasized.

"You can still hunt something you don't intend to kill."

"As long as we're clear on that." Right now, I felt the weight of far more than my weapons on my shoulders. The safety of these animals felt like my responsibility.

"We're clear," he said, "at least on that issue."

I ignored the passive aggressive comment. "I've spotted the wolf twice in this area," I said. "I don't know whether she's tracking me, or if she's laying low out here."

"I thought you said they're being controlled by Addison."

"I think they are, but I don't think they're like remote control cars. Their every movement isn't guided by an unseen hand. Only their influence." I didn't think the lion intended to walk around Fairhaven killing anyone. It was only when the right set of circumstances presented themselves that the collar was triggered.

I was first to spot the wolf tracks. I caught Kane's eye and pointed.

Kane bent down to examine them. "They're recent," he said in a quiet voice.

A low growl alerted us to the wolf's presence.

Slowly Kane turned to get a better look at the wolf. "That's quite the evil eye."

"Don't look directly at it. I don't know what effect it might have on you."

I could try to use my powers the way I used them on the pig, but the wolf was far more likely to kill me before I got a good grip on her. She seemed angry at the world, not that I blamed her.

Kane kept his gaze on the growling wolf. "How do you want to play this?"

"How about your monster form? It might intimidate her into submission."

He cut a quick glance at me. "You think I'm intimidating?"

I snorted. "You're a ginormous creature with wings. Godzilla would find you intimidating."

He grinned.

"It isn't a compliment."

"Are you sure? Because it sounded like one to me."

I gestured to the wolf, who was now salivating and ready to kill us both out of pure frustration and impatience.

Kane removed his jacket with a flourish and hung it on a nearby branch. Then he unfastened his cufflinks and rolled up his sleeves.

"I've seen this routine before," I said. "You might consider changing it up a bit."

He gave me an appraising look before erupting into a giant wolf with griffin wings. His eyes burned with malice as he faced his opponent.

I quickly backed away.

Monster Kane loomed over the wolf. With a few ferocious snarls and gnashing of teeth, Invidia gave it her best effort, but she was no match for this frightening version of the prince of hell. His massive maw opened, and he roared directly in her face, shutting down any thoughts of a she-wolf win.

Her jaws snapped shut. Lowering her head, she started to inch backward where I was ready and waiting for her. I touched her lower back and inundated her mind with red light. The wolf's body relaxed.

Kane gazed at the wolf in awe. "What did you do to her?" he asked in a slightly raspy voice. His monster voice lacked the polish of his usual one.

"I showed her red light, which increases the production of melatonin to help her sleep. She's probably been stressed and unable to rest." I looked at him. "Now you know who to call the next time you can't sleep."

"If you showed up at my bedside, I don't think either of us would get any sleep."

More mixed signals. Terrific. Life was challenging enough; I didn't need the confusion.

"Take her to my house," I said, feeling a strong need to distance myself from him. "I'll keep tracking the others."

Monster Kane slung the wolf over his shoulder and carried her away.

I stepped gingerly through the forest, searching for more tracks and trying very hard not to think about a certain demon whose title rhymed with 'mince of smell.'

I was never so grateful to hear a lion's roar.

I followed the sound, running deeper into the woods to find that Gun and his group had the lion surrounded on a boulder.

"No wonder he sounds unhappy," I said. "Good work, team."

Gun held up a finger. "Nobody feel proud about our accomplishment. I don't want to hunt for pieces of you in the snow." He observed the nature mage. "What's your plan, Peter Pan?"

Brody pulled a vine from a nearby tree and fashioned a whip. He snapped it against the boulder.

Gun stared at the whip. "Did you just make that with your hands?"

"Indeed, I did." Brody lashed the whip at the lion, who roared in defiance.

Gun's eyes widened. "We have a guild you might be interested in, good sir."

"Membership is capped," Cam reminded him.

"If I've learned anything as a very attractive mage with excellent fashion sense and a jawline that could cut glass, there are exceptions to every rule."

"Can we focus on the task at hand?" I said, waving a hand at the lion.

"Not to worry," Brody said. He lashed the whip again, cutting short the lion's roar. "I've got everything under control." Slowly he approached the lion, speaking softly to the animal.

The lion seemed to respond to the nature mage. He dropped to his stomach and yawned.

"I'm feeling woefully inadequate right now, and that doesn't happen often," Gun said.

"Can you transport the lion to my house?" I asked. "Kane is there with the wolf."

"We'll do it," Bert said. "Then I can cross 'carried a lion' off my bucket list."

"You should have a magic user with you," I said.

Camryn raised her hand. "I'll go. My feet are numb."

Gun glanced at her shoes. "Because you wore riding boots. I mean, they look fabulous, but they aren't very practical in the snow."

Camryn turned her leg to admire the boot. "They do look fabulous, don't they?"

"Aren't you supposed to be with West?" I asked her.

"I switched teams. He was too bossy."

"Where's Josie?" I asked.

"She switched teams," Gun said. "She was too bossy."

I stifled a groan.

"How many animals are left?" Gun asked.

"Three," I said. "The snake, the wild boar, and the goat." I tried not to choke on the word 'goat.' I was still mortified that I'd caught the wrong one.

"The snake is on its way to the Castle," Vaughn announced, emerging from the trees behind Gun. "It was a slippery sucker, but I once spent a week in the Amazon rainforest tracking a target. I became very adept at handling large snakes."

Gun snickered. "I think you were an expert long before then."

I started to feel optimistic we could pull this off. "Okay, one wild boar and one goat. Let's go."

We fanned out in the forest. Brody accompanied me in the direction of Sawmill Creek. The snow crunched beneath our sensible boots as we walked.

"I appreciate your help, Brody. You didn't have to get involved."

"Are you kidding? This is the most fun I've had in ages. Feels like a holiday."

"I'm glad we could entertain you during your stay."

"Apparently, Magnarella thinks you're responsible for the magical herd, you know."

"Responsible how?"

"He thinks they belong to you."

I laughed, relieved that the vampire monster remained clueless about my real abilities. "Has he hassled you about not killing me yet?"

"Of course, but I've given him believable excuses." His arm suddenly shot in front of me to keep me still.

I followed his gaze to the bank of the creek where three snarling wolves had Sage surrounded. I wasn't sure what I was witnessing, until I spotted the wild boar tangled in a net hanging from a thick tree branch. Beneath the net stood West.

"Stay back," he commanded.

"Is he talking to us or the wolves?" Brody asked.

West kept his focus on the unfolding conflict. "The wolves," he answered. "They joined us later and didn't have protection in place."

"How can we help?" I whispered.

"They're my wolves. I'll handle it."

I could only imagine the thoughts racing through his mind. He didn't want to hurt members of his pack, but he couldn't let them hurt Sage either.

The largest of the three wolves lunged at Sage. In dodging his fangs, the fae tumbled into the icy creek.

"Sage!" The look on West's face was unmistakable. He didn't just fear for someone's life. He feared for *her* life.

Sage was the woman he was in love with.

The alpha's wolf form exploded from his human one. His massive body cut straight through the trio of wolves and knocked them aside like they were pins in a bowling lane. Water splashed as he ran into the creek. Using his sharp teeth, he grabbed Sage by her coat collar and dragged her to the other side. He covered her body with his, using his fur coat to keep her warm.

Still feeling the effects of the wild boar, the three wolves started to fight each other. Brody quickly interceded, using vines to rope the wolves and tie their paws together.

"How is she?" I yelled across the creek.

Sage nudged the wolf aside and sat upright. "I'm okay. Just cold and wet."

West reverted to his human form. I glanced away before I saw more of the alpha than I cared to.

My phone buzzed in my pocket. *We've got the goat*, Gun's message said. *Does that make us the GOAT?*

"All seven are accounted for," I announced.

West helped Sage to her feet. "I'll take it from here," he said, motioning to the wolves. "Unless you need help with transporting the boar."

"I can help with that," Brody offered.

"You can't risk being seen at my house. I'll take him."

"At least allow me to carry him to your truck."

"I'd rather you didn't. Just because you didn't feel the envy of the wolf doesn't mean you won't feel the boar's wrath if you're around it long enough." And I wouldn't want to be alone with Brody if that happened.

"In that case, my work here is done," Brody said.

"What about Magnarella?"

"Good luck finding me. The vampire doesn't have much influence beyond this area."

"Then why pay his debt in the first place?"

"Because I'm an honorable mage, but knowing what I now know, seems more honorable to defy him." He bowed with a flourish. "'Tis been an absolute pleasure, Lorelei Clay. I do hope our paths cross again someday."

"Only if you're on my team when they do."

CHAPTER 18

I did not want to get out of bed. My body felt like it had been crushed under a steamroller and then hand-tossed like a pizza, not so much from the hunting expedition, but from the wrangling in the house that came afterward. I stared at the ceiling and prayed for mercy. At least I mended quickly—an essential element of the goddess gift basket.

The zoo in my dining room provided the motivation I needed to get out of bed. The animals were getting restless. You haven't been properly annoyed until you've endured the sound of a donkey braying for forty minutes straight.

Although I took my time on the stairs, my hips protested anyway.

"You look like I did right before I died," Nana Pratt said, observing me from the foyer.

"That's a comforting thought. What are you doing in here?"

"You asked Ray and I to watch over the animals while you slept. Don't you remember?"

I had a vague memory of grunting at the ghosts and crawling upstairs to my bedroom. "The donkey is noisy."

"They're hungry. I wasn't sure what to feed them. Do they need nectar or some other special god food?"

I stretched my back, which resulted in a satisfying popping sound. "I'll feed and water them." But first I needed to feed and water myself. It's like they tell you on the airplane —put on your own oxygen mask first before helping others.

Ray appeared in the kitchen as I chowed down on a bowl of Cheerios topped with blueberries.

"That donkey needs to go," he said.

"They all need to go." It wasn't a matter of 'if' but 'when,' and more importantly, 'how.'

"The lion is surprisingly docile," he said. "I thought he might object to being trapped in an enclosure with the others."

"They're not typical animals. They won't bother each other."

"Too bad it doesn't keep the donkey from bothering us," he muttered.

"Is that why you interrupted my breakfast, Ray? To complain about the donkey? Because we can all hear her."

Ray moved closer and hovered next to the table. "Remember those tattoos you asked me to research? I think I found something."

I broke into a smile. "That's great, Ray. Good work."

He floated a little taller. "Independently, the tattoos mean different things. Together, they act as an enchantment called Hidden Door."

The news didn't surprise me. Addison was one big hidden door, and I wasn't sure I wanted the prize behind it. "If I open the door, what will it reveal?"

Ray shrugged. "You're on your own for that one."

My guess was that Addison crafted the tattoos to hide her real identity. As a supernatural, she'd only want to hide her identity from other supernaturals because humans wouldn't have a clue anyway. Which begged the question—why the need to hide from those of us in the small town of Fairhaven?

Unless she wasn't trying to hide from all the supernaturals in town, only one.

Me.

I pushed back the chair and stood. "I'll be back."

"Where are you off to already?" Ray asked.

"You gave me food for thought." I rinsed my bowl and left it in the sink. "Thanks, Ray. That was really helpful."

"What's next?" he asked.

The sound of the donkey's bray carried into the kitchen. "Ever dream of being a zookeeper?"

Ray sighed. "No, but I'll do anything to make it stop."

"I was hoping you'd say that."

With the animals taken care of, I was able to focus on Addison Gray. I wrote a list of everything I knew about her so far. She appeared in town under false pretenses. Cozied up to Officer Leo. Unleashed deities trapped as animals to wreak havoc the old-fashioned way, and then sat back to enjoy the show. I recalled her champagne salute at the Devil's Playground and her compliment at Monk's about my fighting skills. She'd been watching me, specifically. She'd basically admitted this whole 'game' was about me. What would the winner receive?

If she'd wanted me dead like Brody, there were much easier ways that didn't involve killing innocent people in the process. This wasn't about killing me, which meant she wasn't working for Magnarella.

I got a sinking feeling in my stomach. Addison had access to deities that spread the seven deadly sins. Not just access but control. That signified real power—the kind of power that the vampire mafia could only dream of, which left one viable option.

The Corporation.

Swearing loudly, I chucked my pen across the room. I

knew I hadn't escaped Magnarella's fighting ring unscathed. I thought I'd managed to hide my real abilities and credit the god elixir, and maybe I'd been mostly successful—but it only took one keen eye to detect my ruse.

If my theory was correct, that meant Addison Gray was an avatar. I wasn't sure which goddess inhabited her, but I had a couple guesses. She wasn't here to kill me; she was here for information. That had to be the point of her game—to figure out my identity based on her observations. She unleashed the seven vices to see how I handled the crisis—which powers I used, how I worked. No doubt there'd been times she'd been watching me in action when I hadn't noticed. Not creepy at all.

This was bad in every way possible. Not only was my secret in jeopardy, but I'd brought death to Fairhaven. I didn't regret helping Dusty, but I never should've used my powers in the ring. On the other hand, if I hadn't, I'd be dead. Nothing like the dim view between a rock and a hard place.

"Is everything okay?" Nana Pratt asked. She retrieved my pen from the floor and set it in front of me on the table.

I opted for brutal honesty. "No. Would you mind getting Ray? I need to speak to you both."

I gathered my courage while I waited for the ghosts to join me. I had no idea how they would respond to my revelation.

"That snake tried to bite me," Ray complained.

"The snake can't see you. He probably tried to bite the food you had." I leaned back, nearly tipping the chair off its legs in the process. "I need to tell you something."

Nana Pratt clapped her hands together. "You're pregnant! Oh, won't it be wonderful to have a baby in the house?"

My mouth dropped open. "I ... I am 100 percent not pregnant."

The elderly woman held her index finger an inch from her thumb. "Maybe twenty percent pregnant?"

I ran my hand down my face. "I'm not pregnant, Nana

Pratt. I'm a goddess. That's the secret I've been keeping from you."

The ghosts stared at me, appearing perplexed.

"Is this one of those uplifting female things?" Ray asked. "Like you say you're a goddess so we can agree with you and make you feel better?"

"Make me feel better about what?" I shook my head. "Never mind. No, Ray. I'm an actual goddess. An incarnation, which is an uncontrolled birth that happens spontaneously in nature—to human parents."

Ray scratched his translucent head. "That can happen?"

"Yes, but it's extremely rare."

"I've never heard of a goddess called Lorelei," Ray said.

"The goddess is Melinoe," I explained.

"That's a pretty name," Nana Pratt said. "If you have a daughter, you should name her that."

I closed my eyes and counted to ten in my head. "I'm not giving birth anytime soon, Nana Pratt."

"What are your powers?" Ray asked. "Is that why you can help spirits cross over and communicate with us?"

Here came the hard part. "I can do far more than that." I looked at Nana Pratt. "You know how I helped you control the putty knife?"

"Yes, that was very helpful, dear."

"It's because I'm the goddess of nightmares and ghosts. I can control both of those things."

"Control," Ray murmured.

"Yes, like a puppet master. Certain creatures are under my command, and that includes you."

"That's a lot of responsibility," Ray said.

"One reason I don't utilize my powers."

"Did I really want to scrape all the wallpaper, or did you make me do that?" Nana Pratt asked.

"I wasn't manipulating you; I promise."

She nodded, seeming to accept my answer. "I think I need a minute to process this." She winked out of existence.

I shifted my gaze to Ray. "How about you? Need a minute?"

"I'm good," he said. "So, this is your big secret?"

"Yep."

"And this is why you hide?"

"I'm a freak of nature with immense power, which makes me a target for those who'd want to weaponize me."

"And your fella found out what you are. Is that why you two fought?"

"More or less. I have direct access to minds, memories, dreams, nightmares. I can learn a lot about someone in under sixty seconds."

"And your prince of hell wasn't too excited about that."

"He isn't mine, and he has his reasons."

Nana Pratt returned to the kitchen. "Lorelei, I hate to interrupt, but that woman with the tattoos is outside. She isn't even wearing a coat."

"That's because she doesn't feel anything." Only a monster would choose to gather intel the way she had.

I looked at the ghosts. "Are we good?"

They nodded. "Thank you for telling us," Ray said. "I know it wasn't easy for you."

"A lifetime of conditioning will do that." I pushed back my chair. "I want you two to stay away. I don't know yet what Addison is capable of, and I don't want you caught in the crossfire."

I walked to the foyer to peer outside. Sure enough, Addison Gray stood outside the gate wearing only a black tank top, black jeans, and black boots. Judging from her rigid posture, she wasn't happy.

Grabbing my coat, I headed into the cold air to greet her. "Is that you, Addy?"

"Yes." I could hear the ire in her voice. She wasn't just unhappy; girlfriend was pissed.

Good.

She gestured to the gate. "I was just coming to see you. It seems you have a few items that belong to me. Seven, in fact."

I folded my arms. "Haven't you ever heard of finders keepers, Addy?"

Anger flashed in her eyes. Surprise, surprise. The goddess didn't like being told no. "Why would you want them in your house? You've seen firsthand how dangerous they are."

"If they're so dangerous, why do you want them?"

The anger melted from her eyes as she switched gears. "Because it would be very bad if they didn't find their way back to the storage container where they belong."

Storage container? These were living, breathing creatures, not dusty old records. "And where is that?"

"I think you know."

"The Corporation headquarters."

"Close enough. They're kept at an off-site facility."

"Why set them loose in Fairhaven? Innocent people have died because of you."

"Au contraire, snookums. I think you'll find they died because of you. I wanted to see what you're made of."

Wow. Talk about a lack of accountability. "Sugar and spice and everything nice. At least that's what my grandmother used to tell me."

"I think your grandmother forgot a few key ingredients."

"What makes you say that?"

She offered a demure smile. "I heard all about your win in Magnarella's fighting ring."

Disappointment flooded my veins. "From Naomi Smith?" Otherwise known as Eunomia, goddess of law and order. Naomi was The Corporation's intrepid investigator who'd pegged me as another avatar. I'd promised her it was the god elixir at work and asked her to leave me in peace. I'd been both surprised and relieved when she agreed.

"No one from The Corporation. My source is a regular attendee of Magnarella's events. His description of the match intrigued me, so I asked to watch the video. That's when intrigue became genuine interest."

My heart stopped. "There's a video?"

"Not to worry, sweetie. It isn't intended for public consumption. To the untrained eye, everything appears as it should, but I saw enough to decide to vet you myself."

"Is that why you let the wild boar in the nightclub? To see if I sprouted wings or horns?"

She curled her fingers around the metal post of the gate. "I was curious to see how you would handle the situation. I certainly didn't expect that sweet little kitten to breathe fire, so that was a bonus."

"Sunny is an unofficial bouncer."

"Well, she's far more effective than the idiot at the door. One sultry look from me and he completely missed the giant set of tusks that wandered in behind me."

I tried not to be offended that Larry insisted on checking my ID with the laser focus of Superman, yet Addison's smile blocked his view of a giant wild boar.

"If these animals are so important to you, maybe you shouldn't have left them to roam freely around town."

"Honestly, I didn't expect you to round them up and hold them hostage in your house."

"What did you expect me to do?"

She offered a casual shrug. "I assumed you'd try to kill them."

And she wanted to make a note of how I accomplished that. Got it. "What makes you think I didn't kill them?"

"Because you can't. That's why I said 'try.'"

Good to know my efforts would've been in vain if I had decided to off them. "Why are you using an alias and an enchantment to hide your identity from me? Unless you're someone I know, I don't see the point."

She glanced at the sleeve tattoo. "Twenty bucks says you're an only child." Her gaze flicked back to me. "I'm only asking nicely one more time."

"Why ask nicely at all? Channel your inner goddess, barge in, and take them." An idea clicked into place. "You can't."

She bristled. "Of course I can. I choose not to. Send the animals outside before I lose my patience."

I folded my arms. "No."

Addison began to pace outside the gate. "This isn't part of the game, Lorelei. Release them, and I promise I'll explain everything."

"Explain first. Here, I'll even help you get started. You're an avatar. Which goddess, I'm not sure yet. You work for The Corporation, but you've gone rogue. They don't know you're here, and you don't want them to know, hence the fake name and tattoos. You probably didn't go through the proper channels to borrow the beasts, and you're worried if they find out you stole their gods from Pandora's box, you'll be in big trouble—unless, of course, you can tell them something worthwhile that will get you off the hook. Tell me, Addy, what's the penalty for stealing from your employer?"

Addison didn't flinch. "Death, usually. Depends on the value of the stolen goods."

"And which goddess are you?"

"You first, sweetie."

I sidestepped the request. "What do you do for them? Intelligence officer?"

She released a throaty laugh. "Gods, no. I'm much too unpredictable for that."

An unpredictable goddess. That knocked at least one prospect off my short list.

"How did you figure out they were gods?" she asked, sounding genuinely curious.

I couldn't tell her about my entry into the Aztec god's mind. "Magic," I answered.

"Impossible. Those collars are designed to block magic, which means you have a different kind of power that allowed you to bypass the spell." Her eyes narrowed. "Which means you could've killed them, after all." She pressed her face between the posts. "Which begs the question—why didn't you?"

"What makes you think the decision was mine? I had a lot of help."

"Nice try. Why do you think I targeted strangers in town instead of your loved ones? That's right—because you don't have any." She waved a hand at the Castle. "Why not live off the grid in a yurt instead of choosing the biggest house in a small town? You can't manifest the life you want with mixed signals, kitten. You'll only confuse the universe."

"I saw an opportunity to put down roots, and I took it."

"The way you saw an opportunity to save the people of Fairhaven from deadly vices? Face it, Lorelei, you have a savior complex."

I was ready to drag Addison inside and feed her to the lion. "I do not have a savior complex."

"Of course you do. You wouldn't have taken that mage's place in the ring otherwise."

"That was a favor," I insisted.

Whatever I was trying to sell, Addy wasn't buying it. "It's nothing to be embarrassed about, sweetie. I'm guessing it's your childhood that set you up for that. Trauma is as common as the cold. I can tell you why Addison chose to become an avatar. Tragic backstory, that." She eyed me curiously. "But what I'd like to know is why did you become one and, more importantly, how? You're not on the company payroll, and I know it wasn't Magnarella's elixir. The powers didn't match the deity."

"Why go to such great lengths? Why not tell your bosses your theory and let them deal with me?"

"Because I want the credit."

I examined her closely. "I get it now. You're *already* on the outs with them, and you hope delivering me will get you back in their good graces."

Addison opened her arms wide. "What can I say? I'm a rebel at heart. Gets me in hot water on occasion." Her eyes gleamed with malice. "But I always find a way to get myself out of it."

She charged through the open gate and slammed into me, knocking us both to the ground. My teeth rattled as the back of my head hit the paved walkway.

Her fist hurtled toward my face. I rolled to the side, so it only skimmed my hair. Before I could get upright, Addison was on top of me again. As expected, she was freakishly strong. We grappled on the ground, kicking up a mixture of snow and dirt. A flurry of blows landed along my jawline. The taste of blood filled my mouth. This was no ordinary fight. It wasn't even like the fight in Magnarella's ring. This was a true goddess-on-goddess in the real world.

The heel of my boot connected with her nose, followed by a crunching sound. I scrambled to my feet and put a couple yards between us.

"Tell me more about your childhood trauma," I taunted. "Did that involve going uphill in the snow both ways barefoot and with both hands tied behind your back?"

She remained on the ground, and I was pleased to see blood dripping from her nose. "I told you—it was Addison's trauma. I have all her information stored inside." She tapped the side of her head.

"You sound like a robot. Come to think of it, you act like one too. All head and no heart."

She pretended to pout. "Kitten, you wound me. You know

as well as I do that goddesses like us don't have the same lived experience as mere humans."

Except I did, because I was both. I'd always been both, and right now I was afraid that put me at a distinct disadvantage.

I tried another tack. "This doesn't have to be a competition, you know. Women should lift each other up."

Addison sprang forward and rammed her head into my shins. I went sailing through the air, landing on my tailbone with a hard thud. "High enough for you?"

I struggled to my feet as pain radiated down my lower back and my legs. "I give it a five."

She clucked her tongue. "And here I thought it wasn't a competition."

"Why are you holding back? Where are your goddess powers, or is that the problem at work? Was your performance review unsatisfactory?" If I knew her identity, I could formulate a better plan to fight her.

She smirked. "I'll show you mine if you show me yours."

I wiggled my fingers. "Come on, *snookums*. Impress me."

Addison rushed toward me. I grabbed her fist before she could land her next punch and twisted her arm until I heard a satisfying snap. She expressed her displeasure by sweeping my legs out from under me. I fell backward but immediately catapulted myself back to a standing position. She was ready for me with a sharp chop to the throat.

"I've seen you fight in the ring," Addison said. "I know you can do better than this."

"It was the elixir," I rasped.

"Bullshit." She shifted her weight and struck me in the stomach with a roundhouse kick that left me breathless. My left foot slipped, and I noticed I was poised at the edge of the moat. Addison didn't give me time to recover my balance. Smiling sweetly, she poked my nose and said, "Boop."

I fell backward and crashed through the ice that had

crusted over the top of the moat. The frigid water cut straight to my bones. As I attempted to surface, I felt resistance. At first, I thought I'd hit a patch of ice, until I realized it was Addison's hand.

That bitch was holding me underwater.

"You've bored me, Lorelei," I heard her voice say. "Here I thought I'd found a diamond in the rough but turns out you're nothing but a lump of coal."

I could only hold my breath and withstand the icy moat for so long. I clawed at her hand, but she held firm.

I never should've met her outside without weapons. At the very least I could've grabbed a butter knife on my way out to greet her. A regrettable error that just might kill me.

Her hand continued to palm my head, applying just enough pressure to keep me submerged. I tried to pull her in with me, but my strength was quickly waning.

An image of Pops floated in my mind's eye. We were at a lake somewhere in rural Lancaster County. He was teaching me how to hold my breath underwater in case I ever needed to hide. I'd been terrified—that I would drown, naturally, and also that I had to fear someone so much that I'd choose to risk dying over letting them catch me.

I was seven.

My lungs felt ready to burst. I pushed aside the memory and concentrated on the goddess. It was my only way out. I slipped into her mind like it was made of silk. Her thoughts were jumbled and chaotic. A quick sweep of the contents revealed her identity—Aite, the goddess of mischief and ruin. Thanks to her reign of terror over the centuries, there were hundreds, if not thousands, of nightmares in her head.

It was only a matter of selecting the most effective one.

Pain sliced through the numbness of my body as I ripped an image from her mind and thrust it straight into reality. I knew I'd succeeded when the pressure stopped. I shot to the surface and drew a desperate breath. My chilled body refused to cooperate as I attempted to climb out of the moat. I slipped twice before pulling myself to the cold, hard ground.

Addison was on the ground, surrounded by a crowd of men. Some wore tunics; others wore doublets and stockings.

All were angry.

"Who are they?" I asked.

"Men I've led to ruin," she said without remorse. She raised her hand, as though to summon her power, but nothing happened. The circle of men closed in on her.

"What's wrong with me?" she shouted.

She was powerless when confronted by her past actions. Aite's nightmare made perfect sense.

I jogged in place to get the blood flowing again.

"Make them go away," she pleaded.

I stopped to squeeze the excess water from my hair. "Only if you agree to do the same."

I lost sight of her as the maddening crowd tightened around her.

"Help me!" Her desperate plea reached my ears.

Matilda's warning echoed in my head. The Celtic spirit would urge me to let them kill her. I couldn't afford to have Addison run back to The Corporation and report my existence. I could let the angry mob take its course. This was one of the features of my powers that frightened Pops the most—that I could weave someone's nightmare into the fabric of reality. I was the Freddy Krueger of goddesses; except I was a powerful force in both worlds.

And Aite was far from innocent. She wasn't some girl I accidentally bumped elbows with on a crowded street. She was a goddess of mischief and ruin. Of reckless impulse and blind folly. We should've been more evenly matched. Getting inside her head shouldn't have been this easy—unless…

Shit.

I'd been played.

I pushed my way to the inner circle, but the goddess was

gone. Pain exploded in my head, and I fell to the ground in blinding white agony.

"This has been a real blast, but I'm afraid the test is over, sweetness," Addison said.

My head throbbed and my vision was too blurred to see. "Cool. Did I pass?"

"With all the colors of the rainbow. You should be proud."

"The expression is 'flying colors,'" I said. It looked like some of Addison's basic knowledge got lost during the Aite download.

"Whoever you are, you're strong and will likely heal quickly. Goddesses usually do, unless you're Aergia. That donkey is too lazy to heal quickly."

Addison—or should I say Aite—finally came into focus. "You're not taking those gods." I was relieved to hear my voice regain its strength.

Her Cheshire cat smile gave me the creeps. "No biggie. They can be your problem now."

"I thought you stole them…"

"Oh, I totally did. Mischief and ruin, remember? You don't think I'd steal them without planting evidence on someone else, though, do you? I'm a professional, Lorelei."

I spit blood from my mouth. "I thought the only professional bitches were in dog shows."

She leaned down and pinched my cheek. "Have I mentioned how much I like your moxie? Toodles." She blew me a kiss and disappeared in a puff of smoke.

"Cheap theatrics!" I yelled at the empty air.

I staggered to my feet, still reeling from the encounter. My body hurt everywhere, and I was pretty sure my underwear had frozen to my pants, which were in turn stuck to my skin, but that was the least of my problems.

I was now a bargaining chip in a battle that didn't involve me. It was the outcome I'd feared my whole life, the one from which Pops had done everything in his power to protect me.

I'd pulled Aite's nightmare into this reality. It wouldn't take her endless hours of research to figure out my identity. If she followed through on her threat to report my existence to The Corporation, it was only a matter of time before they decided to pay me a visit and make me an offer I couldn't refuse.

And if that happened, there wasn't a ward in the world that could keep me safe.

CHAPTER 19

Kane and I contemplated the cell. The animals had been tranquilized and were slumbering peacefully while we carried out our plan.

"Are you sure you want to do this?" the demon asked.

I surveyed the sleeping animals. "No, but it seems cruel to send them back to The Corporation to languish in a storage container for eternity."

"It seems cruel to unleash them on the world, too."

I cast a sideways glance at him. "Which one of us is a prince of hell again? I'm confused."

His whisky-colored eyes sparked with amusement. "I'm a prince of hell, not the Tin Man from *The Wizard of Oz*."

In other words, he had a heart. Noted.

"How did you even get this thing through the front door?" Kane asked. "It's huge."

"That's what she said," I cracked.

He arched an eyebrow. "You flatter me, Lorelei."

Nope. Shouldn't have gone there. Clearing my throat awkwardly, I turned my focus back to the cell. "It's part of the enchantment. It came in pieces and assembled itself in the room, like magical IKEA."

"But we can't do that with the animals inside." He rubbed his rugged jawline. "The weight isn't an issue—between us we have the strength to carry it to the flatbed, but there's no way it will fit through the doorways without taking it apart."

He was right. "Teleportation magic is our best bet to transport this to the crossroads."

"It's our only bet. Are you sure that's wise, though? What if we're intercepted by your new friend?"

"Addison isn't my friend." Far from it. The avatar was the kind of bad news I didn't want to deliver to anyone, especially myself. "Anyway, I feel confident she isn't coming back right away." I had no doubt she'd return, but today was not that day.

"I can't think of anyone who has teleportation magic in Fairhaven," he said.

Good point. Teleportation required a lot of juice and experience. Phaedra wasn't that accomplished. Neither was Sage.

"I know someone." I dreaded summoning her, though. She would throw a hissy fit when she learned the details of what happened here.

Kane studied me. "Is this someone who knows your secret?"

I nodded. "And she's killed to keep it, so let's just say she's very invested."

"Do you only befriend killers, or is there room in your life for more docile creatures?"

"I don't befriend anybody."

He peered at me. "Do you truly not see yourself?"

The she-wolf stirred. It was time to get this circus on the road. "Would you mind waiting in another room while I summon her?" I'd need a minute alone with Matilda to explain the situation. I knew her well enough to know she wouldn't take kindly to Kane's presence.

"I wouldn't mind a bit of fresh air."

I waited until he was outside to start the ritual. Several lit candles and a chalk circle later, the Night Mallt herself appeared in my living room. The Celtic spirit wore a long silk robe, curlers in her hair, and a mud mask on her face, a far cry from the fierce warrior who rode with the Wild Hunt once upon a time.

"I hope you have a very good reason for interrupting my self-care routine, cariad."

"I do."

She stepped outside the circle. "Where's your cloakroom? I can't see very well. I need to wipe this gunk off my face before I can do anything."

I escorted her upstairs to the primary bathroom and handed her a washcloth and a towel.

"You talk while I do this." She moistened the washcloth and wiped away the thick mask.

I updated her on the menagerie in my dining room and Kane's involvement.

"You can send the devil demon home now that I'm here," Matilda said. "No need to risk exposing your secret."

The look on my face must've given it away, because she gaped at me in the mirror's reflection.

"You told him?" Matilda sounded as outraged as I imagined.

"He figured it out, mostly."

She unrolled the curlers one at a time and tossed each one in the sink with clipped movements to express her dissatisfaction. "A small town was a mistake. You should've stayed anonymous in London. It was safer for you there."

"My secret is safe with him."

She eyed me closely in the mirror. "And why is that?" Gasping, she shrank back. "You two knocked boots, didn't you?"

"There was no knocking of boots." I hesitated. "Only a slight rubbing together of them."

Pivoting to face me, she clucked her tongue. "Whatever

am I to do with you, enaid? Have you no sense of self-preservation?"

"I have plenty of sense. It was the goat that made me take my leave of them." A small but necessary white lie.

"Well, let's see if we can clean up the mess the goddess of mischief and ruin left behind, shall we?"

"Thank you. If it's any consolation, you look amazing."

She turned to admire herself in the mirror. "I do, don't I? My skin is flawless."

We returned downstairs to find Kane in the foyer. They eyed each other carefully.

"Great news!" I said, to break the tension. "The Night Mallt is here."

Matilda lowered her head. "Your Highness." She entered the dining room and stopped short at the sight of the enclosure. "Hell's bells."

"I believe that's my line," Kane said.

"I can see why you summoned me. This is quite a conundrum."

"I told you it was."

"I know, but I thought you were exaggerating. What's the plan?"

"I'd like you to teleport them to the crossroads, and then we'll let them loose."

Matilda moved closer to the pen. "Look at that gorgeous mane."

"Don't admire your own too closely or you might burst with pride," I warned.

A glimmer of mischief glinted in her eye. "In that case, why don't I teleport this one to The Corporation headquarters during a board meeting?"

"I don't want to risk any of the animals being reclaimed and stuffed back in a storage unit."

"Doesn't seem right to keep them trapped in these animal forms. It isn't natural for most of them. What if we transform them back into gods before we release them?" she proposed.

"I didn't think we could," I said. "I tried to remove the collars, but nothing worked."

Kane rubbed the back of his neck. "I think we ought to first consider whether we *should*. They're not innocent people. They're gods of wrath and gluttony and greed."

Matilda's nostrils flared with indignation. "And Lorelei is a goddess of nightmares and ghosts. You're a prince of hell. I rode with the Wild Hunt instilling fear in the hearts of men. Should we be denied the right to freedom and autonomy because of what we're capable of rather than what we actually choose to do?"

Kane appeared properly chastised. Leave it to Matilda to give the prince of hell a severe dressing down.

"Matilda's right," I said. "They only spread their vices because they were compelled to do so. Their collars kept them trapped in animal forms and controlled their behavior. We have no idea how they might behave otherwise."

"Exactly," Kane said. "We have no idea. The alternative could be much worse."

"I wouldn't want to be judged on my providence," I said. "I didn't choose to be a goddess, and I certainly didn't choose the domain of nightmares."

"No, but they did," Kane pointed out. "They're avatars, aren't they? Which meant they made a decision to be inhabited by a god of war and a goddess of envy. Somewhere in their programming, they chose these negative abilities."

I recalled my vision of Macuilcozcacuauhtli and his single word—'help.' "We can't know that for certain," I countered. "And just because they were imbued with negative powers doesn't mean they'd use them. Do you see me running around Fairhaven inflicting madness on innocent bystanders?"

"Not intentionally," he said.

I glared at him. "They deserve a chance, just like you." And a collar and four legs could be my future should The Corporation ever get their hands on me. It wasn't a pleasant thought.

Kane appeared to soften. "Say we release them as gods, then what? We follow them until we're satisfied they're not going to inflict their vices on the world?"

"No." I gazed at the menagerie. "We hope."

Breaking their collars was the first order of business. If we couldn't do that, then the whole plan fell apart.

"I know a smithy who should be able to help," Matilda said, after trying and failing to remove the donkey's collar.

"Someone you trust?" I asked.

"In this world, I only ever work with those I trust. His name is Stellan. He's a descendant of Sindri."

I looked at Kane. "Sindri is the dwarf who forged Mjolnir, Thor's hammer."

"His fascinating pedigree aside, how will he be able to break the collars without magic?"

"Because he doesn't need earthly magic when he has direct access to the divine," Matilda explained. "Makes for an impressive weapons forger."

Kane waved a hand at the animals. "They're gods. They all have access to the divine, don't they?"

Matilda shook her head. "It isn't the same. It's one of the reasons Lorelei is so valuable. She's a natural born goddess. Her powers are direct from the divine and, therefore, stronger than any avatar's. Same goes for Stellan. His is diluted by generations, of course, but it's still in its purest form."

"Do you think he'll help us?" I asked.

"If I ask nicely."

My pulse accelerated in anticipation. "How fast can he get here?"

"Give me five." She patted her curls. "At least I'll look good fetching him. Not a complete waste of a mud mask."

Matilda left the room to return to the summoning circle.

Kane released a small sigh. "Do you think she'll bring him?"

"Matilda's a force of nature. She could lasso the moon if she wanted to."

"Sounds like another woman I know."

We stared at each other without speaking. My heart hammered in my chest like a miniature Thor was trapped inside. The goat bleated, snapping me back to reality.

Ten minutes passed before Matilda reappeared with Stellan. The dwarf's face was barely visible beneath his bushy beard. He wore a short-sleeved floral shirt, khaki shorts, and sandals. Slung across his body was a leather pouch that I would've assumed was ancient if not for the Yves Saint Laurent logo.

He stopped short in the dining room doorway, and deep laughter rumbled straight from his chest. "This is a sight I've never beheld, and that's saying something."

"Can you do it?" I asked.

He moved closer to the pen to examine the collars. "I believe I have what I need."

The dwarf was brisk and efficient. He entered the pen and removed each collar with a tool he called a universalnøkkel.

I didn't recognize the term. "Nothing I can buy down at Hewitt's, I guess."

Stellan kept his focus on the lion's collar. "I don't know what a Hewitt's is, but I'd wager the answer is no."

The transformation from animal to god was nothing short of staggering. They shed their skins—which the snake did literally—and reclaimed their humanlike forms. When the last god exited the cage, the bars collapsed, and the pieces fell on top of each other in a neat pile.

Matilda gazed at the muscular physique of the Aztec god.

"Now that's a thigh sandwich I wouldn't mind being in the middle of."

We thanked Stellan and Matilda returned him to his beach house in Aruba.

"Anybody speak English?" I asked.

Hands went in the air.

"Would you mind telling us how you drew the short straws?" I asked. They looked at me blankly, so I clarified. "Why did you end up in The Corporation's storage unit?"

"The storage unit was a freakin' jar," the goddess of envy replied. "They put me there when I refused their demand to infiltrate a commune. They wanted my influence to be subtle but to slowly destroy it from the inside out."

"Why a commune?" I asked.

"The land is valuable," she explained, "but the commune doesn't know it. The Corporation wanted to weaken them before making an offer."

"Sounds like their kind of tactic," Matilda said.

"I volunteered to become an avatar because I thought I could do good in the world. They told me I would have the power to change lives."

I sighed. "And then they saddled you with the goddess of envy."

She nodded. "They wanted me to change lives, but not in the way I envisioned."

"I don't understand," I said. "Doesn't Invidia fully inhabit you? Why am I talking to the original person?"

"We're failed experiments," the former wild boar interrupted.

"You're a god of wrath, right?" I asked.

He nodded. "I'm Pakhet."

I looked at the Aztec god. "You're Macuilcozcacuauhtli."

His face brightened at the mention of his name.

Pakhet pointed to each of the remaining vices. "The

donkey is Aergia, goddess of sloth. The lion is Tengu, and Rati is the goat."

"Rati is a god of lust," Aergia said, "but I think you already know that."

I suddenly found the grain in the floorboard fascinating.

"None of us ended up working out the way the higher ups intended," Pakhet explained. "The Corporation doesn't like to lose money, though, so they kept tweaking us. Eventually, they figured out they could control us better in animal forms thanks to the collars."

"Then they earmarked us for occasional use," Invidia added.

The Aztec god pumped my hand repeatedly, speaking enthusiastically in his language. I still didn't understand a word.

Invidia smiled. "He says he's grateful you interceded. He's from a small village in Mexico. The Corporation promised to save his people from starvation if he agreed to work for them."

The Aztec god spoke again.

"And he says he would have found another way to save his village if he'd known the price," Invidia added.

Pakhet scrutinized me. "You have decided to let us go, knowing what we are?"

"You're misfit gods," I said. "Find an island somewhere that you can settle down and live happily until your mortal bodies expire."

Kane looked at me. "Expire? They're not cartons of milk."

"It's a euphemism." In my experience, nobody liked to talk about death, and certainly not immortal beings in mortal bodies.

"The Corporation won't let us go that easily," Pakhet said. "They'll hunt us down."

"First, they'll need to figure out what happened to you,

and I have confidence Aite won't be telling that story anytime soon."

"And it's why we're taking you to the crossroads," Kane added. "You'll have your choice of realms. Even if they do discover the truth, at that point The Corporation might decide you aren't worth any further investment."

Matilda continued to ogle the Aztec god. "Do you still need me to teleport them?"

Although it wasn't strictly necessary now, I still thought it was a good idea. With my luck, Chief Garcia would choose this moment to stop by for a chat.

We couldn't all fit in the circle at once, so Matilda organized us into two groups. I traveled with the first group that included Veles, Pakhet, Ratia, and Invidia. Kane accompanied the second group.

Veles looked down at the ground. "Sorry about all the snow. I didn't do it on purpose."

"The kids have enjoyed it," I said. "They love snow days."

Kane pointed to the crossroads. "Second tree to the right and straight on 'til morning."

Pakhet tilted his head upward and closed his eyes. "I feel the energy. It's quite powerful."

The Aztec god offered his arm to Invidia, and she accepted his invitation with a smile. Matilda muttered something unintelligible.

One by one the gods disappeared between the mighty oak trees.

Aergia winked at Kane as she passed by. "Nice abs, by the way. You should go shirtless more often." The former donkey's gaze skated to me. "You, too, hon. The two of you together are…" She licked her finger and made a scorching sound.

I looked away before I could see the expression on Kane's face.

Finally, only Matilda was left.

The Celtic spirit smiled. "I'm off as well. I'll take the crossroads home. I'm spent after that exertion."

"Thank you for coming on short notice," I said. "You know how much I appreciate you."

"'Course you do. Isn't everybody who would risk life and limb for you."

Kane and I watched her leave in companionable silence. The forest fell strangely quiet, as though all the woodland creatures were holding a collective breath, waiting to be sure the powerful beings had vacated the premises.

Kane spoke first. "I understand your reasons for this, but I'm still uncertain."

"Sometimes we have to accept uncertainty. If it doesn't work out, we'll pivot. Choose a new path. That's life." I'd started over more times than I cared to count. It was the price of freedom, and I gladly paid it.

Kane slid his hands into his pockets. "If it doesn't work out when you start a new job, you get a new job. If it doesn't work out because the god of war decided not to turn over a new leaf, you get dead people, and it will be our fault."

"Not all our fault. There would be a lot of names on that list before ours."

He frowned at me. "You seem surprisingly blasé about this."

"I'm not, trust me, but we can't control the outcome. We can only trust ourselves, that we did the right thing with the information we had at the time." I genuinely believed those deities were going to forge better paths for themselves. They'd tasted the negativity The Corporation offered them and rejected the flavor. They may be avatars, but they were more like me than any other gods on the company payroll.

"Is that your grandfather's influence?"

"Pops was a very wise man. He would've made an excellent god." I started to walk, but Kane moved to block my path.

"Before you go home, there's something I'd like to say."

"We don't have to talk about the goat." I wasn't sure how else to reference our almost-tryst.

"This isn't about the goat."

I felt slightly disappointed but refused to show it. "Okay, I'm listening."

"When I first showed you the crossroads and explained their importance, you were shocked to learn there was no crossroads deity to guard them. I told you that the world was too short on gods and goddesses these days."

I nodded. "I remember."

He moved to place his hands on my shoulders but then quickly lowered them again. "Lorelei, what if you're meant to be that deity? What if the universe lured you here for that very purpose?"

I laughed. "You think I'm destined to be the queen of the crossroads?"

He smiled. "I like how you jumped straight to the top of the royal food chain."

"If I'd jumped to the top, I would've said empress."

"These are no ordinary crossroads. It isn't a simple intersection of two realms, remember. This place serves as a gateway to all the realms that are and ever will be."

I glanced at the empty space between the oak trees. "And you want me to be its liminal deity."

"I think you already are."

CHAPTER 20

"It's right there," Ray said. "How can you not see it?"

I looked up from the radiator. "Excuse me for not having the benefit of your eagle eye, Ray."

"Doesn't take an eagle eye to see a crack the size of the Grand Canyon," he muttered. He floated closer and pointed to a spot on the radiator. "Apply the epoxy-resin sealer right there to seal the hole. Do you want me to keep my finger there until you're finished? It isn't like the sealer can touch me."

"Would you mind?"

Ray had persuaded me to fix the broken radiators on my own to save money. He'd offered to apply the sealer himself, but I didn't want to take advantage of his generous nature. The ghosts had done more than enough for me recently. Pops didn't raise a shirker. I had to get back to pulling my own weight when it came to home improvements. I wasn't going to learn if I let Ray and Nana Pratt do the bulk of the work.

My skin started to burn like someone set me on fire. I jumped to my feet and patted my arms to check for flames. I'd have to talk to Phaedra about dialing down the alert mechanism on the upgraded ward.

"Oh, your handsome prince is here," Nana Pratt said.

"He's a far cry from Disney," I replied, as I abandoned the radiator to answer the door.

Kane took one look at my bright green Eagles T-shirt and ratty sweatpants and smirked. "Is this a bad time?"

"I'm fixing the busted radiators."

"I thought maybe Aite had stolen all your clothes." He paused. "And your toiletries."

"Are you here to mock me, or is there a greater purpose?"

Ray and Nana Pratt hovered on either side of me. I was tempted to ask them to leave, but I didn't trust myself alone in a room with Kane—goat or no goat.

The demon produced a bottle from his jacket pocket. "A gift for you."

A tiny thrill shot through me as I recognized the distinctive floral label on the bottle of gin. "Where did you find this?"

"I made a few calls. You were right about its scarcity. Puck's Pleasure isn't easily obtained."

"One of the reasons it tastes so good. Thank you, Kane. This is very thoughtful."

"He's a keeper," Nana Pratt enthused from the sidelines. "Even if he is from hell."

I wasn't sure whether to ask my next question, but I went for it. "Will you have a glass with me?"

He smiled. "I was hoping you'd say that."

I carried the bottle into the kitchen and poured two glasses over ice. We stood at the island, staring at each other like two awkward teenagers.

"This is excellent," Kane finally said. "I can see why you're a fan."

"I think I should leave town," I blurted.

Kane didn't react. He took a careful sip from the glass. "For how long?"

"Forever. I'm going to fix the heating system and see if I

can rent the place."

He choked. "To whom? Count Dracula?"

"I'm serious, Kane. West was right about me from the start. My presence here puts everyone at risk. The supernatural circus proved it. Aite only hatched her scheme because of me."

"West doesn't know the truth about you. He thinks every newcomer to Fairhaven is a problem, which is ironic given his own history."

Kane was being obstinate. I had to get through to him. "Eventually, The Corporation will find out about me, and once they do, they'll try to add me to their roster. And when I refuse, they'll try to persuade me by threatening the lives of anyone I care about." And if they couldn't persuade me, they'd stick me in an enchanted jar or kill me.

"So what's the answer? You let The Corporation dictate your life choices now and evermore?"

I cut a quick glance at him. "Nobody says evermore in this century."

"Don't deflect, Lorelei."

"I never should've come to Fairhaven. It was a mistake."

"But where will you ever find another working moat? You can't possibly give that up." He tried to engage me with a charming smile. That luscious mouth would be the death of me if I let it. I had to resist.

"Plenty of abandoned castles in Europe," I said, forcing my attention away from the deadly mouth. "I can pick one up in France for a song."

"If that were true, you would've already done it."

"No, I wouldn't have. I wanted to come home."

Home. Fairhaven wasn't where I'd been born and raised, but it was the closest to home I'd felt since Pops died.

"You're broke, Lorelei, and nobody in their right mind would buy this heap from you in its current state or rent it for that matter."

"They might now that it has the working moat."

"I hate to be the bearer of bad news, but you're the only person in this century interested in owning one."

"I'll enter the crossroads like the Pandora gods. Go to another realm where they won't find me."

"And likely end up in more danger in a realm where you don't belong," he pointed out.

"Don't you see? I don't belong anywhere." One human foot in this world and one deified foot in the world of nightmares. I was an anomaly that shouldn't exist.

"You can't run and hide," he insisted. "You're too valuable. They'll chase you to the bowels of the earth and beyond."

Now it was my turn to laugh. "You're one to talk. You ran away and hid from hell. You're still hiding."

His face darkened. "It seems we both have a history of escapism. Maybe it's time we stop."

I tilted my head for a better look at him. "What do you mean?"

He clasped my hands in his, and I didn't shrink from his touch. "It seems we both feel the need to protect those who can't protect themselves. Why not join forces and do it together?"

"I thought you didn't want to join any of your parts with mine."

He sucked in a breath. "Oh, quite the contrary. It's more torture than I've ever endured."

Knowing what I knew about his past, that was saying something. "What changed your mind?"

"You did," he said simply. "When I learned your true identity, I feared that my involvement with you would return me to the demon I was."

"I'm a goddess of nightmares, Kane. Those aren't reality."

"But you can make them so. And what are nightmares but our deepest, darkest fears? The primary tools I used for torment and torture." He touched my chin. "But I see you, Lorelei, and I know my concerns were misguided. You and I are alike, yes, but not only in the ways of darkness. Also, in the ways of light."

I slipped my hands away. "And this is exactly why I need to go. You've done well here. If I stay, I'm going to destroy what you've built and the demon you've become. My grandfather warned me I'd be a magnet for trouble. That my presence was too dangerous."

"You, Lorelei Clay—Melinoe—won't destroy anything. Aite will. The Corporation and its minions will. But not you."

"She'll be back," I said. "I don't know when, but she will. And if I'm still here, I'll have to fight her again, not to mention whatever reinforcements she undoubtedly brings. I'll have to protect everyone." It was too much weight on my shoulders. I couldn't handle it. I should've stayed in busy London where nobody noticed me.

Kane's expression was nothing short of fierce. "No."

I cocked an eyebrow. "No, Your Highness?"

"No," he repeated firmly. "Let her come. Let them all come. You're not going to do this alone. *We'll* be ready for her."

Behind him, Ray nodded. "We will."

"Thanks, Ray."

Kane's gaze flicked to the space Ray currently occupied. "Would you mind asking your roommates for a moment of privacy?"

Ray and Nana Pratt disappeared.

"They're gone," I said.

He edged closer to me. "I'm asking you to stay."

"It isn't safe for you."

"I climbed the ranks to become a prince of hell, Lorelei. I can take care of myself." His thumb grazed my lips, tracing their contour. "Stay."

"Is that a royal command, Your Highness?"

"It's a personal request."

"Now that you've collected my secret, I assume you'll lose interest in me."

"Do you really believe that?"

No, I didn't. Whatever we felt for each other was real. The goat had only been an excuse to act on it, and we both knew it.

"You're powerful, Lorelei. More powerful than you've let yourself be. Your grandfather trained you to survive, but that doesn't mean that's all you should do. You deserve a life much fuller than that."

"Not at the expense of others."

"It won't be, I promise." He cupped my face in his hands. "Stay."

I took a step backward. "Sooner or later, there will be fighting. It might be in a year. It might be in two months, but it will happen."

"Then I guess I'd better polish my sword." A sly grin emerged. "I might even let you help with that."

I clutched my chest. "Such a generous offer, Your Highness. How can I possibly refuse?"

He grabbed my shoulders and pressed those velvet lips to mine. My body felt like a pinball machine as my insides whooshed, snapped, and zipped in response. Another second of this and I'd beg him to play me right here on the island. Kane was proving more of a threat than music ever was.

I extracted myself from his grip before I lost control. "We need to take things slowly. I'm talking glacier speed."

"Then allow me to be your iceberg."

I leaned my head against his rock-solid chest. I was going to need all the strength he had to give if I expected to survive what was coming.

"All right," I said. "I'll stay."

ALSO BY ANNABEL CHASE

Midnight Empire

Pandora's Pride

Magic Bullet

Spellslingers Academy of Magic

Federal Bureau of Magic

Lorelei's story continues in *Dead Weight*, Book 5 in the *Crossroads Queen* series.

To join my VIP list and download an extended scene from Kane's POV in Chapter 6 of *Dead to the World*, visit https://annabelchase.com/dead-to-the-world-offer.

Printed in Great Britain
by Amazon